DAY OF THE DEAD

(Joe Hawke #14)

Rob Jones

ISBN: 9781672444163

Other Titles by Rob Jones

The Hunter Files
The Atlantis Covenant (The Hunter Files #1)

The Joe Hawke Series
The Vault of Poseidon (Joe Hawke #1)
Thunder God (Joe Hawke #2)
The Tomb of Eternity (Joe Hawke #3)
The Curse of Medusa (Joe Hawke #4)
Valhalla Gold (Joe Hawke #5)
The Aztec Prophecy (Joe Hawke #6)
The Secret of Atlantis (Joe Hawke #7)
The Lost City (Joe Hawke #8)
The Sword of Fire (Joe Hawke #9)
The King's Tomb (Joe Hawke #10)
Land of the Gods (Joe Hawke #11)
The Orpheus Legacy (Joe Hawke #12)
Hell's Inferno (Joe Hawke #13)
Day of the Dead (Joe Hawke #14)

The Cairo Sloane Series
Plagues of the Seven Angels (Cairo Sloane #1)

The Avalon Adventure Series
The Hunt for Shambhala (Avalon Adventure #1)
Treasure of Babylon (Avalon Adventure #2)

The Raiders Series
The Raiders (The Raiders #1)

The Harry Bane Thriller Series
The Armageddon Protocol (A Harry Bane Thriller #1)

The DCI Jacob Mystery Series
The Fifth Grave (A DCI Jacob Mystery)

Email: robjonesnovels@gmail.com
Twitter: @AuthorRobJones
Facebook: www.facebook.com/RobJonesNovels/
Website: www.robjonesnovels.com

CHAPTER ONE

Nikita Zamkov recalled the day when his family doctor had broken the news of his condition to his parents. He could see their faces, saddened, horrified and yet almost relieved that finally something explained his behavior. Now, when he remembered the words spoken by the old psychiatrist, he heard them clearly in his head.

Dissociative fugue.

A very rare psychiatric disorder inflicting days or even months of temporary amnesia, the condition had lain waste to massive chunks of his life. When he looked back on his past, he didn't enjoy the same way of seeing memories as anyone else. Instead, dark black holes lurked here and there, voids where his life should have been.

Like the moment just before he came around and found himself delivering the killer blow to poor Valentina's skull. His lover was laying on the floor at his feet, blood pouring from her head and a bloody metal pipe was rolling to a stop on her exquisite Kazak rug.

The fugue, he thought, then, with loathing and hatred rising in his throat, *I did this to her.*

Fragments of her crushed skull reflected the low light of the antique oil lamp on the table, like small white rocks on a beach lapped by waves of blood, all tangled in the seaweed-like hair. He gasped and took a step back. His hands were shaking and his heart pounding in his chest. What had she done to him, to make him kill her? Surely, he said, soothing himself, he would never do such a thing without a good reason.

1

But what reason was good enough to break someone's head open?

The fugue – yes, it wasn't him, it was his condition. He couldn't help it. Besides, it went hand in hand with his brilliance. Often he would wake from these dark, blank moments and be inundated with ideas of pure genius. It didn't make the black, unlit forest of his mind any easier to bear, but some of his greatest AI creations were borne of this nightmare.

He looked down at her body and, fully himself again, he knew he had to hide any trace of himself. He worked fast, wiping down fingerprints and scuffing shoe prints out of the rug – these police officers were devils. The slightest thing would lead them to him, and then where would the world be? He couldn't create his AI utopia from the cells of Matrosskaya Prison, he considered with a shudder.

He picked up his wine glass and washed it carefully, then dried it and set it back in the cupboard, holding it with a tea towel to ensure no prints. As he surgically removed all trace of himself from the apartment, he caught himself singing…

The priest had a dog, he loved her,
She ate a piece of meat, he killed her,
Buried in the ground
The inscription wrote:
The priest had a dog, he loved her,
She ate a piece of meat, he killed her,
Buried in the ground
The inscription wrote:
The priest had a dog, he loved her…

It went on and on, a grim never-ending circular nursery rhyme his mother used to sing to him while she rocked him to sleep. The words tumbled from his lips in a bleak, hoarse whisper as he stole her diary and iPhone and laptop and shoved them all in his bag. Then he emptied out her wallet and took the notes and had the rings off her fingers. With luck, those devils would think this was just another robbery.

Certain he had taken care of everything he left the apartment door ajar and jogged down the dark hallway and then stepped out into the swirling snow. He had no memory of killing poor Valentina, but he knew the memory of discovering her corpse right there in front of him, and staging the event to look like a burglary would haunt him until his dying day.

All these years later it was as vivid as the light streaming in through the aircraft window and lighting the dust motes in the cabin. Looking from the window of the private jet, he shuddered, as if trying to shake the guilt away.

Put it behind you, Niki.

After the attack on his compound in the Amazon jungle, he had spent a day or two in Rio organizing the next phase of his attack on humanity, and things were coming together nicely. The next twenty-four hours would change the course of the planet's history forever. Not human history, he mulled, because humans would no longer exist, but the story of the planet itself.

The destruction meted out on Vyraj by the ECHO team had set him back, but not ended him. Things would take longer now, but he could still wipe out humanity and create his perfect AI utopia. All he had to do to trigger the end times was release the supervirus.

His personal chef trod quietly on the plush carpet as he pushed a trolley of his favorite foods to the boss's seat at the front of the plane. Zamkov surveyed the selection greedily, and after choosing a bowl of the Osakan's

3

signature dish, raw kurobuta pork sashimi and dashi jelly garnish, he called his three warriors on the video conferencing facility.

As he chewed on the bloody meat, their faces appeared in front of him, each occupying one third of a giant plasma screen fitted to the bulkhead wall.

"Report, Agent Barbosa."

The bedraggled, unshaven face of Antonio Barbosa stared into his laptop camera with cold, dead eyes. "I'm in a hotel in Kowloon. The vials are ready to go."

"Agent Rodrigues."

Francisco Rodrigues began to talk. "I am in Paris, as ordered, sir. In the Mandarin Oriental. Just awaiting further orders."

"Dove. Make yourself alone."

The Dove was lounging on a wooden deckchair beside a swimming pool. Hair slicked back, he was wearing a bright white hooded bathrobe and holding a cocktail glass. Beside him was a woman in sunglasses and a bikini. Now, he whispered something into the woman's ear. She giggled, ran her finger down his cheek and after kissing him on the lips, she moved out of sight.

"As you can see, I am in Mexico City in a beautiful hotel, but I am also ready and waiting for your orders."

This pleased Zamkov. "You will all receive an encrypted message very shortly. This will provide a code allowing you to activate the timer detonators in the medical bio-cases. You will also see coordinates. These are confidential, revealing the exact location of Eschaton Base, where I am now.

"Why not tell us now?" Barbosa asked.

Zamkov ignored the question, "You will each receive a third of the coordinates, and will liaise to put them together after you have activated the timers. Then you will travel here to Eschaton immediately after activation. When the first wave startsF to die, nothing can stop it, and nothing in human history could ever prepare anyone for how final this will be. You do not want to be around when things go bad. And they will go very bad. Everywhere."

"Everywhere," Barbosa said with a chuckle.

Zamkov sighed. "It was unfortunate that the ECHO team escaped from Vyraj. Dove, is our little surprise waiting for them in Mexico?"

"Yes, sir."

Zamkov smiled. "Excellent. Then good luck, my warriors."

The men nodded and Zamkov killed the camera feed. Outside, the Antarctic coast was a stark, grey scar of igneous rock stretching as far as the eye could see. The scar was bounded on one side by freezing ash-colored water and on the other by thousands of miles of ice fields and snowdrifts. Crossing over the coast and heading inland, the Sukhoi jet was heavily buffeted by a powerful westerly wind. As they descended toward Eschaton Base, the storm grew in strength and knocked the plane around as if it were a toy.

Zamkov's personal assistant, a super-intelligent AI named Yakov, made his way from the cockpit into the main cabin. "Ten minutes out, sir."

The AI pilots had handled the bad weather impressively, and were bringing the flight in to land almost exactly on schedule. Banking hard to starboard as they lined up with the runway, he was able to see the base for the first time.

It was set deep inside a rift valley above a glacier and almost totally buried in thick blankets of snow, and yet to him it was perfection. A mixed team of human staff and robots had been maintaining the base as an auxiliary platform in the event that Vyraj was destroyed. That horror had already passed, but perhaps Eschaton Base had just as much potential.

He saw the runway lights just moving out of sight now as the aircraft manoeuvred for the touchdown. Over thirty thousand tonnes of ice had been cleared to construct it, and crews working on shifts kept it clear of ice build-up around the clock. No one knew when Mr Zamkov would need to use it, and no one wanted to be the one to fail him.

He looked across to his beloved Valentina and smiled. She returned the smile and blew him a kiss. A wonderful creation, he thought, lovingly built with his own hands. Thanks to the laptop and diary and iPhone he had stolen from the original Valentina's apartment, he had been able to recreate her entire personality, likes and dislikes, foibles and annoyances and pleasures. They were all incorporated inside the new Valentina's AI neural framework, and it had worked well. He could barely tell any difference between the two. The physical resemblance was startling.

She laughed the same way, she cried at the same things and she shared most of their original memories. He sighed inwardly when he considered his latest revolutionary concept – scanning specific human brain substrates and transferring them to his AI neural network. This would produce totally identical copies of people inside a simulation, which would then be represented in the 3D world by robots, or even holographic avatars.

Sadly, he needed living brains to do this, and the original Valentina was long gone, cremated and turned to ashes scattered on the Russian wind. That chance might be lost, but that didn't mean the end of the program; it just meant he needed another victim to experiment on. He looked across the cabin at his prisoner, ECHO's Kamala Banks, and realised he had found his volunteer.

Her tears had dried up over Argentina and been replaced with a look of iron-determination to get revenge on him and escape, but he knew what she didn't yet know – there was no escaping from Eschaton Base. Perhaps she would feel more at home when he had cloned her brain and downloaded it into an AI unit like Valentina. How the process would affect her mind, he did not know, but there would be no need for the original Kamala afterwards anyway, so it was irrelevant.

He turned to the porthole. The higher levels of the base were now visible, poking out of the snow here and there. He saw stark concrete blocks and covered walkways which allowed staff the freedom to move around the base even in the deepest and coldest of winters. It was heaven, he thought, and until humanity was scrubbed from the rest of the world, it was now his home; a safe haven while the rest of mankind died the worst of all possible deaths.

The thought made him smile and check his watch.

Only twenty-four hours to go.

CHAPTER TWO

Joe Hawke looked out of the jet's porthole window with a feeling of dread swirling deep inside him. It had taken them nearly two days to get out of the jungle and make their way to Mexico City and they were already tired and on-edge. Nikita Zamkov was a dangerous enigma, and something told him he would get even nastier if he was ever cornered. But cornering him was exactly what they planned to do.

Orlando Sooke had organized a private chartered flight from Manaus to Mexico City, and as it made its way northwest over El Salvador and Guatemala, he had contacted them via videoconference and given them a lengthy briefing about the Russian. Most of it they already knew, but other parts of the intel were fresh, including Zamkov's plan to release the supervirus within twenty-four hours. That had shocked them to the core, as had the Russian's full psychiatric history which Sooke had leveraged out of a contact in Moscow.

That was also eye-opening, to say the least.

But still, no one was entirely sure why the Butcher of Rublyovka had chosen the city for Project Eschaton's ground zero. Speculation was rife. The leading theory was that the city's centralized location in the Americas plus its massive population density would deliver to Zamkov the maximum bang for his buck.

Compounding this theory was that unless their knowledge of the operation was wrong, he had only three men delivering the supervirus. The locations he had sent Rodrigues and Barbosa to – Paris and Hong Kong –

finished off the plot perfectly. Along with the Dove in Mexico, they were a neat troika of maniacs ready to bring the apocalypse to an unsuspecting world.

And ECHO were there to stop them, except ECHO didn't have the reach to meet the threats posed in Paris and Hong Kong, and that was where Hawke's idea, back in the Amazonian ecolodge, came in. As soon as they had discovered the true scale of Zamkov's plan, it was clear they needed more personnel to fight the threat, but they were still on the run and had no recourse to any government for assistance. Hawke's solution to the problem was simple, but daring.

First, Scarlet's Bravo Troop would be dispatched to take down Rodrigues in Paris. This was easy to organize, and Scarlet made the call to Major Clive Hudson on the spot. The moment he learnt about Project Eschaton, he had agreed without hesitation and made calls to the rest of the team, Eddie 'Mack" Donald, Kyra Harpenden and even the permanently ducking and diving Danny Plane. Even without the other two members of Bravo Troop, Scarlet and Camacho, Hudson assured the ECHO team that Rodrigues would be neutralized.

The second part of the plan was harder to pull together. Since Sir Richard Eden's house arrest, Orlando Sooke had been able to offer them a certain amount of surveillance and intel support courtesy of his connections not only to the British SIS but also to a New York-based spy hub known as Titanfort. It was a massive network with connections to every part of the world. The section passing them satellite surveillance was run by a man named Ezra Haven.

And Haven had a team.

That team was called the Raiders. Both Hawke and Lea had heard of them on the underground, but never met any of them. They were a mysterious yet highly respected team of specialists, mostly using their skills to rescue kidnapped people, but they had recently turned their talents to tracking down ancient treasures and relics. Even Ryan had heard all about their daring raid on Cleopatra's tomb against the sinister Occulta Manu.

The Hidden Hand.

Word from Haven took longer to get back. Contacting the man himself was easy enough – Sooke had done it several times during the Orpheus and Hell's Inferno missions, but there was a delay as Haven waited for his team to get back to him. Jed Mason was first to respond. The canny Londoner and former Army boxing champion was always on the lookout for action, and agreed immediately.

The towering former US Army Ranger from Arizona, Caleb Jackson, was next to call back. He was busy on his ranch. Twist my arm. Sure, why not? Count me in. Raiders' IT specialist, Milo Risk was located in San Francisco, and said he couldn't wait to get stuck in. Ella Makepeace replied next. A professional TV hypnotist, she was the team's hustler and organizer. Yes, of course, was the graceful reply, delivered in her top-drawer English accent.

Harder to find was the black sheep of the team.

Zara Dietrich.

Mason had insisted that it was either the whole team or none at all, so tracking the ex-LAPD cop down became urgent. Concerns were voiced. Was she drunk somewhere? Hanging off a bar in downtown LA? Yes and no. Haven eventually found her in the Roxy on Sunset Boulevard, stone cold sober and watching, as she described it, a shitpile of a punk band called the Dumdums.

And was he kidding her?

Hell yeah, she was in.

For half an hour, the teams shared a three-way video conference as they discussed their strategy, all directed by a tired-looking Orlando Sooke from an undisclosed location somewhere in England. It went well, and they agreed to stay in regular contact to provide updates if circumstances allowed, and then they made their goodbyes.

And so Hawke's plan had worked, and the scene was set. ECHO would take on the Dove in Mexico City, Bravo Troop minus Scarlet and Camacho would fly to Paris and eliminate Francisco Rodrigues, and Mason would lead the Raiders into battle against Tony Barbosa in Hong Kong. Then, the teams would unite and find Eschaton Base and destroy whatever hellish playground the Butcher had created down there. After that, Bravo Troop and the Raiders would go their separate ways and ECHO would reunite and prepare for the mother of all battles on Tartarus.

"You think we'll pull it off?" Lea asked.

"We have no choice," Hawke said. "You know that."

She sighed. "I know, it's just that the best laid plans of mice and men…"

He nodded. "And I know *that*, too."

Camacho called out from the back of the small jet. "I hope I didn't just pick up some negative vibes up in first class."

Lea smiled. "I'm just tired, Jack."

"Good – that's what I want to hear. No room for negative vibes around here, right?"

Hawke and Lea replied in unison: "Right."

"Do you two have a hive mind or something?" Ryan said.

"Hey," said Lea. "Don't make me flick a peanut at you, Ry." She shook the little foil bag in her hand. "I'm armed and I *will* fire if I have to. You know I'm not messin'."

"Just pointing out how annoying it is when you two act like one."

"It's cute," Lexi said from the row behind them. "They're like two cuddly little Beanie Boos."

Camacho laughed and he and Lexi shared a high-five. "Nice."

They all heard the fridge door slam at the back of the aircraft, and then Scarlet walked down the center aisle with a bottle of cold beer. "Not one sodding vodka."

"You say that with an unsettling degree of contempt in your voice," Ryan said.

Zeke yawned, reached out and took the beer from her. "I like a lady who says what she means and means what she says. But if you can't appreciate this beautiful cold beer, then I can."

She turned and tweaked his ear, causing him to cry out. "Hey!"

"Beer, Tex. Now."

He lifted the beer back up towards her. "On the other hand…"

Scarlet calmly took the bottle back from him and sank a third of the ice-cold amber liquid in one go. She smacked her lips and sighed with pleasure. "That's not so bad after all."

"God *dammit*, my ear hurts!"

Scarlet ruffled his blonde hair. "Aww, then let's not play with my drinks in future, all right, darling?"

A low chuckle went around the cabin as she finished the beer and began to gather her things ready for the landing.

Ryan popped up over the back of his seat and looked at Zeke. "Did you not go to Sunday School?"

Zeke nodded. "As a matter of fact I did. Why?"

"Then you should know the eleventh commandment."

The Texan smirked. "Oh yeah?"

"Oh, definitely yeah," Ryan said. "Thou Shalt Not Mess With Cairo's Drinks."

Zeke laughed. "Got it."

"Heed the advice, Tex," Scarlet said. "Ryan's had so many ear tweaks he's starting to look like a Vulcan."

A dark smirk crossed Lexi's cherry-red lips "I think he secretly enjoys it."

They all heard Lea groan. "That's gross, Lex."

"Lots of gross things are also true," Nikolai said. Except for a brief conversation about religion with Zara Dietrich on the video conference, it was the first time the sullen Russian monk had spoken on the flight.

"Exactly," Lexi said.

Ryan fought off the blush. "What can I say? I'm secretly in love with Cairo Sloane and one day I will be her…"

"Wife?" Lexi said.

A roar of laughter, and Hawke smiled as the banter went back and forth. But the weight of the mission crushed his shoulders, and as the team raced over the southern suburbs of the city and prepared to land, Lea's words echoed in his head.

The best laid plans of mice and men…

Truth was, there were holes in their plans. For one thing, there was no real way for them to know how many vials of the supervirus Zamkov had escaped from the compound with. And who knew what the Dove, Rodrigues and Barbosa had in store for them?

The flaps retracted and the landing gear came down.

Scarlet finished her beer and said, "Are we sure King Kashala never opened his portal to that parallel universe?"

"Pretty damn sure," Lea said. "Why?"

"Because if Milo Risk isn't the antimatter version of the boy here, I'm a monkey's uncle."

At the back, Reaper grumbled and grizzled and began to pack up his bag.

"I thought you were asleep," Lexi said.

"Moi? Non... I'm too pumped-up for sleep."

"I heard you snoring."

He shook his head. "I was not asleep. I was listening to everything you were saying. I am always on guard, like a ninja."

"Oh yeah?"

"Oui."

"Sure you were," the Chinese assassin said with a smile.

"It's the truth."

"Then what were we talking about?"

"Mostly just... comment dit-on – les banalités..."

"Small talk," Ryan called out.

"Thanks, double-dome," Lexi called back. She returned her attention to the unshaven Frenchman sitting beside her. He had been looking at a picture of his wife and kids and was now sliding it back inside the pocket of his black denim jacket. "Small talk could mean anything at all. It's a get out. You were sleeping. Admit it, you big old bear."

"I was not." He closed his bag and leaned back into his chair. "Reaper's eyes and ears are always open. And what the hell is a Beanie Boo?"

CHAPTER THREE

Hawke weaved through the crowds at Mexico City International Airport, keeping his head down as walked to the nearest exit. The fake passport had opened the country for him, but he couldn't fool the airport's facial recognition system. None of them could, and while there was a chance they wouldn't trigger anything, he wasn't about to bet the farm on it. Being on America's Most Wanted list was not a great place to be, especially when the President was a corrupt megalomaniac with a personal grudge against you.

The team had broken up into various smaller groups to go through customs, but now they pushed through the revolving doors and gathered in the hot Mexican night. It was even busier out here than back in the airport, with thousands of people flying in to spend the Day of the Dead festival with loved ones. The bustling sea of travellers made life a little easier for the team and a little harder for anyone monitoring the airport's CCTV system.

They searched beyond the taxi rank for the two Chevrolet SUVs they had booked under their fake identities. Lea found it first. "I see it, right over there behind the bus station. Who's coming with me? Someone who can speak Spanish better than me, please."

"You twisted my arm," Ryan said, hauling his bag up over his shoulder.

Hawke watched them as they walked through the crowd to the hire company. He couldn't explain it, but he felt a sudden sense of unease in the air. He kept a lid on his fears, and scanned the crowd for anything out of place.

He saw nothing, and reassured himself it was just the stress of such a time-critical mission getting to him.

Worst case scenario was that they had been detected by the cameras back in the airport and that information would rapidly find its way to the White House, but then he heard Lea cry out just as she and Ryan were passing the bus station and his priorities changed in a heartbeat.

Everyone's did.

He climbed up onto a wall running along the front of the departure lounge and looked across the sea of people toward the bus station. Dozens of men were leaping out of the back of three black GMC Savana vans parked up beside one of the coaches. Mostly dressed in torn jeans and leather jackets, some wore no tops at all and were covered in tattoos. Some carried long knives and others gripped handguns.

And they were already on top of Lea and Ryan.

"They're under attack!" Scarlet cried out. Instinctively, she reached for a sidearm, but it wasn't there. With no way to bring firearms safely and legally through customs at such short notice, Orlando Sooke had organized a similar arrangement to when they had landed in Brazil a few days ago. Everything they needed for their mission was waiting for them in a safehouse in the city, but that wasn't going to help them right now.

"Let's move," Hawke said.

Nikolai looked at him. "What about the CCTV?"

"Fuck the CCTV."

Nikolai shrugged. "Sounds fair enough."

Hawke scanned the chaos for Lea, and found her fighting off one of the men. She floored him with a palm strike and ran to help Ryan. He barely saw her, just a glimpse of her leather jacket flicking out behind her and then she was gone again.

16

"C'mon!" he yelled, and followed her into the crowd, weaving and pushing his way deeper into the chaos. Many of the people had painted their faces to look like skulls and others wore giant skull masks instead. Some went further and hid their bodies inside black spandex skull suits.

"Where are they?" he called out. Using his height, he stood up on his tiptoes and started to scan the heaving crowd for any sign of El Jefe's men. The noise coming from the excited crowd was growing louder, and when he called out to Lea, she didn't hear him.

A carnival atmosphere was developing, and fast. Not a patch of sidewalk or road asphalt could be seen beneath the bustling crowd. Squeezed together, shoulder to shoulder, they danced and sang and partied and drank and called for taxis to take them into the city. Hawke was out of his depth.

He felt a hand on his arm and swung around, hand balling into a fist at his side.

"Easy cowboy."

It was Scarlet.

"Bloody hell, Cairo. You nearly gave me a heart attack."

"Your weak constitution aside, all okay?"

"There's no sign of any of Loza's men and I've lost Lea. I think she went to help Ryan."

She raised an eyebrow and crossed her arms over her chest. "So, you're doing your usual bang-up job of keeping on top of things. I respect your consistency."

"Thanks for the vote of confidence. You're a real tonic."

"I aim to please."

Another cry from Lea. Hawke reacted instantly, pushing once again through the travellers that surrounded him as if they weren't there. Looking ahead, Lea and Ryan were still on the back foot. They had done their best, but after a long flight all the way up from Brazil, they were tired and disoriented, and now outnumbered at least ten to one.

Free of most of the crowd now, he sprinted across the parking lot and called out after them, but it was too late. The men had bundled them into the back of one of the Savanas and were climbing inside and slamming the doors. The driver hit the gas and after an impressive wheelspin, he raced the windowless cargo van around in a tight arc and exited the parking lot behind the bus station.

"Jesus!" Scarlet called out. "They've kidnapped them both!"

"How the fuck did that just happen?" Zeke said.

There was no time to answer. The small army of men from the two remaining cargo vans ran toward them, armed with knives and handguns.

Scarlet braced herself, tightening her hands into fists, but she knew there was no hope of overcoming so many men. "We can't fight twenty men with guns and blades, Joe. Not in a place with this many civvies, anyway."

"No," he said, clenching his jaw. "We have to get out of here."

"We can't abandon Lea and Ryan!" Lexi said.

The men were closing on them, screaming insults in Spanish and looking like they meant business.

"We're not abandoning them," Reaper said. "If we stay here and get killed, then we are abandoning them."

Scarlet took a reluctant step back. "Reap's right."

Hawke nodded. "The only way we can save them is by getting after that truck."

18

Zeke sucked his teeth, hands in pockets. "I don't think these guys want us to do that, chief."

"We need some wheels," Camacho said.

"We can forget the car hire place," said Scarlet. "We have to go through those guys to get there."

"C'mon!" Hawke said.

Chaos exploded all around them fast, driving innocent travellers away into frenzied screams as they tried to flee from the armed men. Hawke knew he had to act fast, but they were exposed, outnumbered and without weapons. Seeing an empty, full-size Irizar i8 passenger coach parked up a few yards away, he knew what to do.

"Bus!"

Scarlet was already on it, racing toward the open door with Zeke, Nikolai and Camacho right behind her. Hawke, Reaper and Lexi stood fast, forming a barrier between the men and the bus. The men approached faster now. Those who hadn't drawn their guns, did so. Their leader, a man with a death mask skull tattooed on his face, pulled the barrel of a Magnum .357 from his belt and aimed it at Hawke and fired.

Hawke dived to the floor, executed a forward dive-roll and got back to his feet closer to the bus's door. The sound of the gun firing in the night was incredibly loud, triggering a number of security guards inside the airport to turn and draw their weapons. Hawke ordered the others into the bus and they raced onboard. He climbed up last, and pushed the button to close the door.

Behind them, the bus driver had been leaning into one of the side baggage compartments, presumably trying to find a missing bag for one of the passengers he'd just dropped off at the airport. Startled by the gunshot on the other side of the coach, he peered around to see what was happening. When Camacho turned the engine on, he

19

turned and looked up at the cab with a confused expression on his face.

Inside the coach, Scarlet looked at Camacho with her usual calm eyes. "You know where reverse is, right?"

His response was to slam the enormous bus into reverse gear and floor the throttle. The wheels spun, producing more smoke than any of them had ever seen. The bus surged backwards, nearly knocking them off their feet as he spun the wheel and pulled back onto the slip road heading back out of the airport.

Outside, the bus driver was screaming and waving his hands.

"I can't believe this is happening," Hawke said out of nowhere. "Irony is, first time Lea and I chased anyone it was on a bus. Now I'm using one to save her life."

Scarlet gave him a look. "Eh?"

"Lea and me... we met on a bus." Watching the cargo truck escaping into the night with Lea and Ryan on board, his voice trailed away.

Scarlet rolled her eyes. "Damn, this is *romantic*, then. I'm so glad you pointed that out."

"Do one, Sloane," Hawke said, raising his middle finger.

Outside, Deathmask aimed the .357 at the bus's front window and emptied the remaining five rounds into it. The bullets punctured a row of neat holes in the two broad panes of safety glass. Camacho ducked to avoid the incoming fire, slammed the bus into first gear and stamped on the accelerator once again. "Hold on to your hats, folks!"

"And welcome to Mexico!" Zeke leaned over the seats on the left hand-side and stared out the window. "They're heading back to the trucks, guys. These assholes ain't rolling over just yet!"

DAY OF THE DEAD

Nikolai pointed out the windshield. "And the Savana is getting away!"

"And we have no guns," Lexi said.

Scarlet sighed. "Any more good news?"

Reaper had run to the rear of the coach, and now he screamed out to the others. "Down! RPG incoming!"

"Of course there is..." Scarlet dived for the floor.

"Are you sure?" Hawke asked. He craned his neck and checked the diver's mirror, but Camacho spoke first. "Holy crap, he's right! Rocket grenade incoming!"

"Why do you think I'm on the floor?" Scarlet cried out.

Camacho gripped the wheel and changed up to second, steering around a shallow bend arcing around the side of the parking lot as he searched for the exit sign. Behind him, the others dived for cover in the central aisle or behind the seats. As Camacho raced around the bend, the grenade struck the rearmost window on the left-hand side, ripped through the bus and bursting right back out of the opposite window on the right-hand side.

It ploughed into a billboard at the side of the road and exploded, blowing a giant fireball into the sky and setting off dozens of car alarms in the parking lot.

Scarlet climbed out from behind her seat at the front. "Close enough for you?"

"Close enough?" Zeke said. "It parted my goddam hair!"

Camacho changed up again. Ahead, a boom gate was blocking their path. "Shit."

Scarlet darted a look at him. "What is it?"

"I didn't buy a ticket." He turned to look at her just in time to wink before crashing the bus through the boom gate and tearing it to pieces.

"Fool."

"Who the hell are these guys?" Lexi said. "I mean, they're at the airport the second we arrive, so they're waiting for us, right? They have intel. Not only that, they've got more weapons than some small Asian countries I know."

"We can worry about that later," Hawke said, keeping an eye on the cargo vans through the rear window. "A bigger worry is our *lack* of weapons, and just how the hell we're going to catch up with Lea and Ryan."

"I think that ship has sailed, Joe," Camacho said.

"Eh?"

"I lost them back during the RPG attack." His voice dropped, and was low, quiet and respectful. They all knew why. "I'm sorry, but they're gone."

"And I've got even better news," Zeke called out from the rear. "They're almost on top of us, man! They're much faster than us and they're catching up real quick!"

"No matter what happens, we can't stop," Hawke said. "They'll swamp us. Keep on driving Jack! Lexi and Kolya, you keep him safe at the wheel, whatever comes."

As the Mexican night rushed by, Zeke cried out. "You won't believe it, guys, but the dude with the death mask tattoo on his face is standing on the hood of the Savana and trying to climb in the back window!"

Hawke turned and saw Zeke trying to fight the man away, but then he heard gunshots and the Texan dived for cover behind one of the seats.

"Zeke! Are you hit?"

"No, but they're climbing on board!"

CHAPTER FOUR

Hawke looked down the back of the coach and saw Zeke wasn't exaggerating. Deathmask was already halfway through the blown-out rear window, smoking Magnum in hand, and behind him he saw the bandana-wrapped heads of other men as they launched off the hood of the Savana and pulled themselves inside the coach.

"Evasive action, Jack!" he yelled.

Camacho responded immediately, swerving the coach from side to side as he tried to fling off some of the men climbing in the back. One of them lost his grip, tumbled out of the back and hit the asphalt hard before rolling off to the side of the road. The others were too far inside and fell inside the footwell in front of the rear row of seats.

"Don't stop driving, Jack!" Hawke said. "There are more vans behind us."

"Got it."

"Looks like it's time for fisty-cuffs," Hawke muttered to himself, and rolled up his sleeves as he charged down the aisle toward the back of the coach. "And don't say you weren't warned."

Zeke and Deathmask were brawling on the rear seats as the Texan desperately tried to knock the Magnum from his hands. Behind them, another man armed with a knife was clambering over them, making his way to Hawke. The Englishman didn't wait for an introduction, rushed him and threw his elbow out, driving it into the man's face.

The bus lurched to the right, knocking his opponent off balance. He tumbled off Hawke and slammed into the seats, striking his head on an armrest. Hawke seized the moment and jabbed him in the face with his fist, clicking his head back and driving the back of his skull into the side of the seat one more time.

The man looked like he was going to pass out, but then he shook his head and brought himself back to life for another round. Hawke took hold of his wrist and twisted it until he released the blade, but the man kicked it away, out of his reach.

In the center of the bus, Scarlet was now on her back, raising her legs and swinging her boots up just in time to repel an attacker. She kicked out at him, driving her heels into his face and knocking him out. Further beyond her, Lexi and Nikolai were engaged in a fistfight, awkwardly fighting in the cramped space as they tried to keep two more gangsters away from Camacho in the driving seat.

A final punch from Hawke knocked his opponent out. The Englishman looked up and scanned the coach. The battle in here was over, and ECHO were the victors. "Where's Reap?"

Scarlet crawled to her knees and stepped on her unconscious opponent as she walked over to him. "There."

Hawke followed her pointing hand just in time to see Reaper giving chase to one of the gangsters who was disappearing up onto the roof through one of the smashed windows. Reaper followed him, and Hawke was only seconds behind.

"Everyone else stay in here and make sure no one else get in this bus!"

Clambering through the smashed-out rear window and heaving himself up onto the bus's expansive roof, he saw three gangsters forming a semi-circle around Reaper. Unarmed, they were no match for the Frenchman, not even mob-handed, but these men had switchblades, and a simple strategy: either the former legionnaire jumped off the coach's roof alive, or they would stab him full of slits and kick him off dead.

Hawke made his way up the coach toward his old friend. The Scania Irizar was a big coach, and being on the roof elevated him to fifteen feet off the ground on a vehicle swerving all over the place. If he went over the edge, he was spending six weeks in hospital at best.

By the time he reached the action, Reaper had already thrown two of the men from the coach and was now working on the third. "Maybe you didn't need my help after all."

Reaper shrugged. "The more the merrier."

Reaper was talking to Hawke, but kept his eyes on the gangster. He could see from the feral hate in his eyes that one slip was all it would take for this man to drive the knife into his ribcage. The Frenchman lunged suddenly, smacking the knife from his hand and yanking his wrist forward, pulling the man closer to him.

In range now, Reaper piled a fist into his face, twisted the concussed man around, pinned his arm behind his back and pushed him off the edge of the bus. He crashed to the ground with a dry smack and the bus raced onwards through the city night. With the deadly pursuit rapidly racing east, another busy intersection was fast approaching. Hawke winced as he saw the heavy city traffic criss-crossing the roads up ahead. "We might have a problem, Reap."

The other Savana now pulled up alongside them but Camacho reacted in a heartbeat, swerving the massive coach over to the side and crunching into it. The lighter cargo van was easily pushed off course and skidded over to the side of the road, narrowly missing a high-speed impact with a parked truck.

Not put off, it came at them again, the lights of the city's streets shining dully on its grey hood as it pulled up close a second time. The side door slid open to reveal another armed man. He climbed half out and reached up for the blown-out window on the driver's side of the coach, but Camacho caught sight of him in the mirror and swerved again, crushing the man's legs between the coach's luggage compartment doors and the front wing of the cargo van. He screamed out in pain and tumbled under the wheels of the coach.

A third Savana pulled up on their other side. Scarlet and the rest of the team inside tried to fight them off, but were forced back when a man inside the cargo van raked the side of the bus with rounds from a submachine gun. The barrage continued, pinning them down and providing cover for more gangsters as they climbed up onto the roof.

"Joe!" Reaper called out.

The two men squared up to the gangsters, but Camacho swerved again, this time smashing into the third van and forcing it off the road. The men on the roof crouched to correct their balance and stay on board as the van crashed into a traffic light pole and juddered to a crumpled, steaming stop.

The other van speeded up on their other side, but Camacho was relentless. With an intersection speedily racing up to them, he took the initiative and attacked the cargo van, swerving into it harder than ever. An explosion of sparks spewed into the air as the coach pushed the smaller van off the road and sent it piling into a gas station at the side of the intersection.

The former CIA man watched as the cargo van smashed through one of the pumps and it disappeared inside a colossal fireball. A spark from the crash had ignited the fuel spilling out of the pump and now the entire gas station went up in one of the biggest explosions he had ever seen in his life.

The shockwave rocked the coach and sent Hawke and Reaper and the gangsters up on the roof tumbling over. A thin metal lip ran across the roof to channel rainwater away from the windows, and now the Englishman and the former legionnaire grabbed hold of it to stop themselves sliding off the bus. Gripping onto it for his life, Hawke felt a rumble as Camacho changed down and blew over the junction.

He pulled himself up to his knees just as Reaper was dusting himself off. "Where are our friends?"

The Frenchman shrugged. "Shockwave blew them off."

"Shame, I was starting to enjoy that, and... holy *crap*, look at the gas station."

"What is left of the gas station, mon ami. We'll be lucky if there are no civilian casualties in this explosion."

Hawke was thinking the same thing. He hadn't had time to see how many cars were parked up in the gas station, but it was so late there was a chance it was empty. He hoped for Camacho's sake it was. He knew how hard it was to bear the deaths of innocent people on his shoulders, but there was no time to think about it now. The final Savana had made it through the intersection and was closing in on them.

He followed Reaper back inside the coach where the rest of the stunned team were watching the fireball collapsing in on itself over the gas station now half a mile behind them.

"We still have company," Scarlet said. "So don't think about chillaxing just yet."

27

"Were leaving the main city, guys," Camacho called back.

"Keep going," Hawke said.

"But it's the opposite direction from the safehouse," said Zeke.

"I don't want any more gas stations going up tonight," Hawke said. "Not on our account anyway. We'll lead these clowns somewhere quieter and deal with them there."

The thirteen-litre biodiesel powertrain roared below them, as if they were riding some sort of giant beast, and cars swerved and blasted their horns, crashing off the road to avoid the speeding bus. The Mexican night flashed by in a blur, yellow sodium streetlights streaking past them as they raced east on the highway. An enormous sign above the road read TEXCOCO 20.

"What the hell is that?"

"Gas station."

"Are you freaking kidding me?" Zeke said. "No more gas stations."

Scarlet leaned down over Camacho's shoulder and took a closer look through the bullet-raked windshield. "And this one's blocking the entire road!"

"So we drive through it," Camacho said with a shrug. "Don't worry, we don't need gas."

Looking ahead, she saw cars lined up across the highway. "Every lane is blocked."

"No, the one on the far left is free, but there's a cop car there and something tells me they ain't going to appreciate me driving a bus through at breakneck speed. Am I going through it or what?"

"It's gridlock!" Scarlet said. "This place is worse than London."

"I heard that!" Hawke yelled out. "And I won't have my hometown impugned by the landed gentry, so shut it."

"Hardly landed gentry, darling," she purred.

"Cairo, your brother is a baron."

"Well, yes... there is that, I suppose."

Camacho said, "I need a decision on the gas station, Joe."

"Drive through," Hawke said. "We'll deal with the cops when we've sorted this lot out."

Camacho shrugged. He had nothing to lose. He pushed the pedal to the metal and aimed for the empty lane. The police officers reached for weapons on their hip holsters, but it all happened too fast. He doubted any of them had ever had to deal with a passenger coach racing toward them at top speed before.

The coach powered past the cars lining up in Lane 1 and tore through the boom gate under a hail of gunfire from the uniformed police. Their bullets barely had time to hit the bus, pinging off the metal coachwork into the night.

Hawke peered over the rear seats and saw the same officers dive for cover as the GMC cargo van ripped through the empty lane in pursuit of them. Some of the men in the first van leaned out the open side-door and fired on the police, driving them inside behind their cruiser, but then one of the cops got a shot off and took out the Savana's rear tire.

It exploded and sent the van swerving over the central reservation towards the oncoming traffic in the westbound lane. Clipping the hood of a semi-trailer truck carrying a full load of oil, the Savana stood no chance. It spun around like a toy and tipped over, scraping on its side in a shower of sparks until slamming to a stop in a ditch at the side of the road.

"Looks like we're out of danger," Scarlet said, dusting off her hands. "For now, at least."

"Only if we dump this coach." Hawke watched out of the rear window as police cars swarmed around the upturned cargo van. "Because the boys in blue over there are going to want to breathalyse Jack, at the very least."

Scarlet rolled her eyes. "Let's get to the safehouse. Then we can work out how to find Lea and Ryan and make a start on tracking down the supervirus vials. Time's getting on. We now have less than twenty-three hours before the supervirus is released."

Zeke said two words that chilled everyone. "Tick tock."

Hawke checked his watch. "Yeah, and it's twenty-two hours and fifty-three minutes precisely. We need a back road, Jack, and in a hurry. Then we'll dump this thing and get hold of something a little more city-friendly."

"On it." Camacho changed down and signalled to leave the highway.

"We're headed into a shitstorm, everyone," Hawke said. "The biggest shitstorm we've ever faced."

And with those words hanging in the air, Jack Camacho turned off the highway and headed into the night.

CHAPTER FIVE

Along with just two other men, the Dove held the fate of the world in his hands. It was a heavy burden and a great responsibility, and even if Barbosa and Rodrigues failed in their missions, he would surely deliver his, lock, stock and barrel. This filthy, vermin-infested, shit-heap of a world had given him nothing but an eyeful of spit, and now it was payback time.

He felt no guilt. Looking out from the bedroom balcony across the skyline of the city he was soon to annihilate, he felt nothing but excitement. If life closed every door in your face, then why not slam everyone else's door shut, too? He smiled at the thought, then heard a voice shouting at him.

"Hey, why don't you come down and join the party?"

He looked over the balcony and saw El Jefe on a sumptuous inflatable pool chair in the middle of a vast guitar-shaped swimming pool. Since his arrival at the Mexican gang boss's mansion he had been impressed and mildly disgusted by the ostentatious display of wealth all around him. The giant Les Paul guitar swimming pool crawled over the line into pure tastelessness.

"I'm on my way, Ramiro," he called down. "I need a shower first. It was a long flight."

"No problem, my friend."

"I presume your men have already delivered the packages?"

El Jefe laughed. "Yes, of course. Hurry – we have an even longer night ahead of us. Tonight, we blow a hole through the heart of the Mexico City elite and leave a message that no one screws with El Jefe."

So he thought, the Dove said to himself as he wandered back inside the bedroom. Ramiro Loza was a slug of man, but he had his uses. One of them was being able to supply an endless number of hard-nosed thugs and gangsters to deliver the vials to the locations specified by Zamkov. The other was being stupid enough to believe the cases holding the vials contained nothing more than regular bombs, designed to send the city into a terror-charged panic and raise El Jefe's profile as the nation's most dangerous criminal.

When he finished drying off and changed into his bespoke white shirt, he stepped back into the bedroom, strapped on his gold Rolex and made his way down the impressive spiral staircase. There was, after all, a party raging downstairs, and since Loza's men delivered the vials to their secret locations, it would almost certainly be the last party on earth for a very long time indeed.

*

To Francisco Rodrigues, nothing mattered anymore. His colleague in Mexico was probably still fast asleep, dreaming of the destruction to come and mankind's brilliant new dawn, but here on his balcony in the Hotel Crillon, the magnificent beauties of Paris's Eighth Arrondissement stretched out before him in the real dawn, a glorious golden dawn.

And yet he felt nothing but rage and hate.

It had always been like this, and he knew why. A happy soft-focus childhood ended in a hammer blow the day his father came home and told the family he was leaving. He had met another woman and they were going to live together. He moved out within a week, and his mother cried for a month. Things had never been worse in his short life.

Then Héctor moved in.

On the surface, Héctor Fuentes was a good man. On paper, he ticked all the right boxes. He owned his own banana export company in Panama City and worked long hours to support his new family. He drove a Porsche Boxster and bought his mother the Mercedes she had always dreamed of. He asked them to live in his mansion, in a gated community in Buenaventura.

And he drank.

He drank so hard sometimes, he could barely talk. He raged and cursed and smashed furniture over. He kicked dents in the refrigerator and the dishwasher. When he lost twenty thousand balboas gambling on a boxing match, he wrenched the plasma screen off its wall mounts and threw it around the front room in a spittle-flecked fury until it was in pieces.

And they were the good times. When torrential rain reduced the quality of local crops, the price of his bananas was cut by two thirds. Then the real storm blew in. Francisco cowered in his bedroom, forced to listen to his mother being beaten so hard by Héctor he thought he would kill her. She screamed and cried and tried to fight back but was no match for her powerful husband.

One day, he broke her arm. Driving his broken wife and her son to the local emergency department, he told them both that she had fallen down the stairs in the pool house. If they diverged from the story, he would kill them both.

Francisco prayed her mother would tell the doctors what had really happened; that their lives were tormented by a drunken, enraged monster, a bully who was weak around other men, but who liked to beat women. When she reported the accident, it turned out she had fallen down the pool house steps.

A much older Francisco stepped out onto his balcony and received Paris like Tiberius looking over Palatine Hill. He lit a cigar. He watched the traffic trundling around the Place de la Concorde. He felt the cool, autumn air on his face. No cold like this in Panama. He shivered, but drew comfort from the burning cigar, the warmth of the smoke in his mouth and its fragrant, earthy smoke.

More memories drifted up to him through that expensive smoke.

After Héctor had hospitalized his mother for the second time and started slapping him around as well, he thought about running away, but fate intervened. When the Panamanian National Police smashed their front door down and raided the place, it turned out Héctor had been defrauding the government of millions of balboas. They arrested him and dragged him out of the house kicking and screaming. Deals were struck and strings were pulled, but Héctor still wound up receiving a ten-year sentence.

Then, Francisco and his dear mamá had finally moved out to their own place. Modest but safe, yet the damage was done. Years of abuse had taught Francisco the truth about humanity. He didn't blame people; they were merely apex predator primates who would do anything to protect themselves.

But this time, nothing could protect them – not from Eschaton. He glanced over his shoulder at the matte aluminum medical box and studied it with respect. Behind it, in the corner of the room, an expensive plasma screen was showing a short videotape of the Chinese and North Korean presidents shaking hands.

The world thought these men were powerful, he thought with a laugh. Wrong. Francisco Rodrigues was more powerful than either of them. He was more powerful than even the American president, because inside that small metal box were vials of a supervirus so mighty, its release would mean the end of the human race.

Not only was he going to release the filth inside those vials and poison the whole world, but he was going to enjoy it. His dear mama was long-dead now, and he had no cares for his absent father. Imagining Héctor straining for his last breath made him glow with excitement. Héctor was still alive, and now in the coffee business, but not for too much longer.

He sucked on the cigar and walked back inside the room, closing the ornate double-doors on the outside world and falling down on the sumptuous bed. France24 was still on the television, this time telling the people of France that a storm was on the way.

You have no idea, he thought, and closed his eyes to dream of a clean, new world.

*

Antonio Barbosa looked through the window of his Hong Kong hotel and wondered how many people were walking the streets far below. Thousands, clearly. Tens of thousands was a better guess. Tens of thousands on every street at any time. Walking to every part of the city, to all points of the compass. Not a single one of them knew what was inside the little aluminum box on his table.

Would the others deploy their vials? This had preyed on the mind of the gang boss from El Salvador a great deal. Maybe, he thought, this was all some kind of trick cooked up by the insane raw meat-gobbling Russian.

Maybe, it was a set-up. Maybe, when he opened the box it would explode like some sort of high-tech letter bomb.

Get a grip, Toño. Zamkov might be a megalomaniac, but above all he was a tech-geek. What business would he have creating such an elaborate set-up just to kill Toni Barbosa? He hated to admit it, but he just wasn't important enough to be of any concern to a man like the Butcher. Sure, he ran some violent gangs across the country and things got nasty sometimes; in the whole of Latin America, only Venezuela was more violent and dangerous than El Salvador.

Some of things he had done...

Jesús, mi Señor y Redentor, yo me arrepiento de todos los pecados que he cometido hasta hoy

Forgive me Jesus, for all the sins I have committed up until today...

Good, but would he forgive for him what he was going to do tonight?

He looked down at his arms, covered in gang tattoos. Blue scratches and lines, some fresh and vivid, others old and faded, but each one an important part of his violent and brutal past. His rise to the top of the gang and the pain he meted out to people, sometimes innocent, to let them all know he was the boss, was a long time ago. So was his arrest, and the twenty-one years he spent in the Penal de Ciudad Barrios, usually reserved exclusively for members of the notorious MS-13 gang.

He thought about this release from the prison. His chance meeting with the Dove, and the ensuing introduction to Zamkov. The money he paid an old man like him couldn't be turned down. And then the chance to live like a king in a world swept clean of the ultimate parasites, humanity.

He smashed another neat vodka down the hatch. He'd ordered three bottles to his room upon arrival and was already halfway through the first. Outside, the afternoon was slowly turning to evening, and the good people of Hong Kong were preparing for another crazy, neon night. One of their last, he mulled with little emotion.

But not his. His life was just beginning. Activation of the timer would reveal the location of Zamkov's secret base, and arrangements would be made to get there while the supervirus was starting its long, winding journey into the heart of the planet's most destructive lifeform.

The Russian had told him there would be no one left alive within three weeks, and when he leaned over his balcony and watched the teeming city, he wondered exactly what that might be like. No movement, no noise, just cars abandoned on the road, corpses being picked clean by birds. The sound of the wind blowing through the skyscrapers.

Stillness everywhere, and competition nowhere. No more fighting to survive, just a world of plenty for a few hand-picked survivors. When the dead had rotted away, the entire world would be a playground of limitless choices and pleasures. He lifted the bottle to his lips, took another shot of vodka and began to think about where he might like to live in Zamkov's brave, new world.

CHAPTER SIX

When Clive Hudson had agreed with Scarlet to form a new team this was not what he'd had in mind. Bravo Troop was supposed to be devoted to hunting down long-lost relics and treasures from around the world, both ancient and modern.

Things had gotten off to a great start with the successful discovery of the infamous Nazi gold train during the Seven Angels mission, and Scarlet's brother, Sir Spencer Sloane was already talking about another mission in Mexico that they were excited about.

But Zamkov's Eschaton supervirus was a very different kind of nemesis.

As a former major in the SAS and, at one point, Scarlet's commanding officer, Hudson was more than up for the challenge, and yet the biowarfare element of the operation unsettled him, putting him on edge. That stuff had always freaked him out more than good old-fashioned guns, bullets and bombs. They could be dodged if you were fast enough, but how did you escape something in the air that you couldn't even see? That you didn't even know had infected you until it was too late?

"Coffee, boss."

He turned and saw the man-mountain known to the world as Sergeant Eddie 'Mack" Donald standing in the aisle of their chartered Citation. The ageing Scotsman was gripping two cups of coffee in his gnarled, tattooed hands.

"Thanks, Mack." Hudson took one of the coffees. "The beard's an improvement, by the way."

"I'll say it is," Danny Plane said. The young former SAS trooper looked smugly over to his old friend and grinned smugly. "Now we can't see his face."

Mack sat down opposite Danny and took a slow sip of coffee. "Same ol' bawbag you always were, Plane. About as funny as a day at the dentist."

"He loves you really," Kyra said.

Kyra Harpenden was stretched out on the leather couch running along the aircraft's starboard side. Until she had spoken, Hudson had thought she was asleep. Unlike the rest of the British team, Kyra lived in Washington, having already made a long and tiring flight across the Atlantic to join up with the rest of them.

"Feels weird without Cairo," Danny said, more serious this time. "And what was the name of that bloke of hers?"

"Jack Camacho," Hudson said. "Former CIA."

"I've worked with Cairo plenty of times," the unpredictable young man said. "But not met old Jonny Macho yet."

Kyra sat up on the couch and opened her eyes. Holding Danny's gaze, she gave him a withering look. "I wouldn't call him that if I were you. He has some moves."

"Yeah?" Danny grinned. "I got some moves, too. How old is this geezer, then?"

"Fifties, I'd say," Hudson said.

Danny waved his hands to dismiss any notion of Camacho being harder. "Pfft, he ain't got nothing on a strong, handsome young bloke like me. I could run rings around him with my head up my arse."

"I'd like to see that." Kyra arched an eyebrow. "On second thoughts, scratch that from the record."

"If you talk to him like that," Mack said in a low grumble, "then that's exactly where your head will end up, young Danny."

Danny rolled his sleeve up to reveal a tattoo of the SAS winged dagger. "See that?"

Mack tipped his head to one side and sighed. "We've all got one of them, Danny."

"No, serious now," Danny protested. "Do you *see* it?"

"We all see it," Hudson said. "And I do *not* have one of them, Sergeant Donald."

"Aye, well that's cause you're a fuckin' Rupert, but I want you to know I forgive you for that."

Hudson said nothing, sipping his coffee.

"Still not being heard, people," Danny said, wandering over to Kyra. "Do *you* see this tattoo?"

"Yes, what about it?"

Having got everyone's attention, Danny rolled his sleeve back down and sat down again. "Well, it fuckin' hurt and I'm not having another one."

Laughter filled the cabin, and when it had died down, Danny spoke again, raising a hand and making it tremble. "And please don't tell Jonny Macho what I said. He'll beat me up. I just know it."

*

The Raiders were an experienced team of extraction and rescue specialists. Hired by some of the wealthiest people in the world to retrieve stolen artefacts, treasures or even kidnapped loved ones, there were no challenges they couldn't rise to. Their last mission, the retrieval of the ancient Book of Thoth from Cleopatra's tomb had been mostly successful and led to their being hired by the enigmatic Ezra Haven and his expansive spy hub, Titanfort.

As the Boeing 747 banked to line up with Hong Kong International Airport, their leader, Jed Mason, recalled the mission with mixed emotions. A former British army officer and army boxing champion, Mason had travelled to Hong Kong many times before, but never tired of seeing the jumbles and stacks of buildings and skyscrapers nestling among the subtropical peninsulas and steamy islands.

He wondered if he had done the right thing in agreeing with Ezra to assist the ECHO team by tracking down Antonio Barbosa and his deadly cargo. It wasn't that he was frightened; neither he nor anyone else on his team could be accused of that, especially after what they had gone through in Egypt. What had made him question it was the brutal death of one of their own at the end of that mission.

Virgil Lehman was a good friend and essential member of the team, and he had been shot dead by the enemy in Egypt with the end of the mission in sight. Mason had to consider not only the impact of his murder on the rest of the team, but also how the young New Yorker's absence might affect their efficiency. What if they just weren't ready for another mission like this?

Someone could get killed, he thought. That's what. They had all suffered massively after the death of Virgil, and facing the young man's parents at his funeral was not something Jed Mason ever wanted to do again.

"Woah."

Startled by the sound of her voice, Mason turned and looked at Zara. "What's up?"

Zara Dietrich, the hard-worn former LAPD cop, peered down at the foreign city through the airliner's tiny window. "Never been here before. Looks crazy."

"It's a lot of fun," Mason said.

"You need to speak Chinese or something?"

"Not at all. English will get you through most situations."

"*Most* situations, sure," she said in her usual cocky way. "But what if I'm caught by police standing over a dead body with a smoking gun in my hand?"

"Zara…"

"I'm serious. That shit happens to me."

"Me too," Caleb said. The six-foot-two former US Army Ranger from Arizona stretched in his seat and grumbled about the lack of leg room. "I attract that shit like nails to a magnet."

"Then you need to change your polarity and start attracting peace and happiness instead."

They turned and looked at Milo Risk, smugly smiling with his eyes closed, just across the aisle. In the intervening months since seeing each other, the young man had grown his hair long and was looking more like an old rocker than a young IT specialist.

"He's right." Ella Makepeace was the team's voice of reason. When she spoke, they usually listened, but this time she got a different response.

"You can't believe all that shit about sending out positive mental energy?" Caleb said.

"I actually do."

"Me too," Zara said. "I learned it at a monastery once."

"Is *that* what you were doing in Japan?" Ella prompted.

Zara nodded. "Yeah, but I'm not convinced it works. I'm thinking about asking the monks for a refund."

Mason chortled. It wasn't what the team were talking about that amused him, more that they had gelled together so easily after such a long time apart. Technically, they worked for Ezra Haven now, at Titanfort, but the truth was a little different. Most of them never saw each other from one month to another. It was also good to see that Virgil's death wasn't stopping them from making jokes and getting along. That was important on a mission like this.

He checked his watch and changed it to local time. It was late afternoon in this part of the world, and he wanted to get checked into their hotel, cleaned up, fed and ready to go before nightfall. As he remembered it from previous trips, the sun usually sank into the sea just before six in the evening at this time of year.

"Everyone ready to get moving?" he asked.

"Not right now," Milo said. "For one thing, if I try and leave this aircraft at this exact moment in time, I think it might cause the other passengers a certain amount of consternation."

"All right, very good," Mason said. "You know what I mean."

"We're all ready, Jed," Ella said, scowling at Milo.

"Good, because we've got less than two hours before nightfall and we need to get out on the streets as fast as we can. We don't know where Barbosa is yet, and you all heard what Ezra said in the briefing. If Zamkov gets any word that the authorities are aware of the threat, he might detonate all the vials."

"And that right there," Caleb said, "is not only the end of this mission, but the end of our lives, and the lives of everyone else on this planet."

"So we have to keep this to ourselves," Mason said. "I guess the timers are set to give his men time to deploy the vials and get safely away, but he *could* release the supervirus at the drop of a hat if he thinks there's any chance of the authorities finding them and closing them down."

"So, it's down to us," Zara said. "How reassuring."

"We'll do it," Mason said confidently. "There's not just a world to save, but something more important than even that."

Caleb smirked. He knew what Mason was talking about. So did Zara and Ella, but Milo looked confused. "What could be more important than saving the world?"

"Proving our reputation as even better than the ECHO team and Bravo Troop," Mason said. "Not only are we going to find the vials in Hong Kong, but we're going to find them first and with less fuss and bother, too."

Zara smiled. "I'm liking the introduction of mindless competition in this, Jed."

"Me too," Ella said. "It's unprofessional, but yeah."

"Milo?" Mason asked.

"Oh, count me in. If it means beating Bale's arse then I'm all for it. After our conference call I got the distinct impression that dude thinks he's better than me."

"A better nerd than you?" Zara said. "Never."

"Thanks, Z. I knew I could count on you."

"And I know I can count on all of you," Mason said. "Even Caleb, providing he gets enough sleep before the big fight. Right, Cal?"

The older man's heavy snoring was the only reply.

CHAPTER SEVEN

The comfort of the Mexico City safehouse hadn't lasted long. After a long drive around the city in a stolen SUV, they had arrived at the empty haven, taken showers and selected a mini-arsenal of weapons. But Hawke and the others were missing Lea and Ryan badly, and making contact with Sooke and taking another briefing from him had changed the mood starkly.

We don't know where they are.

The words had hit Hawke like an ice pick through his heart. What they had thought was the worst crisis they had ever faced had just got much worse. Maybe it had been reckless, but like the others he had presumed Sooke would be able to requisition a satellite or bribe an old MI6 friend or do something, anything to find where the kidnappers had taken them.

"What else does he say?" Hawke asked.

Scarlet was on the phone to Sooke, and now she cupped the receiver and spoke in low tones to everyone in the toom. "Some of his work has paid off, but only partly. They know the identities of the men who snatched Lea and Ryan. They're called Las Serpientes, or the Serpents. They're Mexico City's most dangerous gang. Involved in everything from people trafficking to drug smuggling and contract killings, not even the Mexican Government has dared to confront them."

"Great," Zeke said.

"It gets worse," Scarlet said. "No one knows where the Serpents are holding Lea and Ryan, and... wait, sorry Orlando, I'm back."

Hawke sighed. This was like cutting the head off the Hydra to find another two had grown back in its place. The seriousness of the situation could hardly be overstated, and glancing at the faces of his friends told him they all knew it, too.

Hawke walked to the window and checked his watch. After chasing the cargo vans through the city, they now had only twenty-two hours to locate and destroy the Eschaton virus or millions of people across the Americas would be infected with the lethal pathogen within days. Two weeks after that, the entire western hemisphere would look like something out of an apocalypse movie.

And if Hudson and Mason failed in Paris and Hong Kong, that movie would be showing not just in the Americas, but across the entire world. If that weren't bad enough, Kamala was being held by Zamkov in an unknown location and Alex, Brandon and President Brooke were still being held captive by Faulkner on Tartarus. His head spun when he realized it had now been five days since their arrest and detention.

In the reflection of the window, he saw Scarlet cut the call with Sooke and toss her phone down on the bed. She looked exhausted. Frayed nerves and sore, red eyes. Was she even eating these days? He couldn't remember the last time he'd had a proper meal. When was hers?

"What else did he say?" he asked her.

"It gets worse, Joe. Titanfort don't have much about what's going on either," she said. "They know the Dove landed here a few hours ago and that he drove straight to the home of Ramiro Loza, otherwise known as…"

"El Jefe," Camacho said. "The Chief."

Scarlet frowned. "Right – you know him?"

Camacho frowned. "Is that what you think of me, Cairo Sloane?"

"You know what I mean. Do you know *of* him?"

"That's a different question, and the answer is yes. El Jefe is one of Mexico's most wanted drug lords, and you're not going to like this next bit."

"He's the boss of the Serpents?" Hawke asked.

"Got it in one."

"Bloody hell," Scarlet said. "Loza must be connected to the Dove and Zamkov."

"But why the hell would he be involved with a plan to wipe out humanity?" Nikolai asked. "This does not sound like the actions of a gang boss."

Camacho nodded. "Kolya's right. Loza is wild, dangerous and unpredictable. He was born in 1966 and inherited a vast criminal empire from his father, who was shot and killed by a rival gang twenty years ago. There's a five million dollar bounty on his head offered by both the US and Mexican governments. But he's never shown any interest in the kind of psychopathic insanity required to take out an entire global population. He likes power games, fighting with other gang lords. The supervirus doesn't fit his profile at all."

"Tell us more, Jack," Hawke said.

Camacho shrugged. "He's well-known in the underworld for his extortion and kidnapping, not to mention his predilection for disposing of his victims in a concrete factory, but what is less well-known is that he's decided to take out all his rivals and expand his empire."

"Which might explain why he's hosting the Dove tonight," Scarlet said.

"Where is El Jefe's place?" Hawke asked.

"It's a colonial mansion in a district called Lomas de Chapultepec."

"Which is highly desirable and very exclusive," Camacho said. "We're talking twenty-thousand square foot houses with seven bedrooms, ten bathrooms and luxury swimming pools. That sort of thing."

Lexi pouted. "And my mummy told me crime would never pay."

Hawke, who had been peering through a greasy, smudged window looking out on the rear of the property, suddenly got everyone's attention. "Heads up. Looks like Sooke's man is on the scene."

Moments later, a short, overweight man in a badly fitting suit opened the back door and stepped through into the room where they were sitting. Lexi had already drawn her freshly selected SIG Sauer and taken up a position behind the door, but when Scarlet recognized the man, she stood down.

"Alby!"

The man's tired, unshaven face suddenly lit up. "Cairo? Is that really you?"

"In the flesh, darling."

As the former SAS officer gave the portly man a tight hug, Hawke glanced at the rest of the team and shrugged. "I take it you two know each other?"

"We do indeed," she said. "This is Alberto Castillo, a former CNI officer."

"CNI?" Nikolai asked.

"Centro Nacional de Inteligencia," the man said with pride. "I'm pleased to meet you all."

Zeke whistled. "Cairo – you know everyone, dammit. I guess you met him during some cool undercover operation in Acapulco or something?"

"As matter of fact," Castillo said, almost apologetically, "we met at a casino in Cancún."

Cairo smirked. "You lost a ton that night, Alby."

"And, as usual, you almost broke the house."

They laughed, then Castillo made a quick call on his phone. Slipping the phone back in his pocket, he said, "I have a colleague waiting out in the car. I'm retired, but Franco is still in the Agency. He can help us."

The man stepped in through the rear door moments later.

"Please, everyone, this is Manuel Franco."

The man smiled goofily and gave a casual wave at the packed room full of awkward fugitives. He was the same height as Castillo but stick-thin and dressed in a similar suit. When he saw them standing side by side, Zeke chuckled. "All you two need are a couple of bowler hats and you're good to go."

Castillo and Franco looked at each other with expressions of confusion.

"Guess you guys never got Laurel and Hardy down here, right?"

"He means," Scarlet said, scowling at the Texan, "thank you both for coming out tonight, and he also apologises for being a stupid berk."

Zeke's broad, toothy grin suddenly appeared. "I don't know what the hell that means."

"Berk," Scarlet said. "It's Cockney rhyming slang, darling."

"Still don't get it."

"Apples and pears – stairs, Barney Rubble – trouble, and so on."

Now, nearly everyone was confused.

She sighed. "Look, there was a famous fox hunt in Berkshire, England, and so Berkshire hunt…"

"Yes, thanks for that, Cairo," Hawke stepped in. "I can see why you chose the SAS and not the diplomatic service. Now, getting to business."

Scarlet arched an eyebrow and pulled out her cigarettes. "Their loss, I'm sure."

"Yes, to business," Castillo said, pulling up a seat. When he collapsed down on it, his entire body seemed to sag, and he gave a long sigh of relief as the chair creaked. "Orlando gave us a full briefing, and we have agreed to help you, and also, reluctantly, not to involve the Mexican authorities."

"Thanks, Alby."

"This is not an easy decision, especially for Franco, but we believe it is the right one, and we also believe we can deal with this problem quietly. As a matter of fact, we should be able to move much faster without the Agency on our backs."

"Do you have new information about Lea and Ryan?" Hawke asked.

"Sorry, but so far, only what you already know. They were snatched by members of El Jefe's gang, *las Serpientes*, and taken to an unknown location somewhere out of the city. We believe they were snatched to be used as bartering chips to keep you away from the supervirus."

"Out of the city?" Hawke said, feeling the fear rising. "That's new."

"Then I have already been of some assistance, but there it ends."

Camacho squeezed his right hand into a fist. "Bastards! They're using them as human shields, making us back off away from the supervirus or they'll kill them!"

Castillo gave a sad nod. "You have it."

"None of that's going to happen," Hawke said flatly. "First, we're not backing away from the mission, and second, we're not leaving Lea and Ryan in the hands of those scumbags."

Scarlet blew out a long column of fragrant, blue smoke and leaned back on the table beside the window. Three lean lines of cold moonlight broke through the venetian blinds and striped her face. "Are you thinking what I'm thinking, darling?"

"Always," Hawke said. "We break into two teams. Team One is going after the supervirus and Team Two is getting our people back and teaching the Serpents what happens when you piss about with the world's best special ops team."

"Hell yeah!" Zeke said. "I like fighting talk."

The burst of enthusiasm quickly settled down when Hawke asked Castillo if they had any way of breaking into the dark underbelly controlled by the Serpents. "After all," he said. "We know the Dove has already met with El Jefe, so as far as both the supervirus and Lea and Ryan are concerned, all roads lead to Rome."

Castillo nodded, but looked doubtful. "Yes, and both of those roads are guarded by the Serpents."

"But how do we get to those roads?" Nikolai asked.

Castillo had an answer. "We know the kidnapping was arranged by a man named Vicente Alonso."

"That's also new," Hawke said.

Castillo sighed. "You might have met him already – he has a tattoo of a skull on his face."

"We had the pleasure, yes," Scarlet said. "Do we have a lead on him?"

"Si," Castillo said. "Much of El Jefe's wealth comes from a vast empire of nightclubs and bars that he runs all over the country. One of those nightclubs is called El Armario, or The Locker, and yes, it's a real meat market."

"Don't tell me," Zeke said. "Old Deathmask just happens to work there?"

"He does more than work there. Vicente Alonso runs the entire club for Loza. He is the best chance we have of tracking down the location of your kidnapped friends, and if you're going to find him anywhere in this crazy city, then you will find him in El Armario."

"That's Team Two sorted then," Hawke said. "I'll lead it, and I want Lexi, Kolya and Zeke with me. Three should be enough to take out the Serpents."

"You must also take one of us with you," Castillo said.

"No problem. That makes four."

"I'll go," Franco said. "I've been wanting to nail that son of a bitch Alonso for years."

"Then now is your chance," Zeke said.

"What about the vials?" Hawke asked. "Do we have any lead on those?"

This time, Castillo was less confident. "Yes and no, my friends. All we know is what I have already told you, which is that when the Dove landed, he was picked up by Loza's driver, Gustavo Cavazos, and driven back to his mansion. We do not know if they have been deployed or not, and certainly we have no idea of the locations they are using."

Scarlet stubbed out her cigarette. "Then let's get what we need straight from the horse's mouth."

"Agreed," Hawke said. "First, we need more than sidearms. This safehouse has a good armoury, so we need to raid it bigtime – machine pistols, grenades, ammo, duct tape, binoculars, you name it. Stuff your bags. Then I want Cairo leading Team One, which means Reap and Jack."

"And me," Castillo said, heaving his bulk up out of the seat.

Scarlet smiled. "And Alby," she said. "I'd never forget you, darling."

"Okay, we know what we're doing." Hawke smacked a fresh mag in the grip of his gun and slid it in his holster. "Let's get this thing on the road."

CHAPTER EIGHT

A sharp burning pain woke Lea from unconsciousness. The back and side of her skull was throbbing and it felt like bolts of electricity were crackling down her neck. She tried to reach up and rub her head, but her arms wouldn't respond. When she opened her eyes she saw why; both of her wrists were taped down to the arms of the chair she had been dumped in, and her ankles were taped to the legs of the chair.

Dazed, she looked around the room. It wasn't office space or industrial, but looked like part of a residential property. A blend of colonial wooden paneling and the pastoral artwork expressed in the décor, combined with a heavy silence outside the window made her think the place was rural, a ranch maybe, or some other kind of country property. But where, was anyone's guess. She just prayed they were still in Mexico.

She heard a groan. Turning to her right, she saw Ryan. He was in the same situation, with his arms and legs taped down to his chair and his head slumped forward. He was still out cold, dried blood caked around his nose and mouth. It looked like he had tried to resist after they knocked her out and been given a good beating for his trouble.

Keeping her voice to a low whisper, she called out to him. "Ry! Wake up!"

No response.

"Ryan!"

Another groan, and now his head started to lift up. "Where am I?"

"Some sort of ranch, I think."

"Damn, it feels like Reaper used my head as a boxing speed ball."

"I think they drugged us after they knocked us out."

Ryan tried to pull his hands free of the tape, but they were stuck tight to the wooden arms and wouldn't budge an inch. "No shit. I've got a very bad feeling about this, Lea."

She pushed back against a feeling of helplessness which had started to rise up when Ryan was talking. That kind of thinking wouldn't help either of them get out of here.

"Don't be stupid. We've been through worse, and at least we're together."

"We *were* together," he said.

"That's not what I meant, Ry. I mean we're *here* together, if the worst happens."

He let the words hang in the air and time seemed to slow down. After a long, sad silence, he said, "Why *did* we break up? It was so long ago I can hardly remember."

"You want to talk about that now?"

He shrugged. "I'm all dressed up with nowhere to go."

"We weren't a good fit, is all," she said. "I don't regret a minute of the time we were married."

"Liar."

Even now, she couldn't resist a smile. "All right, maybe there were some ups and downs."

"Some ups and downs? Our marriage was like being strapped into the Kingda Ka roller coaster, but for years instead of thirty seconds."

"Yeah, there is that."

Now, he gave a low, wistful laugh. "But the good times were great."

"They sure were," she said. "Both of them."

55

He laughed again. "Funny, but then we always could share a laugh."

They shared another long silence, but this one was easier. Lea thought back to what he had said about the roller coaster, and he was right, but there had been good times, just as he had also said. They were young when they met. Now, looking back, she knew they were too young. Their individual circumstances had flung them together, each of them vulnerable and hurting, and they had sought solace in each other, and found it.

Crazy, drunken nights out on the town and lots of friends had created a false impression of their relationship, but it had been enough to keep them together for many years. The inverted dynamic of her military background and his IT background had helped as well. For a long time, they made each other stronger, but then she outgrew him.

Not that she would ever tell him that.

And then she met Hawke. He was a much better fit. Even now, less than three hours since the kidnap at the airport, she missed him, and she worried about him.

Ryan finally broke the silence. "You think you'll have kids with Joe, then?"

"Maybe. He'd make a good father."

A long pause. "Yeah, he would."

"You'll find someone."

"Me?" He huffed out a bitter laugh. "I'm too much of a fuck up, Lea. You know that. It almost worked with Maria, but then she was taken away, too. I'm destined to go through this world a lonely man – and that's supposing we even get out of here."

Lea thought back to what Ryan had said about having a bad feeling about the situation. She felt the same, but that too, she would keep to herself. "Of course we're getting out of here. Joe might be able to shoot a bad guy off the top of a cable car from a thousand yards, but have you ever seen him trying to pay an electricity bill?"

"Funnily enough, no."

"He's hopeless. He needs me, and if…" She felt her voice waver, and stopped talking before she gave away her fears.

Ryan changed the subject. He was good like that, she thought. "You say you think this is some sort of ranch?"

"I think so, just from the way the place is decorated, plus we're right next to a window, and I know it's shuttered, but we'd hear something going on out there if we were in the city."

"I agree, but we're not too far out. We were at the airport just a few hours ago, so even if these guys drove like maniacs, we can't be that far away from the city, right?"

"Wrong. We could have been put on a plane. We were knocked out."

"Thanks for that."

"Just sayin'."

The quiet, sullen conversation was cut short when someone unlocked the door and booted it open. A man with another skull tattooed on his face walked into the room, silhouetted by a stark light in the hall behind him. At first, Lea thought it was the man they had seen at the airport, but now she saw he was someone else with a similar tattoo. Behind him were two other men, both holding handguns, but Skullmask was unarmed.

"Buenos noches," he said, and chuckled. "And welcome to Buena Vista Ranch. I hope you're enjoying your time here."

Lea braced herself, determined not to show any weakness. "Who are you?"

"I am Vicente Alonso," he said calmly. "I work for El Jefe. I help him run Las Serpientes, the most feared gang in Mexico."

"Why have you taken us?"

Alonso stepped forward. "You are bait."

Ryan said, "Bait? I don't understand."

Alonso sneered at him. "You don't have to understand. It's like I said – you are just a little bait fish. A little Mexican bonito."

He laughed and the men behind him joined in.

"Are you working for Nikita Zamkov?" Lea asked.

The joke ended. "Que?"

"Nikita Zamkov," she repeated, raising her voice. "The Butcher. Are you working for him?"

"I never heard of him in all my life, but he sounds interesting. The sort of man I could do business with. I work for Ramiro Loza... El Jefe!"

Lea's mind raced. How much did this man know? Did he know about the vials? Was he working for the Dove, and Zamkov, or just for this Loza? She tested the waters. "You must have a lot of family here in Mexico."

Alonso's face stretched into a grimace. "What damn business is it of yours if I have family here or not, *puta!*"

"Watch your mouth, Tattoo."

Ryan regretted the words as soon as they left his lips. Alonso stepped over to him and without saying a word, delivered the heaviest backhanded slap Lea had ever seen. The force of the impact knocked Ryan and the chair clean over and he crashed onto the floor.

"Ry!"

"The boy is out cold," Alonso said. "Now, why are you so interested in my family?"

Lea pulled herself together. Her only ally was unconscious, and the way his head had struck the flagstone floor, she had serious concerns he might have sustained a fractured skull or maybe something even worse. Now, the man with the tattooed face was leaning into her so close, their noses were almost touching.

She fought through the stench of cigars and tequila and foul breath and replied. "Because they're all going to die when those biobombs go off and spray their supervirus cargo all over the city."

The man straightened up, but as he rose to his full height, he reached out with his right hand and clenched her jaw. The grip was like iron, squashing her cheeks up until she was almost stopped from speaking.

"Que?"

"The little package you delivered for Loza," she said through the grip. "It comes from a man named the Dove who works for the Butcher. It contains a lethal biological pathogen that's going to wipe out not only the entire population of Mexico, but all of the Americas, and eventually the entire world."

He released his grip and pushed her head back. "Bullshit."

One of the men behind him spoke up. "What if she's telling the truth?"

"She's not telling the truth," he spat. "She's a lying *puta*, trying to get us to turn on each other." His eyes were still fixed on her. "A lying whore. They're simple bombs. Loza told me."

"We can't take the risk, Vicente!"

Alonso silenced the man with a raised hand, but she could see he was thinking through what had been said. "I'm going to leave you in the dark now, to cool off, and the next time you see me, I will find out whether you are lying or not. Believe me, I have ways of getting to the truth."

He walked across the room, slapped the light off and slammed the door. Lea felt a wave of terror tingling up her spine. "Ry? Are you all right?"

No response.

She was alone, and in near total darkness. She closed her eyes and prayed Joe Hawke knew where the Serpents had taken her, because for the life of her, she had no idea how she was going to get out of this one.

CHAPTER NINE

The son of a bitch base commander Blanchard was playing mind games. The last time he had spoken with him, the colonel had said he was going to force him to watch the torture of his daughter, Alex. They had dragged him, kicking and screaming all the way to Mr Mahoe's torture block, except when he got there, he saw no sign of his daughter. Instead, they had strapped him into the dental chair and Mahoe went to work on him.

On the third tooth extraction, it was obvious Brooke would not be coerced, and Blanchard ordered Mahoe to stop. The disappointed Hawaiian psychopath had thrown his tools down and pleaded with the colonel to let him remove the whole set of teeth, but Blanchard ordered him to stand down.

"Why did you tell him to stop?" Brooke had asked.

The Air Force officer sighed. "Dammit, Brooke, why don't you just confess? You think I want to do this to you?"

"You've changed your tune."

He shook his head. "Don't ever think that, Jack. I will obey my orders and do whatever it takes to get the confession."

"Then why stop Mr Happy Smile in mid-flow?"

"I wanted to give you a chance to think it over."

Brooke spat a wad of coppery blood into the little stainless-steel bowl at the side of the chair. "You know I'll never confess."

Blanchard drummed his hands on his knees. "I have a daughter, Jack. She's about the same age as Alex."

Brooke suddenly understood. "You don't want to let that maniac rip Alex's teeth out? Is that what you're trying to say?"

"I'm trying to get a confession out of you the easiest way I can. Jack, from one military guy to another, just make the damn video confessing to treason and then all this ends. Please, don't test me on this. Alex is the next stop, and this time I won't end the show at three teeth like I did today."

"You're a son of a bitch, Blanchard, but thanks for saving Alex from what I just went through."

"She'll go through a hell of a lot worse if you don't confess. I'm giving you a few more hours to consider it, and then I have to order Mahoe to torture her until you confess. The dental work is just the first course, Jack. I've seen what he can do, and it burns a scar on your mind."

It burns a scar on your mind.

In the darkness of Brooke's cell, the words echoed in his mind. How long ago had Blanchard told him that, anyway? He was starting to struggle with keeping time. Hours came and went like smoke in a cheap bar. Minutes meant even less.

He paced his cell, hands in pockets. He might not know what time it was, or even if his daughter was still alive, but one thing was for sure – these guys weren't bluffing. Faulkner was playing a deadly game and it was the kind where there could only ever be one winner. Right now, he was having fears for the first time that it might be his old rival after all.

He had to admit it to himself, but things were starting to look bleak. In the dark silence of his cell he closed his eyes and visualized Alex. It was hard to picture her anywhere other than right here on this god-forsaken base, alone and frightened. He curled his hands up into two tight fists and lashed out at the wall-mounted bed with his shoe, kicking it so hard he hurt his toe.

"Damn it, Jack!" he cursed under his breath and collapsed down on the bed.

His head was in his hands now and his only company was his own shadow. Maybe he should make the video confession and just tell Faulkner what he wanted to hear, and then—

Never. Not only would it be lying to the American people and the world, but he knew better than to trust a man like Davis Faulkner. There was no way that bastard would give either him or Alex freedom, even if he *did* make the false confession. He was just too dangerous to keep around, with too many friends in the wrong places. And saying he knew where the skeletons were was the understatement of the century.

He blew out a deep breath. Truth was, whether he confessed or not, neither he nor his daughter were getting out of this place alive. It wasn't hard to see the news. Former President and his daughter killed in accident. Former President and his daughter killed while escaping from detention center and killing guard. The possibilities were endless.

Faulkner could say what he wanted. He controlled the media. He decided what came out of the pipelines and what the world heard. What the world knew. Truth, after all, was a malleable thing, like modelling clay. It could be shaped and moulded to fit any agenda, and Faulkner was the sculptor.

He got up and started pacing again. Never before had he felt so weak and helpless. Things were as low as they could get.

And then he heard the key in the door. That dry, metal scraping sound he had learned to fear more than anything else in the world. When it opened, a pool of greasy light spilled down onto the floor of his cell, a soldier stepping into the middle it. His long shadow crossed the floor and stretched all the way to the far wall. There was another soldier behind him.

"Get up, Brooke. Blanchard has something to ask you."

Brooke leaned up on one elbow and twisted his head toward the guard. "Thanks, but no thanks. You tell the colonel I've already had one marriage and we all know how that ended."

The man moved into the cell and pulled him off the bed. Brooke crashed onto the floor but was unable to get to his feet before one of the soldier's boots smashed into his ribcage. He cried out in pain, but his anguish fell on deaf ears.

"Get on your feet and get out of this cell or I'm gonna let the guys come in here and beat the hell out of you."

Brooke obeyed, hobbling forward to the door with one hand wrapped around his bruised ribs. Glancing at the soldier's chunky diving watch, he saw it was just after nine in the evening, and something told him this was going to be a long, dark night.

*

Thousands of miles way in Mexico, Agent Cougar barely rested her left hand on the steering wheel as she cruised away from the airport. Her right hand was twiddling the tuner on the hired GMC Sierra's radio. A lot of it was talk radio, and after so many years, her high school Spanish only helped her catch the odd word here and there. She'd really have to brush up on it before she moved Matty and herself down to live with Justin in the villa in Los Cabos.

Los Cabos.

The words meant more than just a part of the Baja Peninsula. Dangerous but exciting, it meant liberation from a life of misery and suffering. It meant a new beginning for her and Matty. It meant never having to do the bidding of Pegasus and the men behind him, hidden in their smoke-filled rooms. It meant the end of killing people she had never known or knew the first thing about.

Would a new life in Los Cabos bring her redemption? She thought just maybe it might. If she stayed on the straight and narrow. If she looked after Matty and Justin and did the right thing from now on. No more violence. If she stopped inflicting pain on others, then would she stop feeling it inside her?

She squinted and turned her head away from the bright lights of a row of vehicles in the other lane, catching sight of her sniper kit down in the passenger footwell to her right. It was relatively compact considering what it could do to a person. One precision rifle, a handful of optical scopes and field glasses, her monocular, and the box of ammunition.

Each one of the bullets in that little box was engraved with the name of its victim. She'd had the idea when she was young and cocky. She wouldn't think of something like that now, but it had become her calling card, and more, it had become a ritual. A superstition. Cougar never missed, and she half-believed this was because of the engraved names.

She blinked and rubbed her eyes, focussing on the road ahead.

All this would soon be behind her. She had only a handful of men and women to take out before the contract was delivered, and then she could walk away without any loose strings keeping her tied to men like Garcetti and

Faulkner. They'd miss her. She was the best there was in the business and they all knew it.

She guessed they'd find someone else. There was aways someone ready to step into Number One's shoes. She thought maybe Paul Garrett or Gary Schultz might get the top job, but neither were anywhere near as good as she was. She cracked a coke and took a sip. None of this shit was her problem anymore.

She had a way out. She had a chance. Just one shot. She had a box of high-velocity rounds sitting beside her, and a list of names in her head that would stay there until the job was done.

And then, she could fly into the sunset with Justin and her boy, and start over.

It was all she had ever wanted to do.

CHAPTER TEN

Zamkov felt her hands first, sliding around his waist, and then her chin on his shoulder. One of the hands went north, slipping under his shirt and gently brushing against his skin until reaching his chest. The other went south, sliding underneath his belt before stopping abruptly.

He really had to reprogram some of Valentina's etiquette protocols. Like all of his AI systems, she was able to write her own programs, but only within the boundaries he had already established. He also had to work on her body temperature. She still felt *wrong*. Too cold, and not soft enough. The artificial skin was still not quite there.

And of course, there was no breath. If she was the real Valentina, the one he had murdered in Moscow all those years ago, he would be able to feel her breath on his neck by now, but instead he felt nothing but the pressure of her robotic chin against his skin. Listening closely, he could hear the hum of her insides – processors, fans and discs. All of this had to change, and yet…

He had to confess, he found himself increasingly aroused by her presence so close to him, here in the master bedroom of Eschaton Base. Just the two of them, and a one hundred-foot-long window wall looking out on the expansive, snow-filled rift valley outside compound.

It was November, and that meant light twenty-four hours a day down here – a cold, pure, hard light bouncing off the sharp white landscape. Out there, nothing but a hell of frostbite and snow blindness, but in here, the warmth of the enormous central fireplace and the gentle adoration of Valentina Kiriyenko.

He considered the question he had wanted to ask her from the very first moment he had created her. He moved to say it, but the words froze in his throat. He had created Valentina with one thing in mind, but he was just too scared to ask her. Now, staring into her organic LED display eyes, he felt an instant connection to her soul. She had to have a soul, he told himself. She was alive. She thought for herself, she solved problems with her own solutions, and she knew she was alive. She even felt a kind of pain, at least, she knew when she was damaged.

He had to ask her. He leaned closer, and held her hands in his. He licked his lips. He swallowed, even though there was nothing to swallow. He looked away from her eyes and found a patch of floor to stare at. Studied the way the crisp Antarctica light hit the parquet tiles. The grain of the red oak and the sheen of the varnish.

Anything but ask her the question he feared to ask more than anything else.

"What is it?" she asked.

"Valentina, I have something to ask you."

"Yes, милый."

He gasped when he heard the word *Milyy*. It meant sweet, or sweetheart. Russians used it instead of darling, but he had never programmed her to say it. She had written it into her own vocabulary and decided on her own that it was an appropriate way to address him.

"You called me sweetheart," he said.

"That's what you are to me."

Hydraulics whined as she moved a hand up to his thigh, and his arousal returned.

"And you are my милая."

Milaya. The same word, but addressing a woman.

68

Her skin blushed, but it was uneven, with a heavier rouge on the right cheek. He had to improve that, too.

"What do you want to ask me, sweetheart?"

"I..." the words wouldn't come. He felt his throat constrict. "I wanted to ask you something very important. It means a great deal to me."

She smiled. The smile was good. He was proud of her perfect smile. "What? You can ask me anything."

Yes, he could ask her anything, but it was the answer that kept him up at nights. What if she said no? He could program her specifically to say yes, but that would render her reply totally meaningless. If she said yes, it had to come from her heart, from her soul. From her own self-written AI neural network. She had to *mean* it for it to be real.

He leaned in to kiss her, but stopped. Instead, he stroked a trembling hand over the smooth artificial skin, the gentle slope of her synthetic shoulder. Pulling her top down to reveal more of his creation, she gasped and looked into his eyes.

"You felt that?" he asked.

She looked confused. "Of course."

He was pleased. The sensor upgrade was a success. The new optical waveguides he had incorporated inside her, just beneath the skin, had worked like a dream. The slightest pressure on the skin had severed special elastomeric optics and triggered her sensors. The touch, the most tender and loving of brushes, had been felt.

He felt almost overwhelmed; she really was almost identical to the real thing.

And now, he wanted to get closer, to feel her more, and to kiss her.

He wanted even more than that.

He wanted to—

"Sir."

Yakov's voice was speaking to him from across the room. He hurriedly removed his hand from Valentina's shoulder and looked at him. Was he imagining it, or was that a look of jealously in Yakov's eyes? That might have to be checked out.

"What is it?"

"Update from the Dove in Mexico City, sir."

"Thank you, Yakov."

Zamkov got to his feet and activated a giant monitor with voice-control. Slowly, a vast plasma screen descended from a slit in the ceiling, blocking part of the window wall and greatly reducing the light in the room. It flickered to life to reveal the Dove's perfect, tanned face and his bright white teeth.

"You have something to report, my loyal friend?"

"Things are going well." The words rolled off his tongue like honey. "El Jefe is reliable and has provided many men to help us. We have made good progress, and his men have deployed the supervirus in the city's most popular areas exactly as you ordered."

A wave of excitement rushed to Zamkov like a tsunami. "You have done well. What about ECHO?"

"I'm handling them. Loza's men snatched two of the team and if ECHO get in our way, they will execute one of them and dump the body in public as a warning."

"Good, very good."

"Is there word from Paris and Hong Kong?"

"No further updates than when we spoke last, my friend."

Valentina rose from the side of the double bed and sauntered across the room. Standing beside Zamkov, she reached down and held his hand. Zamkov relished the touch. Maybe the body temperature was more realistic than he had thought.

Almost identical.

Without prompting, she focused her LED eyes on the screen and spoke to the Dove. "Can El Jefe be trusted?"

The question surprised both men. The Dove frowned and his eyes narrowed. He looked irritated at being questioned by the robot. Zamkov took it another way. To him, Valentina asserting herself in this way was yet another step forward for her.

"Well?" the Russian said to the Dove. "She asked you a question. Answer her."

She squeezed his hand, and the Dove leaned back in his chair. "Yes, I believe he is loyal."

"Is he suspicious of the true meaning of the Eschaton mission?" Valentina asked.

"Not at all. He believes the boxes contain a new type of high explosive, and that when they go off they will simply explode like bombs. The chaos of multiple terror attacks across the city excites him greatly."

"And what would happen if he ever found out what was really inside them?" she asked.

She hears the answers, Zamkov thought. She processes the data. She evaluates all the possibilities and weighs the risks.

Almost identical.

"El Jefe is the most dangerous man in Mexico. If he found out what we were really doing, he would kill me on the spot and then set his cartel empire after all of you, too."

"He cannot harm me," Valentina said. "And if he tried to hurt Niki, I would kill him on the spot."

Kill him on the spot. Zamkov was disappointed by her repetition of the Dove's phrase, but the sound of her promising to exact revenge on anyone daring to harm him made him glow inside. He believed with all his heart they would truly be a twenty-first century Romeo and Juliet.

"When you return from Mexico, my friend, you will be most welcome here at Eschaton Base. Valentina and I look forward to your return. There will be no need to worry about El Jefe. The virus will kill him and all his cartel within a few days and there will be nothing to worry about."

"What about the American woman you are holding hostage?" the Dove asked.

"She is not your concern. But as it happens, she is already assisting me with my latest project and I hope to be able to present the results very soon. I think you will enjoy them."

He ended the call and as the plasma screen retracted back up into the ceiling, he felt Valentina's arms slip around his waist. She pulled herself closer to him, bringing her hands up his back until her arms were draped loosely over his shoulders.

"Did you mean what you said about killing anyone who tried to harm me?" he asked.

She said nothing, but drew in closer to him and opened her mouth.

When Zamkov returned her kiss, he lost himself completely.

CHAPTER ELEVEN

Two things struck Hawke as he pulled up around the back of El Armario and switched off the engine. The first was, no one partied like the *chilangos* – four in the morning and it looked like things were only just beginning. The second was, the clock was ticking and the other team had less than twenty-one hours to track down the supervirus. Never before had they had to work to such a tight schedule, and he was starting to doubt they'd make it.

Hawke stared at his wristwatch in disbelief. "We've only got a little over twenty hours left." The small group of friends sat in the SUV in the hot Mexican night, helplessly watching the minutes slip from the present into the past. Each single one of those minutes had never been so valuable as they were right now. More precious than all the gold in the world.

They watched the club, lost in the heart of a strange city. Cabs rattled past, windows down and music blaring. Young men and women tumbled out of the front doors and out onto the boulevard. One of them held onto the trunk of a palm tree for her life as she threw up in the gutter. Above it all, a wild grove of stars fought to be seen against the light pollution of one of the biggest metropolitan areas on earth.

Zeke rolled up his shirtsleeves and opened his top three buttons, exposing the upper part of his chest. "So, that's the locker."

"Welcome to Mexico City," Said Franco wearily.

"Judging from the look of what they're wearing," Lexi said, "maybe they should rename it the Meat Locker. If those women wore any less they'd be naked."

"Yeah," Zeke said, lost in a dream. "Naked."

Lexi's eyes widened as a muscular man in a black shirt climbed the steps and walked into the club. "Tell me about it."

Hawke pulled the keys from the ignition. "Snap out of it, both of you. We're not here to discuss what the natives wear. We're here to get a lead on where El Jefe is holding Lea and Ryan. Any screw-ups and they could die, and we're not going to let that happen."

"You're right, Joe," Zeke said. "But so's Lexi. If they wore any less they'd be *naked.*"

Lexi and Zeke shared a high five as the team climbed out of the SUV and made their way across the parking lot toward the club. Bright arc lights lit their way as they approached the four-storey building's front entrance. It was typically colonial in style, with blue-painted plaster and stone balustrades running along balconies in front of shuttered windows.

Two heavy-duty men were working the door, both dressed in white shirts, with little earpieces tucked inside their ears. The club was situated close to the Fuente de las Cibeles, one of the busiest roundabouts in the city, and now a cacophony of angry car horns echoed in the night as they reached the door.

The doormen closed ranks and held out their hands, touching Hawke on the chest. "ID."

A bass beat thundered from somewhere inside the club. "What?"

"Everyone shows ID to get in," the other said.

Hawke looked down at the man's hand and then back up to his face. Without another word, the bouncer removed his hand. Hawke made no comment and reached for the new, fake passport Orlando Sooke had arranged back in Turkey.

The doormen both studied it, then handed it back and waved him through. After showing their fake ID, Lexi, Zeke and Franco followed the Englishman into the club's foyer and into another world.

Suddenly, everything was red and black, except for the neon blue fairy lights hanging over the entrance to some downward stairs. Just ahead of them, a group of young women were putting their IDs away and making their way down the plush, carpeted steps.

Seeing Zeke watching the woman, Hawke pulled him away by his elbow. "We're looking for the offices."

"I don't see any offices," Zeke said.

"That's because you're not looking for them."

"Access to them must be downstairs in the main club," Lexi said.

"Damn it!" Zeke said, checking out the women walking down the steps. "Why do bad things happen to good people?"

Hawke stuffed his ID in his pocket and headed for the stairs. Looking around at the clientele, he was feeling decidedly past his best. "C'mon."

They stepped beneath the fairy lights and made their way down the staircase. Halfway down, the bass beat they had heard at the door turned into a song – Guns and Roses' *Right Next Door to Hell*. Hawke swung open the double doors at the base of the stairs and emerged into his own version of hell. "Shit," he said, shaking his head. "I feel about two hundred years old."

Lexi stood beside him and slipped her hand through his arm. "Huh?"

"I said this place makes me feel old. Look how young they all are."

"Yeah," Zeke said. "I noticed that."

"Me too," Lexi said, eyeing up the man in a black shirt for the second time. "I'd love to check out that guy's business portfolio."

"Lex…"

"Sorry."

"It's all right for you, you're still young." He turned his unshaven face toward the Chinese assassin. "Don't forget – I'm nearly old enough to be your father."

"Hardly."

Zeke pushed past them and scanned the crowd. "Behold the Promised Land."

"Hey, Joe's right," Lexi said to Zeke. "So remember why we're here, clacker bag. El Jefe has Lea and Ryan, and his goon Alonso happens to manage this club. This could be our only chance to find our friends, so stop thinking with that little sausage of yours and keep your eyes peeled."

"Woah!" Zeke said. "I'm just getting the feel of the place. My mind is on the job."

They weaved through the noise and lights and sweat and screams until reaching a door marked in Spanish saying STAFF ONLY. "Looks like our next stop," Hawke said, and opened the door.

They walked into a carpeted area and saw a man sitting behind an old table. He was listening to music on an iPod and now glanced up and saw them. He waved them back into the club, but Lexi closed the heavy, sound-proofed door and a clean silence fell over the small room.

"We're looking for Señor Alonso," Hawke said in Spanish.

The man was on his feet now and pulling the little white buds from his ears. He said in Spanish, "He is not here, now fuck off back into the club."

"Where is Alonso's office?" Zeke asked in English.

"I said fuck off, or things are going to get nasty."

Hawke said nothing. He stepped forward, ripped the iPod from the man's hands and threw it hard against the wall, where it smashed and fell to the carpet. Before there was a response, he grabbed two chunky handfuls of the man's leather jacket and lifted him six inches off the floor. "I think my friend here asked you where the boss's office was."

Shocked by the former commando's unbridled strength, the man caved. "It's down there, but he's not in," he mumbled. "I swear I was telling the truth. But it's down there, like I said. The office suite is down that corridor behind the desk. You can't miss it."

"Neither can you."

"I don't understand."

"The wall," Hawke said. "You can't miss the wall."

Before he could respond, the Londoner threw him against the wall as hard as he could, smashing his head against the exposed brickwork, knocking him clean out. Dusting his hands off, he turned to his friends. "You know, I really have to start lifting weights again. For a few seconds there, I thought I was going to put my back out."

"Jesus," Zeke said, peering down at the unconscious man. "That guy was no stranger to the street taco and look what you just did! He must have weighed two hundred and fifty pounds!"

Franco was horrified. "That was a brutal assault!"

Hawke shrugged. "See if he's armed."

Zeke gave a distracted nod, still shocked by what he had just seen. "Sure thing, Joe. I'll get on it right quick."

After a quick search, he pulled a Beretta from a shoulder holster. "Good job he didn't pull this on you."

"Good job for him, yeah," Hawke said. "You keep the gun."

"Got it."

They followed the man's directions until reaching Alonso's office. Hawke kicked the door down and padded inside. Lexi, Zeke and Franco rushed in behind him, guns raised into the aim and ready to fire but found something none of them had expected. A man and a woman were having sex on a chair behind the desk.

Seeing them, they broke apart. She scrambled for her clothes and the man reached for the desk's top drawer.

"Leave it," Hawke said in Spanish. "Or you'll get three bullets in the chest before you reach the handle."

The man instantly raised his hands. "I'm unarmed."

Lexi peered over the desk at his naked body and raised an eyebrow. "You can say that again, Vaquero."

The woman was still stumbling around pulling on her clothes and trying to claw back some dignity. Behind the desk, the man was trying to roll his chair forward to hide his naked body under the desk.

"Not so fast," Hawke said. "As hard as this is for both of us, you're going to stand up and get away from the desk. We don't want any nasty surprises."

"I think that ship sailed out of the harbor a couple of minutes ago," Lexi said, wincing.

"What the hell is this?" The man grabbed a cushion and covered himself before obeying Hawke's order, stepping back away from the desk. "If you're trying to rob the club, then boy, did you pick the wrong place to knock off. You know who owns this place?"

"Yeah, Ramiro Loza, and we want to talk to his little monkey Alonso," Hawke said. "I'm guessing you're not either of those men."

"No, my name is Enrique Murillo, and I work for Vicente Alonso."

"Wrong," Hawke said. "You work for me, and your first job is to tell me where Alonso took our friends."

A look of understanding washed over the embarrassed man's face. "Ah, now I get it. This is about the kidnapping."

"You're a bright boy," Lexi said. "Which is just as well considering what you keep in your underpants."

The man shifted the cushion around, blushing heavily. The woman was now dressed and sitting in the corner with her hands in the air.

Murillo said, "I swear I don't know where your friends are, but Vicente does. He organized everything. If you speak to him, you will find your friends… if he doesn't kill you first."

"There's no chance of that," Zeke said. "Believe me, I've seen these guys in action."

"Where do we find Alonso?" Hawke said.

"His address is…"

"Write it down," Lexi said. She picked up a pen and tossed it at him.

He reached out with both hands and caught it, dropping the cushion and exposing himself once again in front of everyone. Lexi gave another wince, and turned away while Zeke chuckled and shook his head. "I ain't touching that pen or the paper, neither."

"You have a point," Hawke said. Turning to Murillo, he said, "Get dressed, because you're going to drive us out to Alonso's place."

CHAPTER TWELVE

Scarlet Sloane leaned on the hood of the SUV and scanned El Jefe's opulent mansion and sprawling grounds through the pair of binoculars she'd picked up at the safehouse. They were parked up at the side of the road on a hill half a mile to the north of the property, hidden behind a wild tangle of undergrowth and tree branches.

As she swept the binoculars back across the house and grounds, she gave a low whistle. The property was a testament to the old saying about money being able to buy everything except good taste. Smooth white stucco walls wrapped around the main three-storey house, and sitting directly above a grand portico entrance, a long balustrade ran around the front of the master bedroom's balcony.

Peering inside through the open French doors, she saw a world of Talavera tiles and Moorish murals, and the top of a pink granite staircase flanked either side by a roaring jaguar, carved out of something like limestone, with pink marble accents.

Outside, high pressure pop-up sprinklers were spraying a fine mist of water over freshly cut lawns, and to the north, she saw some tennis courts. Swivelling to the east, she saw some outbuildings, including a garage block where things got even got worse. Down at the garage block was a long line of luxury supercars, including a Bugatti Veyron, a Ferrari California and a Jaguar F-Type, all of them painted a brash metallic pink.

"Wow," she said. "I wonder if they belong to Mrs El Jefe."

"There is no Mrs El Jefe," Alberto Castillo said. "And even if there were, she would be La Jefe."

Scarlet grinned. "So our man just likes pink?"

"And black. In that garage block he has a brand-new Mercedes Maybach and a Lamborghini Sian, both in jet black. Not bad for a life of organized crime and murder, no?"

Reaper gave a sigh of despair and lit a roll-up. "Mon Dieu, this world…"

"You can say that again, my friend," Nikolai said.

Scarlet tossed the binoculars into the car. "So, we'll put the pink down to whimsy then."

Castillo sucked his teeth. "I'm not so sure whimsy is a trait commonly associated with people whose favorite pastime is leaving decapitated heads on the lawns of his rivals."

"No, I think you might be right. Either way, not much going on inside the house and judging from all the noise, I'd say the Dove's welcoming party is around the back."

Castillo chuckled. "Ah – the back yard! If you like pink Ferraris, you're going to love his swimming pool."

"What about it?"

He laughed and slapped her on the back. "You'll see, my old friend."

"He has a pink swimming pool?"

"It's so much more than that."

"This, I have to see. Let's go get 'em."

"Hey, wait just a second," Castillo said. "Aren't we going to make a plan of attack?"

She looked at him with sympathy. "We already have one, darling."

"What is it?"

"We tool up, kick his front door in and introduce him to the true meaning of the word *devastation*."

"But this is El Jefe! He will have at least a dozen armed men in there, maybe more if there's a party."

"And most of them are going to be drunk or trying to get their legs over. It's already well on the way to dawn and the last thing any of them is going to expect is a direct attack on the heart of Loza's empire."

Castillo looked uncertain. "I know you are reckless, Cairo, but this seems like a leap even for you."

"Pfft," she said, climbing into the car. "Last one at the bar is a scaredy cat."

Castillo turned desperate eyes to Jack Camacho, who simply shrugged. "She usually gets things about right."

"This is true," Nikolai said.

"Oui," Reaper said. "C'est vrai, mon ami." He flicked his roll up into the gravel at the side of the road and slid inside the front seat, making the entire car rock up and down on its shock absorbers. Camacho followed him inside and slammed the door.

Scarlet fired up the engine and revved the car. "Coming, Alby? Or you going to stand around out here all night, sticking out like a bulldog's bollocks?"

Castillo shook his head, cursed and walked over to the car. "I hope I don't regret this, Cairo Sloane."

"Don't be such a big girl's blouse, Alby. You used to love this sort of thing – or were all those stories you used to tell me at the blackjack table nothing but cock and bull stories?"

"What stories?"

She pulled away off the side of the road and headed down to El Jefe's mansion. "The counterterror raids, the drugs raids, the undercover missions in El Salvador... I could go on."

He sighed heavily. "All true enough, and there are many more I kept to myself."

"So what's changed?" Camacho asked.

"Time is a cruel master, Jack," he said wearily. "I was a young man then. I worked out. I ran before work. Now, I'm double my fighting weight and I get out of breath tying up my shoelaces."

"Ever thought of slip-ons?" Cairo said.

"I'm being serious, Cairo. Maybe I'm jeopardizing the mission simply by being here."

"Rubbish, you're as sharp as you ever were." She glanced down at his gut. "Even if you are expecting. When's it due?"

"Funny… very funny," he said, sucking his stomach in and straightening himself up in the chair. "Maybe we'll see how funny you think it is when you are my age and you start to put on a little weight."

"It'll never happen," she said. "I take care of myself too much."

Camacho laughed. "Sure."

"What? You still work out?" Castillo asked.

"No, I smoke too much. It's an appetite suppressor – ah! Here's the turn to El Jefe's Nightmare in Pink. Everyone ready? We have a supervirus to contain, after all."

"We sure do," Camacho said. "Weapons ready folks, because we're going in and we're going in hard."

"Said the bishop to the actress," Scarlet said, using Ryan's old joke.

Reaper chuckled, but then a silence fell over the car. Scarlet said, "And we're going to get Ryan back, too, and Lea."

*

The gates at the front of El Jefe's mansion were closed and locked, but the fence running around the property was mostly just for show and easy to climb. Everyone managed it easily enough, except for Castillo who struggled until Reaper and Camacho helped him over.

Inside the grounds, Scarlet led the way. None of the five of them was a stranger to infiltrating an enemy location covertly, and they soon made their way across the gardens, using shadows and undergrowth for cover until they had reached the main house.

They chose the west of the property for their ingress point, as this was furthest away from the drunken revelry unfolding in the back garden. Moving with professional ease and swift and confident actions, they prised open a window and slipped inside the old colonial villa totally unnoticed. Finding themselves inside a large and ornately decorated dining room, Scarlet paused and turned to the rest of the team.

"We all set?"

Camacho drew his gun from his holster and nodded. "Always right behind you babe."

"Ryan wouldn't be able to let that go," Scarlet said. "But it's good to know, Jacky Boy. What about you, Kolya?"

The Russian monk nodded, but left his gun in the holster. "I am ready, but prefer to fight with my hands."

"Alby?"

The ageing Mexican was already checking his gun. "I'm ready, and if it's the same with you guys, I prefer to fight alongside my fifteen nine mil friends in this gun."

Scarlet smirked. "That's the spirit, but for now it's guns away please, folks."

"Huh?" Camacho asked.

She walked over to the drinks cabinet. Pouring herself a large vodka, she gave the team a wink. "We have a party to go to, after all."

*

"Zeke would love this." Camacho weaved through the throng of people dancing to a deafeningly loud stereo system parked up at the poolside. He picked a glass of martini off a tray being carried by a waiter. "Too bad he's not here."

"But Loza is," Castillo said. "That's him over there by the pool house."

"The *pink* pool house," Scarlet said. "And oh *my*, I see what you mean about the swimming pool. Is this thing shaped like a guitar?"

Castillo nodded. "It used to belong to an American rock star. And you know what's even better than that?"

"Enlighten me."

"Last week, my wife and I finally paid off the mortgage on our three-bedroom house in San Ángel. It took us thirty years."

Scarlet gave him a sweet look. "Alby, these people are scum. You're an angel compared with them."

He shrugged. "I know – wait, is that the Dove?"

Scarlet turned and looked through the crowd. People were diving in the pool and others were standing around a barbecue, but through them all, in front of the pool house, she saw the Brazilian hitman stroll over to Loza. He was in swimming trunks and had a crisp white towel flung casually over a shoulder.

"Yes, that's him. God, he's *ripped*."

"I'm standing right next to you, baby."

She turned and saw Camacho pulling an olive off a cocktail stick. "Just saying, Jack"

He nodded and grinned. "Sure thing, and those babes over in the bikinis are..."

Her face darkened. "Are what?"

He swallowed the olive. "Paying no attention to pool safety *at all*."

Reaper chuckled, turning away to watch Loza and the Dove.

She smirked. "That's what I was thinking, too. The young today."

Reaper laughed. "This from the woman who once skinny-dipped in the Lincoln Memorial Reflecting Pool."

"Huh?" Camacho said. "You never told me that."

"It's a long story." Reaching down and tweaking his backside, she winked and gave him a kiss. Then, lowering her voice so only he could hear, she said, "You're the only one for me, Jacky Boy. I mean it."

"I know, babe, and that goes both ways."

She knew it, too. "Okay, let's nail these bastards."

CHAPTER THIRTEEN

They walked around the pool and drew closer to the pool house, but two men in black suits closed ranks and blocked their path. "This area is off limits. Go back to the party."

Scarlet said nothing, but stood her ground. Behind her, she felt the reassuring presence of Reaper, Camacho, Nikolai and Albert Castillo, and she knew they were all armed.

The second man took his hands out of his pockets. "My associate told you to fuck off. It's good advice. Take it, or I will throw you into the street."

The man came closer, but Scarlet didn't move an inch. She knew what had to be done. Behind the guards, Loza and the Dove were engaged in conversation, surrounded by more women in bikinis and trays full of canapés and cold drinks.

When the man was almost nose to nose with her, she fired her right hand up in a sharp tiger punch. Driving her knuckle bones up into this throat, she felt his larynx crush and give way. He instantly fell to his knees, desperately bringing his hands up to his throat and struggling to breathe.

Camacho rolled his eyes and slid his hand inside his jacket until his fingers felt the grip of the Glock he was packing in there. "Crap, here we go again. You can't take her anywhere."

The first man stared at his friend with wide eyes, took a step back and reached for his gun, but Scarlet was already two moves ahead. She lifted her right leg up and spun around in a circle, three-sixty degrees, stopping momentarily to deliver the heel of her boot into his face and driving him off his feet. He fell back and cracked the back of his head against one of Loza's ornamental plant pots.

A woman screamed and dropped a tray of daiquiris all over the concrete.

Scarlet stared as the cool alcoholic drinks spread out in strawberry-scented pools. "What a scandalous waste."

Loza and the Dove looked up to see what was happening.

Nikolai spoke quietly. "And the chaos starts in three, two…"

"One of you will pay for this!" Loza screamed. "Who dares come into my house, beat my security and draw a weapon on me?"

His words were hard, but his body language was telling another story. He had scrambled up from his sun lounger and was taking a step back toward the safety of the pool house. The Dove joined him. Almost naked apart from the tight trunks and the towel, he had already calculated that discretion was the better part of valor and was only one step behind his host.

"Cairo Sloane," she said. "That's who dares, fucknuckle."

The Dove's eyes widened. "ECHO!"

"In the flesh," she said to the Brazilian. "Where is Zamkov's little doomsday device?"

"You're too late," he said. "The Serpents have already delivered them all over the city."

"Them?" Scarlet felt her skin prickle when she heard the word. "What do you mean, *them*?"

The Dove grinned. "You thought there was just one device? Maybe you're not as good as they say you are.

Project Eschaton has been deployed all over the city in several top secret locations and there is no way you have the time even to find one of them, never mind all the others. Face it, you lost this one."

Half a dozen men moved through the crowd, all carrying MP5 compact machine pistols and slowly surrounded Scarlet and the rest of the team.

"Lower you weapons," Loza said. "Or die."

"Like hell I will," Camacho said. "I'm pointing this right at your ugly ass of a face, Loza. You tell these guys to stand down or I'm giving you a third eye socket."

"Well, it seems like we have a Mexican standoff," Scarlet said.

Camacho rolled his eyes again. "Dammit! Can't you take anything seriously?"

"I suggest you stand down and fly away," Loza said. "The Serpents are holding your people, and if you do not back off, one of them will be executed. If you contact the authorities, they will be executed. If you persist, I will order the death of the other."

"Harming either of them is signing your own death warrant," Scarlet said.

"We will see about that, Sloane."

A gun fired. Driven by years of training and experience, ECHO hit the deck and rolled into the cover of a stone wall dividing the pool from the back garden. Castillo reacted almost as fast.

"Where?" Scarlet called out.

"On the balcony," Reaper said. "One shooter."

"It's one of the Loza's men," Castillo said. "I recognize him from the files."

"Talking of which," Nikolai said. "Loza is gone, and so is the Dove."

Scarlet looked over the top of the stone wall. "Bugger!"

The party had melted into chaos. People screamed and ran in every direction, desperate to flee the flying lead, but up on the balcony, the shooter was returning Reaper's fire. The Frenchman fired back and clipped his shoulder, spinning him around and sending him tumbling over the balustrade. He fell to the ground, almost hitting a man running for his life, and smacked into the concrete.

As Reaper reloaded, Castillo rolled over to them. "I hate to say this, but I hear a chopper."

"This is turning into a clusterfuck, Cairo," Camacho said.

Castillo shrugged. "I said we needed a plan. No one ever listens to the old guy."

"They're firing again!"

"Then fire back!" Scarlet yelled.

A short fire fight with the men armed with the MP5s ended in a bloody victory for the ECHO team. The machine pistols were superior to their sidearms, but the men behind them were no match for former SAS commandos, covert CIA agents and French legionnaires.

"They're dead," Nikolai said.

Scarlet cursed. "Yeah, but they did their job and kept us pinned down long enough for the boss to get away."

Above their heads, the helicopter carrying Loza and the Dove rose gracefully above the pool house, turned in the air and zoomed away over the treetops surrounding the villa.

"Great, we lost both of them," Camacho said. "You think they'll move the supervirus?"

Scarlet shook her head. "Not a chance. They know we don't know where they are or we wouldn't be here trying to find out, and they're cocky bastards, too, both of them."

"What now?" Castillo asked.

She got to her feet and holstered her gun. "If I'm not very much mistaken, the dude over there who just swan-dived off the balcony is still alive. Let's see if he's in the mood for a chat."

The others followed her as she walked over to him. The man was young, and dying. His broken body was in a pool of expanding, congealing blood, and he was moaning and struggling to breathe.

Castillo muttered a short prayer and made the sign of the cross as Scarlet knelt beside him and grabbed him by the shirt.

"Where are the supervirus devices, chumpy?"

His bloody lips began to move up and down as he mumbled a response. Reaper recoiled his shovel-hand to deliver one of his persuaders, but Scarlet stopped him. "Easy, Reap. One of those in his condition and he's out cold till he dies."

The Frenchman lowered his fist. "But his face is so smackable."

"Is that even a word?" Camacho asked.

"Don't look at me," said Nikolai. "English is my ninth language. It comes after ancient Greek and Latin as far as fluency goes. Why do you think I say so little?"

Camacho shrugged. "I thought you were just the strong, silent type."

The Russian monk gave a solemn nod of his head. "Of course, this is also true."

Out of time, Scarlet reached down and squeezed the man's balls hard. In response, he gasped and grunted and writhed.

"The last few moments of your life don't have to feel like this, scumbag. Where did they put the devices?"

"All right, all right… I'll talk, please, just let go of me."

"With pleasure." She released him and wiped her hand on his jeans. "Gross."

"I only know where one of them was planted, the one in my team. The others went with different teams."

"Where?"

"The Palacio del Bellas Artes."

"The Palace of Fine Arts?" Castillo said. "That's not too far from here."

Scarlet saw the man was fading and leaned down closer to him. "How many other teams were there planting the bombs?"

"Four teams."

She let go of him, throwing him back on the ground. "Fuck it. Four teams, Jack? We barely have enough time to track down one of them."

"We'll never know if we don't try."

Behind them, they heard sirens, and then, flashing on the trees at the front of Loza's gatehouse across the lawn, the blue and red lights of what sounded like a small army of police cars.

Nikolai looked at the bodies strewn around the swimming pool. One dead man was even bobbing up and down over the top of Loza's lounger in the middle of the deep end. "Getting arrested and charged with these deaths is not a good idea."

"He's right. We have to go," Reaper said. "Alberto, how far is this *palacio*?"

"Not far, we can be there in less than twenty minutes."

The Russian monk checked his watch. "Less than twenty hours, and we have a whole fine art museum to search?"

"Not if we use our heads," Scarlet said. "Come on, let's go."

CHAPTER FOURTEEN

Located in the famous historic quarter of Mexico City, the Palace of Fine Arts is a dramatic neoclassical building positioned at the eastern end of the Alameda Central park. Its famous brass-colored ceramic dome is seen for miles around the city, each year enticing hundreds of thousands of visitors to come inside and see its many attractions.

Scarlet Sloane didn't notice the dome, or any of its nouveau architectural designs when Castillo approached the building at speed and swerved the old SUV to a halt on the Avenue Juárez. Her mind was too preoccupied on the threat lurking within its mighty stone walls, and exactly what she was going to do about it.

Her fears back at Loza's villa had been right; there was no way she or anyone else was going to track down the vial and whatever IED it was attached to in a place this size. She could only guess its size, but it would be no bigger than a very small suitcase, and maybe even no larger than a laptop case. Starting at one end of a palace and working through to the other would take weeks.

And she only had hours.

"What's the best way in, Alby?"

"We could speak to the security guards."

"No. No contact with anyone. Any of them could be in Loza's pocket, or they could radio into their HQ which might have been infiltrated. Remember what they said about Lea and Ryan – if we contact the authorities, they're dead."

A mischievous smile crossed the Russian's face. "In that case, it's time for what Zeke might call the old bait and switch."

"What are you talking about?" Reaper said.

Nikolai clapped his arm on Castillo's shoulder. "Exactly how old and tired are feeling right now?"

Castillo looked confused. "Very."

"Good," the Russian said with a smile. "Very good."

*

When Alberto Castillo collapsed in front of the Palace's rear entrance, he made sure it was in view of the security guard station, but just out of view of the CCTV camera above the door. Nikolai's plan was hasty, but it was all they had, and now it looked like it was working. As he coughed and spluttered and clutched his chest, the guard inside swiped a card through the door and ran over to give him assistance.

"Are you all right, sir?"

"I'm… it's my heart…"

The security guard reached for his radio. "I'll call an ambulance."

"He doesn't need an ambulance," the gruff voice behind him said. When he turned, he saw a mountain of a man rising up above him. Black beanie hat pulled down low, a week's silver stubble on his lean face, and a Harley-Davidson t-shirt under a tatty denim jacket. "But you might."

Reaper piled a meaty fist into his face and instantly knocked him out. He fell backwards into the loving arms of Jack Camacho, who caught him and dragged him back inside the building as Castillo got to his feet. Dusting himself down, the Mexican was again concerned by the level of violence.

"He is an innocent man," he mumbled. "He works nights, Cairo. We shouldn't have done this."

"You think he would have just let us in here tonight without asking his boss? We could be anyone."

He shrugged. "If I was still in the CNI, I could have shown him my badge."

"But you're not, darling. You're retired, and if you want to continue enjoying that retirement then you need to let us do our thing. If we don't find the vial, Sleeping Beauty over there, and everyone else in this city – this country and the wider world – will be dead in a few weeks."

He conceded the point, but with a lingering look over at the unconscious man. "Okay… okay, fine."

"It is a necessary evil," Nikolai said. "It had to be done."

"Now we've got that clear," Scarlet said. "Let's get on."

They moved over to the guard's desk and rummaged around until they found a pile of floorplans. "Here," Scarlet said, "where's the main security suite?"

Castillo pored over the plans. "Looks like it's at the eastern end of the building, on the first floor."

"Then let's get there as fast as possible."

As they made their way inside, the art nouveau exterior gave way to a softer, classier interior of art deco. Long carpeted corridors lit with low amber lighting opened onto individual exhibitions spaces full of paintings and photographs and sculptures, but none of the team were here for the culture.

"We're almost there," Castillo said.

"But what are we looking for when we get there?" Nikolai said.

Scarlet sped up the pace. "If Loza ordered his men to put the vial in this building, then he must have done it after the Dove arrived in the city. We know that was just a few hours ago, so that means we have a specific timeframe to work with. There's no way he got in here and moved around without being picked up on the CCTV system, right?"

"Ah."

"So we search through the CCTV until we find a shifty bastard with a case of some kind and then we follow him to wherever he put the vial."

"Sounds like a plan," Camacho said.

Castillo frowned. "But what about the other vials the dying man told us about?"

"One thing at a time, Alby," Scarlet said. "Ah, we're here."

Peering through the small porthole window, Reaper sighed. "Oui, but so are another two guards."

Castillo cursed. "They're not making this easy for us... maybe we could—."

It was too late. The former SAS officer kicked the door in and drew her weapon. The guards staggered to their feet but they had no chance. Reaching for their weapons, they froze in mid-air when Scarlet tutted and clicked back the hammer on her gun. "I wouldn't if I were you."

With their shoulders visibly sagging, the two men deflated on the spot and raised their hands in the air.

"Jack, Reap – see to it our two friends are incapacitated for the rest of the night."

Reaper pulled a roll of duct tape from his bag and gave the men a sympathetic look. "Je suis désolé, but what the lady wants, the lady gets. Now, there is an easy way, or there is my way. Which do you prefer?"

"The easy way," one of the guards said.

"Tres bien. Then, sit down. *Maintenant.*"

Reaper and Camacho taped them to their chairs, not stopping until they had used the entire roll of tape.

"They look like Egyptian mummies," Nikolai said.

"Oui," Reaper said with a devilish smirk. "But I am the daddy, n'est-ce-pas?"

Camacho laughed. "Nice work, Reap."

"Et toi, aussi."

"Now what?" Nikolai said.

"Now is already history, darling," Scarlet said without looking up from the guards' cluttered desk. "Me and Alby are already going through the CCTV for the last eight hours."

"You find anything yet?" Camacho asked.

"Give me a break, Jacky. I've been looking for two minutes."

Under the sad, impotent gaze of the two mummies taped up in the corner, they walked around the desk and peered down into the grainy black and white CCTV monitors. Scarlet and the Mexican agent were working fast, taking alternate cameras and fast-forwarding through the footage as fast as it would go.

After another ten minutes of searching, Scarlet saw something. "There! Look – in this corridor over here, I see someone holding a case."

"Is he staff?"

"Ask King Tutankhamun over there."

Nikolai wheeled one of the guards over to the monitor bank, and Castillo spoke to him in rapid Spanish and pointed at the screen as Scarlet zoomed in on the figure. When the guard shook his head, they had their answer.

"He says he does not recognize him as staff, and the timestamp shows this part of the palace was closed to visitors at that time."

"I think we have our man," Scarlet said, pausing the screen. She looked at the small black case in his hand and felt a shiver go up her spine. All that destruction, all that death and suffering in something so small and innocuous.

She resumed the videotape and they followed the man along the corridor again until he turned left and headed into another narrower corridor. At the end of it, he pushed through some double doors. Moving onto another monitor now, they watched him walking down an aisle in a large theatre. He approached an enormous stage, but instead of climbing up onto it, he opened a hatch in the front and disappeared inside.

Camacho rubbed a hand over his face. "Where the hell did he go?"

"Under the stage," Nikolai said.

Scarlet was staring at the screen, but now she turned to face the Russian. "It's called the trap room, darling. Do you not know the theatre?"

Nikolai returned her gaze without blinking. "I was a priest in an ancient religious cult who spent most of my time in an isolated monastery, but yes, the Oracle used to take us to shows on Broadway all the time. I think he enjoyed *Cats* the most."

"I take the point," she said.

"He isn't coming back out," Castillo said.

"Yes he is," she said coolly. "Here's the little mouse now – and without the case."

"Looks like we found vial number one," Reaper said.

Scarlet turned to Castillo. "Ask His Majesty where this stage is."

*

The theatre was much more impressive in real life than on the security monitor, and when they stepped inside, they entered an epic auditorium, with white and pink marble columns and dozens of rows of comfortable seats stretching down to a large orchestra pit. Sumptuous balconies and boxes punctuated walls of yet more marble, and at the center of it all was an enormous backdrop at the crossover of the stage depicting a giant moonlit sphinx surrounded by palm trees. On the stage, giant cardboard columns painted to resemble marble were positioned carefully in a row running along the back, and beautifully painted carboard palm trees lined up on either side of the stage, giving it the appearance of a forest.

"Looks like we're in Egypt," Camacho said.

Scarlet stared up at the backdrop. "It's from the Magic Flute."

"Huh?"

"It's a Mozart opera about the Freemasons, darling. They must be putting on a production here. You really must read more."

"Funnily enough, nineteenth century operas about Freemasons wasn't big on the syllabus when I was at Langley."

"That's too bad," she said. "And it was eighteenth century."

"I do apologize."

"There's always time to learn,' she said, leaning over and kissing his cheek. "We'll start you off on Puccini."

"Gee, *thanks*," he drawled. "I can't wait."

"You can see why he chose this place," Castillo muttered. "They have thousands of visitors every day – but why the stage?"

Scarlet shrugged. "Hiding it somewhere like the cafeteria is only going to hit the people in the cafeteria. That might only be a few hundred people. Just look at the size of this place, and imagine all the people packed in here. What's the capacity?"

"It seats just under two thousand people," Castillo said. "And tomorrow night is the last night – it will be packed. After that, it's the opening night of Tosca."

"And what is that?" Camacho asked.

"It's Puccini again, darling," said Scarlet. "It's about Napoleon's attack on Rome."

"My god." Camacho passed a hand over a stubbly jaw. "If this thing blows up in here when it's crowded with two thousand people, there won't be any stopping the infection."

"So let's get it under control and secure the vial," Scarlet said.

They walked down house-left until they reached the apron of the stage. There, Reaper leaned down and ripped off the hatch leading into the trap room beneath the stage. He peered inside, straightened back up and shook his bag off his shoulder. "It's dark in there. We'll need a flashlight until we can find the light switch."

At the exact second the Frenchman switched on his flashlight the entire auditorium was plunged in darkness.

"Impressive," Nikolai said. "Do that again."

"We're in trouble," Scarlet said.

A flash of light sparked up in the gallery as a bullet ripped a chunk of carboard from one of the trees just above their heads.

"Shit, he's still in here!" Scarlet said. "Everyone take cover!"

CHAPTER FIFTEEN

With a gun pointing into his ribcage, Enrique Murillo drove the rest of the team in an old Mercedes southeast to Alonso's address. Beside him, Hawke rolled the window down and hung his arm outside, resting it on the warm steel as Alonso's goon cruised through the hot city streets. One look at the area they were driving into told the former SBS operative that tonight would be no picnic.

Iztapalapa was a densely populated part of the city, known for its sky-high crime rate. Here, the streets were as mean as they came, with rape and violence against women being commonplace, and drug trafficking, prolific. He also knew it had some of the highest rates of car-jackings and robberies in a city notorious for them, especially among taxi drivers.

They drove on, passing through some of the area's worst districts. They cruised past a knife fight in the parking lot of a pizza house in Santa Martha Acatitla, and saw another gang drive a taxicab off the road in Citlalli. Crossing into Xalpa, they passed a Baptist church, before turning left into a warren of narrow side streets.

The tires rumbled over broken, crumbling asphalt as they made their way toward the address. A small group of young men were standing beside a viburnum tree planted in the center of the sidewalk, their thin, hate-filled faces lit in the ghostly glow of a nearby streetlamp. One of them tracked their car, hiking up his t-shirt and pointing at the grip of a handgun stuffed inside his pants. He winked at them and blew a kiss.

"Seems like a nice guy," Lexi said.

They drew closer to Alonso's place. Telephone cables hung over the street, strung from pole to pole like black spaghetti, and below them endless houses were tucked away behind decorative concrete breeze blocks. Tattered Mexican flags fluttered in the humid night sky from several front yards.

"We're here." Murillo pulled up outside a property on the right hand-side of the street and cut the engine. The road surface was more uneven here, covered in a grey patchwork of asphalt laid at various times over the last thirty years. The houses on either side of them were mostly obscured by walls, and piles of household junk were stacked up on the sidewalks, spilling out into the street. A dog barked and scuttled across the road, running into the shadows. The entire street looked like a hurricane had just ripped through it.

It was not yet dawn, but this was the sort of neighborhood that never slept, and Hawke was anxious. He would have been happier with better intel before the raid. Titanfort had proved the quality of its intelligence during the last mission in Brazil, but this time it was all down to Alonso's sweating minion sitting beside him.

"So what now?" Murillo asked.

Lexi replied by coshing him around the back of the neck with the grip of her pistol, knocking him out cold. "That's what's next for you, *bèndàn*."

"I take it that was no compliment?" Zeke asked.

"You could say that. He'll be out for hours."

They climbed out of the car, quietly closing the doors. Hawke rested his elbows on the car's roof and scanned the decrepit old colonial villa. A dog barked and howled behind him as he scanned the broken-down old building. Missing roof tiles and peeling paint were the order of the day, and the bermudagrass lawn had gone to seed sometime around the turn of the century.

Swivelling to east of the property, he saw a rusted pickup truck, jacked up on concrete cinderblocks with dry, yellow grass twisting through the spokes and empty lug holes. A pile of empty Pacifico beer bottles was stacked up in front of the garage door, some of them smashed with the brown glass strewn out over the paving.

The soundtrack to all of this was the constant, low rumbling of a bass beat, booming out of an open window obscured beneath the veranda. The smell of cannabis smoke drifted out of the window and blew over to them on the early morning breeze.

Hawke took a deep inhalation. "Nothing like some dank *cro* to get your motor whirring first thing in the morning."

Lexi gave him a look. "If you call me *blud* you're getting a slap. Fair?"

He nodded. "Seems fair to me."

"The good news," Franco said, "is if those guys have been up smoking dope all night, they're going to be seriously impaired."

"Which puts them on an equal footing with Zeke," Lexi said.

"Stop, or my sides will be aching too much to fight."

She arched an eyebrow. "You can fight?"

A light went on and a scream of rage echoed through the open window. The light went out and all went silent again. Zeke reached for his weapon, checking the magazine was fully loaded. "I hope I don't have to use this thing."

"These guys are some of the worst scumbags in the city," Hawke said. "They're not going to roll over and let you tickle their tummies."

"No, they most certainly are not," Franco said. "This is a dangerous *barrio*. Here, life is about bootlegging, mugging, pickpockets, muggers, robbery, rape, murder and kidnapping."

"But that's way too much to put on the tourist posters," Zeke said. "You're going to have to come up with something much snappier."

"This is no joke, my friend." Franco's eyes misted with hate and sadness. "I have lost good friends working this neighborhood. This place is as tough as it gets. There is a reason why all the best boxers in Mexico come from places like this part of town and Tepito."

"Sorry, chief," Zeke patted his arm. "Didn't mean anything by it."

Hawke checked his gun. "Time to focus, everyone. We go in hard and fast and we find Alonso. If he's already slipped the net we get the next man down. One way or the other, we're not leaving these guys alone until we have the location of Lea and Ryan. All good?"

A round of nods.

"Then let's go."

They moved up the path, drawing guns as they approached the property. The flagstone walkway bent to the right a little, leading them into a tunnel made by mature fruit trees hanging over the path.

Hawke ran into the lead, keeping his head low as he darted across the overgrown front lawn and headed toward the house. Lexi, Zeke and Franco fanned out but kept up with his pace, all of them approaching the property at the same time.

They walked on, checking around them all the way for any sign of trouble. At the double front door now, and a decorative metal grille over the glass made it harder to see what was inside.

"Can't see shit from here," Zeke said.

"We'll get a better view inside." Hawke hit the front door like a hurricane, almost kicking it out of its frame and bursting into the hall in a shower of wood splinters. Gun raised into the aim, ready to take out any threat in a heartbeat, he swept the hallway. "Clear!"

The rest of the team followed, fanning out once again and working their way through the front of the house. They reached a sitting room at the back less than ten seconds after putting the front door in, and were met by a handful of startled, doped-up faces.

"Alonso," Hawke said, gun muzzle sweeping over their faces. "Where is Alonso?"

One of the men reached for a weapon and Hawke fired three rounds into him. A double tap in the chest and one in the forehead. The dead man fell back into his easy chair in a cloud of blood mist and skull fragments.

Franco held his gun firm, but his startled face told another story.

"Where is Alonso?" Hawke said again, firing on the stereo and killing the music.

The other men both raised their hands. "Vicente is not here! He is not here! Please do not shoot!"

A car sounded in the garage.

"Who is that?"

"Gustavo. It's just Gustavo."

"Who is he?"

"Gustavo Cavazos," one of the men said, all trembling hands and blinking eyes. "He's Alonso's right-hand man! He just went out for ice. Only he knows where Alonso is."

"He's going to get a lot more than ice."

Lexi fired on the men, killing both of them stone cold dead. The team raced for the door leading out to the garage, but Franco froze on the spot.

Lexi saw his hesitation. "Franco, we have to go now."

"You murdered these men!"

"They would have told Alonso we're on his tail."

"But..."

"Forget it, Franco," Zeke said. "They were scumbag gangbangers, dealing dope and crack to kids, and they would have gotten us killed if they had a chance to draw their weapons or tell Alonso about us."

"It's still murder!"

"No time for this," Hawke said. "He's backing out of the garage and he's the only chance we have to find our friends. You're either with us or against us."

"I'm with you, but..."

"Good, then let's go."

By the time they hit the garage, Cavazos was reversing out onto the street in an old reconditioned Cadillac. He was driving erratically and too fast, and it was obvious the last thing on his mind was ice. "He knows who we are," Hawke said. "We can't let him get away."

"Already on it." Zeke was running out to the street and heaving Murillo out of the driver's seat. Dumping him on the sidewalk, he started the engine and swerved over to the rest of his team. "Anyone feel like a little night-time ride around Chilangolandia?"

Hawke was already up front beside him, and now Lexi was slipping into the back seat. "You read my mind." She patted the black leather and looked up at the dazed Mexican agent. "Keep me company, Franco?"

He looked over his shoulder at the silent house. "Count me in."

"Good," Hawke said. "Because we have one shot to save our friends and this is it."

Zeke slammed his foot down on the gas, sending the Mercedes racing into the night.

CHAPTER SIXTEEN

At the wheel of his beloved Cadillac, Cavazos mumbled a prayer to his god and loaded his gun. He pressed his foot half-down on the throttle and spun the wheel around. The tires squealed and belched out a cloud of burnt rubber smoke. The smell of gas fumes seeped into the cab through the air vents in the dash.

Off the sidewalk and on the street, he floored the throttle. The power of the Cadillac's mighty engine pushed him back in his seat as he scanned the crossroads ahead for a way to escape the scum who had just raided his house. Who the hell were these people? It took some nerve to raid an Alonso property and think you could get away with it, but to kill three Serpents in cold blood without batting an eyelid? Whoever they were, they spelled trouble.

At first he thought they were gone, then he heard a horn blowing loudly in the night, just off to the south of the Baptist church parking lot. Looking in his mirror, he caught a glimpse of the front of a Mercedes screeching around the corner behind him. That was what those sons of whores had parked up outside the house a few moments ago.

And they were on his tail.

He felt his chances of seeing the sunrise rapidly dwindle, and desperately navigated the classic car through the back streets as he considered where offered him the best sanctuary. Just maybe, his best chance would be to stand and fight, but that was a last resort. For now, better to live and fight another day. Besides, when Alonso heard about this, they would be cut up into little pieces and dumped out for the vultures.

Knowing the roads and traffic better, he quickly put some distance between them, but was it enough? He gripped his gun harder now – perhaps it was his only salvation. Looking at the speed gauge he saw he was passing eighty miles per hour. This was an insane speed in a built-up district and if he hit something the crash would be fatal.

He checked his mirror once again and saw they had gained on him and now they were swerving out to the left to overtake him. He cursed, and steered his car into them but they regained control and smashed back into him. The driver's side wheels rammed into the kerb and produced an ear-bending scraping noise and showers of sparks.

Cavazos struggled to control the car and dropped the gun on the passenger seat. When he looked to his side he saw they were alongside him yet again. A Chinese woman was raising a gun and aiming it at his head. He hit the brakes and they shot ahead of him. His gun slipped off the seat and crashed onto the thick red carpet in the footwell.

They attacked again, and the Chinese woman fired. He swerved and the bullet punched a hole in the back door. He stamped on the gas, weaving around a busy junction and only just missing a Pepsi truck crossing ahead of him. By the time they had caught up with him, he was already lifting the heavy gun from the passenger seat.

All the way across the other end of the expansive red leather bench seat, the passenger window was rolled up. He cursed himself for not thinking about winding it down earlier. The classic car was built long before electric windows were standard, and now he had no choice but to shoot his own goddam window out. *Needs must when the devil drives, Gustavo, and when you kill them, you can take their wallets. They will pay for the window.*

The sound of the gun firing in the Caddy's cab was almost deafening loud. The buffalo bore heavy round left the Magnum 44 at just under 1500 feet per second, turning most of the window to glass powder. His ears rang in the chaos, and he had missed. The bullet had hit the pillar between the Merc's front and rear doors and ricocheted into the night.

The son of a whore at the wheel was still in control of the vehicle and the woman was raising her gun into the aim again, this time directly at his face.

Her window, he noticed, was rolled all the way down.

He hit the brakes and the other car surged forward a second time.

They hit the brakes too, and then the Merc executed a perfect, high-speed one-eighty degree turn so they were now facing him.

Cavazos rolled the driver's window down and aimed the heavy handgun at them. He fired a burst of three rounds. A neat little triplet of high-velocity hell now drilled into the Merc's windshield. One, two, three spider-web fractures appeared, causing the driver to lose control.

The Merc swerved to the left, but Cavazos saw the two vehicles were still headed for each other. He spun the wheel but it wasn't enough. The two cars clipped each other on their passenger's side headlamps and the impact was sufficient to plunge both of them into a high-speed flatspin.

The Mexican's head spun as he wrestled with the wheel, desperately trying to steer into the skid. He felt dizzy and sick. The car smashed through a dumpster and finally came to a stop when it collided with a raised kerb outside a laundry. Cavazos didn't have enough warning to stop it happening; he leaned over to the side and threw up in the passenger footwell.

He wiped his mouth and cursed the scum in the other car. Where was his gun? He searched the cab and found it in the footwell covered in vomit. Another curse as he reached forward and snatched it up off the floor. His beautiful red carpet was ruined, but he had the gun. It felt slimy now, but its weight made him feel safer. Where were the scum? He carefully craned his head above the level of the dashboard, careful not to be seen.

Smoke was pouring out of the sides of his hood. No, he realized with relief it was just steam – the crash must have broken the radiator. His head hurt like hell, and he blinked as he scanned the parking lot for the Merc. Last seen colliding with him at a combined speed of probably around one hundred miles an hour, there was no sign of it.

Part of him – the part he was would never tell El Jefe about – was relieved they were gone, but another part of him was consumed with rage. Who the hell were these bastards? Just who the goddam hell thought they had the right to break into Alonso's house, murder three Serpents and then chase him all over his hometown? When El Jefe heard about this, they were dogfood.

But then he heard a car's tires squealing loudly in the dark. His heart began to beat hard in his chest and his tongue dried up like a dead lizard. The smashed Mercedes spun around the corner and raced over to him. He lifted his Magnum and fired.

Three shots split the night, but the car absorbed the impact of the massive rounds. All he had to show for the fireworks display were another three neat holes punched in a line across the thick safety glass, and the car kept on coming, heading right for him.

He clambered out of the car, ran for cover behind the trunk and raised his gun. It was a mistake. The man driving the Merc piled into the front end of the Caddy and spun it around one-eighty degrees. The crash wrecked both cars and knocked Cavazos into the air with a broken hip.

He crashed down onto the parking lot with a grim smack and felt an instant wave of dizziness and nausea flooding over him. He heard the people inside the Merc climb out of the car and walk over to him. Turning his head to see them, the bones in his neck made a dry grinding noise, and then he saw his pursuers, the scum who had hunted him through the night like an animal.

A tall, well-built man was in the lead, and the Chinese woman who had fired on him was beside him. Behind them, he saw two more people. Another big man with blond hair and what his nose told him was a local cop. He was right. The last man kicked his gun away, introduced himself as Special Agent Manuel Franco of the CNI, and then read him his rights.

He groaned in response as the big man at the front crouched over him, and put his boot on his chest. "Where is Alonso keeping the people he kidnapped?"

"I don't know what you're talking about."

Franco was on his phone.

Lexi looked at him. "What are you doing?"

"This man needs an ambulance."

She took the phone from his hands in a split second. "No, he doesn't."

Hawke moved the boot up to his throat. "Tell me where they are, now, or this gets very painful for you." Pushing down on his windpipe, the man gasped and spluttered, giving in faster than any of them had thought.

"Please... *por favor*...take your boot off my..."

Hawke obliged. "Where, Cavazos? Now."

"He has a ranch just to the west of the city."

"Name and location."

Cavazos croaked out the details, and Lexi checked it on her phone.

"It's called the Buena Vista ranch," he said, his groans slowly fading. "If you go there you will face an army of Serpents. They will kill you in your boots and hang you out for the vultures."

Lexi nodded. "There is such a place where he says."

"You're wasting your time!" he said. "Your friends are already dead."

Zeke paled. "Huh?"

"Bullshit are they," Hawke said.

"At least we have the address," Zeke said. "That's a start."

"Not until it's verified," Hawke said, pushing down on the man's throat and scanning the parking lot for any sign of more Serpents. "Franco, get onto your database and confirm it."

Franco gave Lexi a look. "May I have my phone back?"

She threw it over and he caught it with one hand. After a short conversation, he slipped the phone in his pocket and nodded. "The ranch is owned by Vicente Alonso."

"Doesn't mean to say that's where Lea and Ryan are though," said Lexi.

"It's all we have," Hawke said.

Franco was pulling his phone back out again. "And now this man needs an ambulance."

"No, he doesn't," Hawke said.

Franco threw his hands in the air. "Not this again! We are *not* murderers!"

The Englishman took his boot off Cavazos. "He doesn't need an ambulance because he's dead, Franco."

"Too bad," Lexi said. "Guess the kids of Iztapalapa will have to go somewhere else for their crack."

"That's their problem," Zeke said.

"And we need a car in a hurry so we can get out to the Buena Vista ranch," Hawke said quietly. "That's our problem."

CHAPTER SEVENTEEN

High up in El Jefe's Anzures District penthouse suite, the Dove watched the television with grim satisfaction. There was nothing on the news, and no news was good news. After the attack on Loza's mansion by the ECHO team he was concerned how fast they would be able to locate the vials, but according to his Mexican host, they were all still in their hiding places, ready and waiting for zero hour.

He sipped a cold drink and started to relax. The assault on the colonial villa had shaken both men, but Loza's gang had given them the time they needed to escape, and a few short minutes after the guns started firing they were already touching down on the downtown skyscraper's helipad. Now, he had nothing to do but wait.

The devil makes work for idle hands. He laughed out loud and pulled a cigarette from a pack on the table. His mother would be proud of him, he thought. She raised him well. Taught him to look after himself. If she were alive today, she would approve of what he was doing. He was fighting for his survival in a world of bastards dedicated to his destruction.

He inhaled the cigarette smoke, making the tip glow in the low light of the hotel room. Looking into the large window, he saw not the streetlights of Cuauhtémoc, but his own reflection. Lean, fit and tanned. A head thick with blue-black hair, slicked back away from his face and held in place by grease. A straight, aquiline nose and strong jaw, freshly shaved and splashed in expensive aftershave. Apart from his black heart, he was almost perfect, he

ROB JONES

thought with a grim smile. Apart from all the killing and hurting.

"Hey, come over here."

The woman was talking.

He padded over to a sumptuous double bed and slid down next to her on the sheets. She was smoking, too. He looked at her long legs, smooth and silky in the soft, orange headboard lights. Her black satin chemise reached down to her knees, but now he took his right hand and pulled it up higher, revealing more of her. If the Dove had one weakness in this world, it was beautiful women.

How that sad old technoperve Zamkov could get his rocks off over steel, bolts and artificial nanotech flesh was a mystery to a man like the Dove. The Brazilian might have had what it took to scrub an innocent life in return for a few thousand dollars, but he still had a beating heart, and when he kissed a woman, she had to have a beating heart, too. No hard drives and data processing units for him, no sir. He lusted after the real thing, not some depraved facsimile.

The woman giggled and play-slapped his hand. "Not now, darling."

"Yes, now."

She returned serve, sliding her hands down inside his pants and then she went further, sliding them down inside his boxer shorts.

"Tell me." He leaned closer, fragrant smoke twirling up from the tip of his cigarette in wispy tendrils. "What was your name again?"

She feigned offense, then stubbed her own cigarette out and turned to look in his eyes. "You might forget my name, *corazón*," she slipped her hand inside his half-open shirt and ran a fingertip down his chest, "but you won't forget tonight."

116

No, on that you're dead right.

*

Thousands of miles across the Atlantic, Clive Hudson was driving Bravo Troop through the streets of Paris in a hired BMW 7 Series. Mack was sitting up front with a canvas bag full of handguns and ammo in between his boots, and sitting in the back, Kyra Harpenden and Danny Plane were discussing how much they annoyed each other.

As they turned onto the Boulevard Saint Germain, Danny broke off from the light-hearted insults to ask Hudson a question. "We got a location for this sodding vial yet, boss?"

"As a matter of fact we have not," the former SAS Major said.

Danny sniffed and stared out of the window. He saw a woman packing away empty bread baskets in the window of a bakery. "Great stuff."

"Nil desperandum," Hudson said.

"Eh?"

Mack's hand was hanging out of the window in the cold air, a cigar drooping between his fingers. "He means stop panicking, you little bawbag."

"Tell me, Mack," Danny said. "Why did you never bother to learn English?"

"You don't want to know what I think about the English, Danny."

"That explains it then."

Mack sucked on his cigar. "Explains what?"

"Why you talk like you've got a bag of bollocks in your mouth."

Mack cracked a smile, but turned away to hide it from Danny. "You know, there's one thing I really love about you, young Dan."

"Oh yeah? What's that then?"

"That one day you'll be dead."

They all laughed as Hudson cruised over the River Seine and headed into the First Arrondissement. The brutal banter was a staple among Bravo Troop missions. The rules were simple: anything went and if you couldn't take it, then you couldn't dish it out.

Hudson changed gear in the car, and in the conversation. "You might like to know that my old CO *has* however managed to get us a lead."

"Oh aye?" Mack said. "What's that then?"

"She has some intel relating to our man Francisco Rodrigues. After landing at Charles de Gaulle, he checked into the Hotel Crillon. We don't know if he's still there, or if he intends to spend the night there or not. Maybe he just checked in to dye his hair and shave his handlebar moustache. Who knows?"

"So what else do we know?" Kyra asked.

Hudson navigated around the Place de la Concorde with the easy confidence of a man who knew the City of Lights like the back of his hand. "We know his room number, so that's where we're starting."

"And we need to get a move on, boss," Mack said. "Cause the fucking ECHO team have a good head start on us." He turned pleading eyes to his former CO. "We cannae let the bastards beat us on this one, Clive."

"I hear you," Hudson said with a smile. "So it's just as well we're here."

"Ah," Mack said, blowing out a thick column of smoke, "the serendipities of life."

They parked up in the taxi rank and walked to the bay tree-flanked door. It was an unassuming entrance, considering the grandeur of the hotel, and they quickly stepped into the opulent lobby and over to the elevators.

This was a world occupied by the richest of global society. Elegant women sat on suede easy chairs and sipped couture cocktails as they leafed through glossy magazines. Men in Armani suits ordered from a list of over one hundred and fifty champagnes at the plush Ambassadors' bar. The entire place was a white marble and gold-flecked paradise.

"Fuckin' 'ell," Danny said. "Look at them prices!"

"You're so classy, Daniel," Kyra said. "If we get the chance to tour the city, I want you to be my guide."

"You wouldn't like the parts of Paris I know about."

"It's on the second floor," Hudson said. "We're in and out as fast as possible, all right?"

Kyra winked at Danny. "Sounds like our first date."

"Easy darlin'," the young SAS trooper replied. "You'll get me all hot and bothered."

Up they went, and when the elevator pinged and the doors swished open, they found themselves looking down a long, richly carpeted corridor. "Let's move."

They walked down to Room 21, stopping on the way at a janitor's cupboard. "Sergeant Donald," Hudson said. "I wonder if you wouldn't mind facilitating the lady's entrance into this cupboard?"

"Aye," Mack grizzled, chomping on his unlit cigar stub. "I thought it would be down to me to do the heavy lifting."

The burly Scot persuaded the door to open with his size-thirteen riot boot, and a moment later Kyra was leading the way down to Rodrigues's room with an armful of freshly laundered linen and towels. At the door, the three men pulled their weapons while Kyra tapped on the door.

"Room service."

No reply.

This time, Mack didn't wait for the order, and easily kicked the door in once again. They burst into the room, guns raised, but after a quick search of the suite it was clear Rodrigues had moved on.

"Damn it!" Hudson holstered his weapon.

"Over here!" Kyra was kneeling by the wastepaper basket, pulling out some crumpled balls of hotel stationery.

"What have you got?"

"Looks like he wrote something down on the sheet above this one and then tossed the whole pad in the bin," she said. "If you tip it toward the light at the right angle, you can see something written down."

"What is it?" Mack asked.

She gasped. "It's an address!"

"Blimey," Danny said. "The old ways really are the best."

"Where is it?" Hudson asked.

She shrugged and handed the paper to Danny. "Somewhere called Gros-Caillou. Is that anywhere near the knocking shops you frequent?"

"I do *not* frequent knocking shops," Danny said.

"Let me see it," Hudson said. "I know the city."

Mack checked the corridor and holstered his gun. "All clear out here, boss. Do you know where we're going?"

"Yes, it's a nice little district south of the river on the Left Bank. We can be there in half an hour. Looks like a residential address."

"How the hell can that help us?" Danny said.

"I don't know," Hudson said. "But if Rodrigues wrote it down on this pad, he had a reason to do so. The only way we're going to find out its significance is by getting our arses over there. All good?"

"You know me, boss," Danny said. "I'd follow you into the depths of hell itself. Well, to the entrance at least."

"How reassuring," their commander said. "Let's get out of here, everyone. We have a continent to save and time is running out fast."

*

It was just after eight o'clock in the evening in Hong Kong, and night had lured the city into its neon embrace. As their SUV cruised through the streets, Jed Mason rubbed his jaw and wondered when he had last shaved. He couldn't remember. Definitely not since Ezra Haven had made contact about the Eschaton threat, but how long before that? No matter, he thought. Ella had once told him he looked better like this, anyway.

"Any word on Barbosa's whereabouts?"

It was Zara, and he knew her well enough to know she was getting an itchy trigger finger. For now, he'd have to disappoint her – he'd just come off the phone with Ezra back in Titanfort and the news wasn't exactly what any of them wanted to hear.

"Not a direct lead, no, but Ezra gave me the name of one of his contacts here."

"And who might that be?" Caleb asked.

Mason checked the notes he had just made on his phone. "A woman named Maggie Lai."

Milo shifted in the back seat of the SUV. "And what does Maggie Lai do to bring home the bacon?"

"She's a former British SIS agent with twenty years under her belt at Six."

Mason was referring to MI6, the British external intelligence service, similar to the American CIA.

Ella sat up. "But former?"

"Early retirement, apparently," Mason said casually. "She wasn't fired for being a double agent or anything like that, so there's no need for alarm."

"I'm not sure they fire you for being a double agent," Milo said. "I think it's more likely you have a terrible accident in your car one night."

"The CIA would *never* do anything like that," Zara said, and everyone laughed.

"So she can be trusted?" Caleb asked.

"Ezra isn't in the habit of putting our lives at risk," Ella said quietly.

"Exactly," said Mason, pulling up outside a house in Kowloon. "He says she's solid."

Caleb glanced suspiciously up at the tower block. It was a large building, but quite usual for an area where most people lived in small apartments in the many tower blocks dotted all over the hillsides.

"C'mon!" Mason said. "No time like the present. Rodrigues is still on the loose."

They followed him up to the door where his knocks were greeted with a rapturous explosion of shouting and screaming in Cantonese.

Milo took a step back. "I'm scared. I want my Teddy."

Zara nudged him in the ribs. "Zip it, Miles, and don't embarrass us."

A slim, middle-aged woman appeared in the door. Her hair was tied back and she was wearing a baggy track suit. The aroma of star anise, chilli and lemongrass drifted over her shoulders and out into the night, carried on a cloud of billowing steam.

"You're Jed Mason?" she asked.

"I am indeed, and if you're Maggie Lai, I'm pleased to meet you."

"Come in," she said. "And please don't mind the mess. My sister and her family are staying and that means... well *this*."

Mason looked down at a hallway strewn with toy cars, dolls, plastic tiaras and dozens of other pieces of bright pink and purple plastic. It looked like a bomb had gone off in Toys R Us.

"Don't worry about it," Mason said. "Milo's room is worse."

CHAPTER EIGHTEEN

In the Palace of Fine Arts, Scarlet had drawn her gun and fired on the shooter in the gallery three seconds after his first shot. Camacho and Reaper were nearly as fast, and the three of them had spent the last quarter of an hour engaged in a heavy fire fight with the unknown gunman.

After driving him into cover, Castillo led Nikolai into the trap room. They began searching for the supervirus vial and the device that would blast it all over the unsuspecting audience the next day, but then the shooter stopped firing on them.

"It's gone very quiet, Jack," Scarlet said.

"If he's got night vision we're all dead," he said, anxiously sweeping his gun into the darkness at the top of the theatre.

"If he had night vision we'd already be dead," she said.

Another shot blasted in the dark. The bullet missed, ricocheted off the fly rail above their heads, ripped into the stage and chewed out a large chunk of wood.

"Shit!" Camacho said.

Reaper moved his gun down a few degrees. "Down there!"

The second shot's muzzle flash had indicated the shooter's new position, much lower than before.

"Bastard's in the circle!" Scarlet cried out. "I'm after him."

"And me!" Camacho called out in the darkness.

Halfway over to the door leading up to the circle, Scarlet turned and shouted out to her old friend. "Reap, get somewhere out of the line of fire and cover Kolya and Alby."

"Pas de probleme," he called back, and tucked himself down inside the orchestra pit.

On the other side of the theatre, Scarlet barely felt her legs as they powered her up the stairs to the upper circle. She moved so fast, and with such determination to take out the shooter, it was almost as if she was sprinting on autopilot. Behind her, it sounded like Camacho wasn't having the same experience.

"You okay, Jack?"

"Sure," he wheezed. "Just what I needed to lose a few of these unwanted Christmas pounds."

"Christmas was nearly a year ago, Jack."

"Yeah, I know." More huffing and puffing. "Don't judge me."

Reaching the upper level, they took cover either side of a curtained gangway. She turned to him, barely making out his face in the low green emergency lighting. "Ready for some action?"

He sucked his teeth and moved to unzip his fly. "All right, but if it was up to me we'd take out the shooter first."

It was enough to raise a smirk, but not a laugh. "I love you, you fool. We're go on three, two, one…"

They burst through the curtain, their guns raised into the aim. Scarlet saw movement on the far side of the circle and vaulted over the first row of stalls to give chase.

"He's trying to climb into the box!" Camacho yelled.

"I see him!"

She crouched, taking cover behind another row of stalls and unleashed a deafening volley of fire on the man, now desperately trying to claw his way across to one of the boxes closer to the stage.

The muzzle flash was savage, lighting up the fleeing shooter like a strobe. In the stark, intermittent flash of the gunfire, they both saw the seven bullet holes in his back. He released his grip on the box and crashed down into the aisle beside the orchestra pit.

Camacho walked over to her and put an arm around her shoulder. "Holy shit, that was something else."

Scarlet said nothing, holstered her weapon and looked down at the dead man, sprawled out arms and legs akimbo on the carpet below.

"You okay?" Camacho asked.

"Sure, I'm fine. Don't like shooting people in the back, that's all."

"He was getting away."

"I know. I've done it before and I'll do it again, but I'm not a robot, Jack."

He looked at her, seeing something different in the way she was looking back at him; something unusually vulnerable. "Sure, I know that."

She nodded and called down to Reaper. The Frenchman was climbing out of the orchestra pit and making his way over to the corpse. After giving him a hefty kick in the ribs to ensure he was dead, the former legionnaire looked up at them both. "Il est mort et bien mort, mes amis. Bien mort."

"What did he say?" Camacho asked.

"He said he's as dead as a doornail, Jack. We'd better hope Kolya and Alby found what we're looking for in the trap room or we're at square one."

"We did!" Castillo called up. He was climbing out of the trap room, and behind him, the sombre Russian monk was holding the suitcase they had seen earlier on the CCTV.

"Hold on," Scarlet called out. "We're on our way down, so don't start another bubonic plague just yet, please."

When they reached the stage, the five of them gathered around in the emergency lighting and Camacho checked the suitcase over. "My experience tells me this thing is rigged." He held it up and showed the others.

A long sigh from Scarlet. "It needs a code. Check his phone."

In the eerie emergency lighting, Castillo padded over to the dead man and lifted up his jacket. "I have his wallet."

"That's not a phone, Alby."

"No, but it IDs him." Castillo stared down at the man's driver's licence. "Joaquin Lopez," he said with disgust. "I recognize the name. He's a long-time member of the Serpents and one of Loza's most loyal lieutenants."

"He's a dead lieutenant now," Nikolai said.

"And the phone?"

The old-time Mexican agent was a step ahead of her. "Catch."

Scarlet's hand darted out and she caught Lopez's phone. Within seconds she had bypassed the passcode and was flicking through his personal messages.

"Woah, you can get into an iPhone that quick?" Camacho said. "I never knew that."

"When you've dated some of the men in my back catalogue, darling, it's a necessary requirement."

"Well, you have nothing to worry about with me."

"I know," she said coolly. "I audited your phone just a few days ago."

Reaper and Nikolai shared a chuckle as Camacho's jaw fell open. "I'm not going to lie, babe. I feel violated."

Scarlet gave him another wink. "Ah, here we go. The password is in here – sent in an email from the Dove a few hours ago."

As she read out the numbers, Camacho entered the code and the locks flicked open. "Double woah."

Scarlet peered inside, shining the little light on Lopez's phone down into the case. "Ugly."

"You can say that again," Reaper said.

Castillo gave a low whistle of surprise. "Thank god we found it."

When Scarlet looked at the device, she felt her blood turn to ice. She was expecting something much bigger, much more powerful, but what she saw was no more than an aluminum medical case fastened to a compact IED with duct tape. Yet, its small size was exactly what horrified her the most.

"You're the best bomb disposal expert we have, Jack."

The American CIA man wiped his hands on his jeans and looked at her with a nervous smile breaking on his face. "You're too kind."

"So I've been told."

He peered in and saw a simple IED constructed from a pack of explosives. It was connected to a timer placed beneath a row of metal cartridges, each with its own timer.

"It's ingenuous," Scarlet said. "A virus is killed by anything hotter than seventy degrees Celsius, so this is designed to blast the vials out into the air in these bomb-proof cartridges before their own mini timers cause them to break open."

"Ensuring the vector-borne biological pathogens are dispersed over as wide an area as possible," Camacho said. "Bastards."

"Like some sort of sick fireworks display," Nikolai said.

Camacho took his time to study the device from all angles, peering through the makeshift casing and studying the little bundles of wires inside. He gave a long, weighty sigh and turned around to face the others.

"The device itself is not that impressive, but the problem is that the vials are not only connected to the timer, but…" he paused. "Looks to me like they're connected to the timer in such a way that any attempt to cut them will trigger their activation."

"And look here," Reaper said, pointing a fat sausage finger down into the nightmare of wires and circuits. "Looks like a GPS transmitter, so the Dove and maybe even Zamkov can track their location."

"We should destroy this right now," Camacho said. "But first we need to disconnect the propellant mechanism to stop it launching the cartridges into the air. Looks to me like only the timer can do that, when it runs down to zero, but I sure ain't taking any chances with the shit inside those vials."

He leaned down and carefully disconnected the cartridges from the small motor designed to propel them into the air when the timer ran out. "All right, we're good to go."

"Hang on a sec," Scarlet said. "What are these numbers here?"

Camacho and Reaper peered down once again, seeing several numbers on the timer screen. Static, and not counting down like all the other numbers, they stared back at them, almost daring them to work out what they were.

"It's not clear what they are," Camacho said at last.

"But they must have some significance," Scarlet said.

"I don't like it," Castillo said. "If I don't understand it, I don't like it."

"They're not part of the timer," the American said.

The Frenchman agreed. "These are not part of the timer, non."

"Then what?" Nikolai asked. "They wouldn't be here for no reason."

Scarlet snapped a picture of them on her phone, slipped it in her pocket and pulled her gun out. "All right, time to blow this bastard to kingdom come. We need somewhere to contain the explosion. Alby?"

"When we were in the trap room, I saw a steel grate in the floor. It must be some sort of conduit leading down to the sewer system."

"Then off we go."

They walked into the trap room, lighting their way with the small lights on the phones, and found the grate. Scarlet angled her beam through the steel mesh, seeing a twenty-foot drop and then some water. "Okay."

Reaper wrenched the grate out of the ground and Castillo moved to drop the case down into the hole.

"Wait." Camacho opened the case, pulled out the transmitter and threw it down into the back of the trap room. "Better they think this baby is still live and ready for action."

"Good call, Jack," Scarlet said. She spied down the sight of her weapon and pulled the hammer back.

Castillo looked at her with pleading eyes. "And you're sure this virus will be burnt to death in the explosion."

"Judging by the amount of C4 in this thing, when this goes up it's going to reach nearly three hundred degrees. It's dead at seventy. With the propellant in place, the cartridges would be fired away from the blast and then open, but now Jack has cut them, they'll just go up with everything else in the case."

"If you say so," he said, taking a step back.

"All right, everyone out of here."

They followed her orders, and then she was alone. She dropped the case into the water and fired a single shot, sprinting for the trap room hatch as soon as she squeezed the trigger. The detonation was violent, and channelled by the concrete tunnel, it directed a lethal column of white-hot fire up into the room in seconds.

Chased all the way by the roaring fire and smoke, she dived though the door, hitting the carpeted orchestra pit and rolling to a stop just as the explosion reached its peak. With smoke billowing up into the auditorium, she looked up at Jack.

"Did the earth move for you, darling? Because it moved for me."

He reached his hand out. "Get up, you fool… and good work."

"That's one down, and two to go," she said, dusting herself down. "I think you'd better call the fire department, Alby."

"Already done it," he said. "They are on their way."

"Which means we are out of here," Scarlet said.

Nikolai nodded at the trap room. "But we still need to find three more of those *things*."

Scarlet tossed Castillo Lopez's phone. "First send a message to El Jefe saying everything is good at the theatre. Then go through this as we go back to the car, Alby. And I want some good news before we get there."

As they hurried to the fire door and burst out into the night, the seasoned agent was still flicking through an endless stream of emails and text messages, stuffed full of Mexican slang and gang talk. "I think I found something. There is a short conversation here talking about delivering the package to the…" his eyes widened. "My god!"

"What is it?" Nikolai asked.

"I think they put one of the devices somewhere in la Feria Chapultepec Mágico."

Scarlet turned to him. "Significance?"

"It's an amusement park, and one of the most popular attractions in the entire city. With today being the Day of the Dead, it will be even crazier. And there's more – it looks like they have left men there to guard it, like here."

Thoughts turned to Lopez's twisted, blood-soaked corpse.

"Didn't work out so well for them here, though, did it?" Camacho said.

"This is terrible." Castillo passed a trembling hand over his face. "It's nearly dawn! If the supervirus explodes there, it will instantly infect tens of thousands of people."

Scarlet reloaded her gun and slid it into her holster. "Then we'd better hurry up. Hold on to your balls boys, this could get dangerous."

CHAPTER NINETEEN

The Dove took breakfast on the balcony.

He was enjoying a glass of chilled grapefruit juice and flicking through the fresh copy of *El Universal* that one of Loza's men had delivered to his room a few moments ago. It turned out nothing very special was happening in the news today. The usual cartel kidnappings and murders were pushed out of the way behind some boring, technical article outlining the latest free trade agreement with the economic giant to the north.

But things changed when he switched on the TV. A newsreader was cutting to a reporter standing outside the Palacio del Bellas Artes. There was no sign of any smoke or fire, but a number of large fire trucks were parked up outside it, and a chaotic scene of firefighters and police officers was unfolding by the second.

"What the hell is this?" he muttered.

"We had a problem last night."

He turned and saw Ramiro Loza standing in the doorway leading out to the balcony. In the light of day he looked different. He was a big man, unshaven for at least three days and wore a thick salt-and-pepper moustache under a fat, squashed nose. He was perspiring freely, despite the cool air inside the room from which he had just come, and when he sat down at the Dove's breakfast table, he let out a long sigh of relief.

The Brazilian kept his body in fighting order, but he guessed taking three hundred pounds of weight off your feet probably felt pretty damn good. He sipped his grapefruit juice and watched Loza reach a fat hand across

133

the table to grab one of the croissants. He tore the end right off and began chewing hungrily as the shower of pastry flakes fell onto his black shirt.

The Dove folded his newspaper and dropped it down onto the table. "After all the excitement last night, I was hoping for some peace before the big event. Now, I wake up and see the Palacio on fire. I trust you have good reason for interrupting my morning routine, and that this reason will include an explanation about what happened here?"

"Si." When he spoke, he blew out more croissant crumbs. "But there is good news as well as bad news."

The Dove had known right from the start that El Jefe would be difficult to work with. He had a well-deserved reputation for his bloody ruthlessness when dealing with enemies and traitors, but he was also known for his casual arrogance. No matter – he would be dead like everyone else in a matter of weeks.

"Then, give me the good news first. Bad news interferes with my digestion."

"The good news is that three of the bombs are still in place, just as you ordered."

The bombs, the Brazilian thought. *If only he knew.* "I presume the fourth one in the Palacio was eliminated by this team?"

"Yes."

"This displeases me, Loza. If that's the good news, what is the bad news?"

The fat Mexican swallowed the croissant down then reached for the cigar jutting out of his top pocket. He bit the cap off, spat it over the balcony, then sloppily slid the head into his mouth and fumbled for his lighter. After spending a few long moments wafting a flame across the cigar's tuck, it came to life. He sucked noisily and the embers glowed a deep, warm orange, then he exhaled the smoke away from the Dove, over the balcony.

A wise decision, the Brazilian considered.

"Have you finished digesting your grapefruit juice?" Loza asked.

"I'm ready for the bad news, if that's what you mean."

"Good, because my man failed to take out the team last night when they neutralized the Palacio bomb."

"So they're still on the loose. Very disappointing. How did they get this information?"

"It's hard to say, but maybe from one of the men last night at the villa."

"You're making me angry, Loza."

The Dove kicked the table leg and knocked the glass pitcher over, spilling grapefruit juice all over his newspaper. The Mexican pushed his chair back a few inches to avoid getting the fruit juice in his lap.

"And it gets worse," Loza said.

"Explain."

"One of my men, a good man named Gustavo Cavazos, has a place out in Iztapalapa. It's not a good part of town, but he grew up there, like a lot of my men. He's a good fighter. Brave. Tough. A hard man who spent more time in prison than the next ten of my guys put together."

"So?"

"So, last night this team broke into his house, smashed it up real bad and took out at least three of my men there. The cops found Gustavo's body in a parking lot not far from his house."

"What are you saying?"

"Gustavo knew we were holding the hostages at Buena Vista ranch. Maybe they beat it out of him."

"I see."

"You want me to move them to another location?"

135

The Dove gave the matter some thought as he watched the cars trundling up and down the busy avenues. If only they all knew, he considered, they would take the day off and enjoy themselves. "No. If they have the location then we are forewarned, and forewarned is forearmed. When they get to the ranch, I want your men ready. An army of men, got it?"

"I get it, but these guys were good, and I mean razor-sharp. Joaquin called from the theatre before they murdered him. He said they move like real pros, and they're totally ruthless. Plus, they must have been in and out of Gustavo's place in minutes and they meant business. No screwing around."

"Why are you telling me this?"

Loza shifted in his seat and squinted his eyes as he sucked on the cigar. He took his time, eying up the Dove while he blew out a long, thick cloud of smoke. The Brazilian had seen that look before. It was a killer's look.

"I'm saying, maybe you should have told me if you have guys with skills like this chasing after your ass, because now they're chasing after *my* ass, too."

"Until the attack on the villa last night, we thought they were dead."

"Wait a minute." Loza's face darkened. "You mean you know who they are?"

The Dove nodded. "Welcome to the ECHO team."

"And who the fuck are they?"

"Mostly special ops, and easily the best in the world."

Loza tossed his hands in the air. "Well, this is just great, isn't it?"

The Dove saw movement off to his left, in the periphery of his vision. When he turned to look through the balcony door, he saw the woman from last night. She had turned the TV volume down and was walking from the bed across to the bathroom. The breeze from the open door caught the intricate lace hem of her chemise and lifted it up over her knees. She turned and smiled, giving him a sleazy wink before disappearing inside the bathroom.

"Tell me more about these assholes." Loza asked. "If my men are going to fight them at the ranch, we need to know."

"Like I say, they're an international special ops team called ECHO. They came to my employer's compound in the Amazon jungle and wiped it out. If you were impressed by what they did to Gustavo, you'd be blown away by what they did down there, believe me."

"I knew they were trouble. My men don't get easily rattled."

"No, I'm sure they don't."

Loza's brow furrowed. "I'm not too happy about my men going up against a special ops team. I want more money."

The Dove looked at him sharply but then softened his approach and smiled. What would it matter how much he paid Loza and his goons? He could pay him all the gold in the world and it would mean nothing, but then again, asking the fat gangster to name his price would be a mistake. Loza was nobody's fool, and if he thought for one minute that the Dove's employer would pay whatever he asked, he would become suspicious. The Dove decided to haggle.

"We already agreed a price, Loza. Los Serpientes deliver the bombs to the locations specified by my employer and I supervise the operation. When the task is completed and the bombs go off, you will be paid one million US dollars for each of the four bombs."

"I know this."

"Four million dollars is a lot of money for placing some explosives and guarding them, not to mention you have already screwed up and allowed ECHO to take out one of the bombs. Maybe Mr Zamkov should only be paying you three million dollars?"

Loza tapped the cigar on the table and knocked the ash into the croissants. He was being deliberately provocative, as the Dove knew he would be. There was no need to put him in his place. His place was dead in the streets with the rest of the people of this city, and he would be in that place soon enough.

"You think you can play hard ball with me?" Loza said. "Because you can't, my friend."

"How much do you want?"

"My price just doubled."

"You want eight million dollars?"

"You think I'm some kind of idiot? I know who Nikita Zamkov is. He's one of the world's richest men. He controls hundreds of billions of dollars across all the global markets, not to mention his famous gold reserves. Now…" he leaned forward and locked his eyes on the Dove. "I don't know why your little Russian boss wants to blow up my city, and I don't care about it either. All I know is, when you forget to tell me about your little team of special forces maniacs, you put my life and the lives of my men in danger, and you need to pay a price for that."

"No way is Mr Zamkov going to sanction eight million dollars. He's very astute with money. How do you think he has so much? Not by spending it."

"So how much would he agree to?"

The act was nearly over.

"Six million. We already talked about it."

Loza's stern face broke into a smile and then a deep, belly laugh. "You already agreed to go to six million dollars, but thought you would try out four first? I like you, Dove, you are a man after my own heart. I'll take the six, payable when the bombs go off."

The Dove nodded. "On one condition."

The eyes narrowed once again. "Oh, yeah? What's that? That I squeeze you some fresh grapefruit juice, too?"

"No, that you kill the ECHO team."

"Now I know what I'm up against, I can arrange that."

"And Loza?"

"What?"

"Exercise extreme prejudice."

The fat Mexican raised his palms, exposing sweat rings on his shirt. "When dealing with my enemies, I know no other way, amigo."

"Good, now get off my balcony. You're ruining the view."

Loza pushed the chair back, barely concealing the hatred he must surely have felt for the easy-going, carefree Brazilian in his crisp white shirt. "Next time we meet, I will expect you to be carrying six million dollars in cash, and I expect you to throw in the little suitcase that's holding it, too, for free – just for that remark."

"You'll get what you ask for," the Dove said as Loza waddled back into the room and headed for the other door.

And what you deserve, too.

*

In the white world of Antarctica, Valentina Kiriyenko wished she could remember life before her accident. Her only memories were being in her apartment alone when a man had attacked her. She had no memory of him at all and could not picture his face, but she knew he hit her very hard in the head.

Whatever he did to her was bad enough to have induced a debilitating and comprehensive amnesia that had, with the exception of some important childhood memories, deleted most of her life from her birth up to the night of the attack. Now, her life began when she saw Niki running into her apartment and saving her life.

He had cradled her head in his arms and stared down into her eyes with such sympathy. He had called an ambulance and been there for her when she was discharged from hospital. He had taken care of her. He had taken her under his wing. He had given her a new life to replace the old one the attacker had stolen from her.

She owed him everything and she would do anything for him. Lately, she had started to dream of marrying him and having a child with him. What was it he had wanted to ask her earlier today? Was he going to propose to her? She felt her cheeks flush a little. Why would a genius billionaire like Nikita Zamkov ask a penniless woman with no past to marry him? She felt a rush of excitement.

No one deserved to be this happy.

She looked at herself in the bedroom mirror and sighed. Maybe she should grow her hair a little longer, or try a different shade of lipstick. Something to shake things up a bit. She had no idea how long they would be trapped down in Antarctica. Niki told her it was just for a few weeks while the virus worked its way around the world.

Her thoughts stopped dead in their tracks.

For a moment, she had wondered if they were doing the right thing. Niki had explained to her all about the overpopulation of the world and the ever-diminishing resources. He told her about how mankind would soon destroy not only the planet, but also itself. *What we're doing is a mercy, Valya,* he had said, brushing his hand against her cheek. *We're saving them from themselves; we're sparing them from wars and famine and plague and from a slow, agonising death.*

Yes, Niki was always right. This was the best way. Only this way would humanity be spared from the punishing brutality of its own selfish actions. And she was privileged to have been chosen by him to survive. The two of them could live after the apocalypse – two of a handful of people left, creating a new world populated by his AI creations.

Just the two of them.

Man and woman.

Adam and Eve.

CHAPTER TWENTY

Hawke, Lexi, Zeke and the Mexican secret service agent cruised down the western slopes of the Sierra Madre mountains with the rising sun at their backs. Today, the breaking of the dawn was a bad sign, and one look at the dashboard clock told them exactly how bad.

Over seven hours had passed since their arrival at midnight and progress was slow, and when Lexi's phone buzzed and she held up the screen for him to see the message, Hawke's mood grew darker. It was from Scarlet. The good news was they had taken out the supervirus, the bad news was the Dove had broken up the supply and there were three more devices hidden around the city. The text also said that they were on their way over to the Chapultepec amusement park right now, following a possible lead.

"Where is Chapultepec, Franco?" he asked.

Lexi was sitting in the front beside Hawke, and now she turned and showed Nikolai and the Mexican the same message.

"To the west of the city," Franco said anxiously. "The amusement park is also close to many very important and busy tourist attractions, including the country's most famous zoo and several museums, not to mention the famous Chapultepec Castle. The castle is set in parkland around seven hundred hectares in size."

"Seven hundred hectares?" Hawke said. "That's three times bigger than the City of London."

"Because of all these attractions, the entire park is one of the busiest places in the city. It's always full of people, families and children, you name it. I have to call my superiors."

"No." Hawke's tone was unusually harsh. "I can't let you do that, Franco."

"But if a bomb goes off in the park, literally hundreds of people could be killed – perhaps even thousands. The CNI can get an undercover team out there at once and begin evacuating the museums and zoo, at least. They can start a search for the explosives with specially trained sniffer dogs."

"I said no," Hawke said, even more firmly this time. "Nothing has changed since we briefed Alberto and you back at the safehouse. The terrorists behind this attack are the most technologically-advanced enemy we or you have ever faced."

Franco reached into his pocket. "This is madness. If we do not act, innocent people will die."

Hawke saw the Mexican agent moving in the rear view mirror. "Zeke, take his phone."

The Texan tank commander moved fast, snatching the phone from Franco's hand before it was even fully out of his jacket pocket. "Sorry, but you're not making that call."

"Give me that back!"

"No," the Texan said as he wound down the window. "Again, accept my apologies."

"No!" Franco watched helplessly as Zeke tossed the phone out of the window into the desert. It smacked down with a plastic clatter in the dry, dusty gravel at the side of the road and then was gone.

"You will be reimbursed by ECHO," said Zeke. "At some point."

Franco's face reddened and his hands curled into fists. "How dare you do that to me? I am an ally in this war. I could have helped. And that was my personal property."

Hawke turned down the volume on the radio and lowered his voice. "I already told you in the briefing, Franco – two of our teammates are being held by the Serpents. They told us any contact with the Mexican authorities would result in their immediate execution. We took a big enough risk speaking to Alberto and you, but having a team of bomb disposal dogs running around Mexico City's biggest park is sort of taking the piss, wouldn't you agree?"

Franco's shoulders slumped. "It is wrong to put the lives of two people ahead of the safety of the general public, to save two lives if it means putting the lives of hundreds, or maybe even thousands of people, at risk."

"They're not at risk," Lexi said coolly. "Not while Cairo Sloane is on the case, so just chill down and take it easy. You're making me agitated. I'm kind of wishing we didn't bring you along."

Franco laughed. "Then let me out right now, and let's see how far you get. This is my country and these are my hunting grounds. I have spent my life putting men like Los Serpientes behind bars. I know how they think. I know how they operate. You need me more than I need you."

Lexi's dark eyes flashed with anger, but she controlled her temper and kept her mouth shut. Whatever she was going to say was unnecessary – the look in her eyes was enough to make Franco sink down in his seat and turn his head to stare out of the window.

"Tell me," Hawke said. "I'm guessing this road is usually pretty quiet."

"Yes," Franco muttered. "Especially at this time in the morning, and the further away from the city you get, the less busy it gets, of course. Why?"

"Because we've been followed for the last three miles." Hawke added hastily, "And don't anyone turn around to look, please. We don't want to give our friends behind us the heads up."

Lexi tipped her head and glanced in her side mirror. "The 4x4?"

"That's the one."

"Could be anyone," Franco said.

"No," Hawke said. "Something doesn't feel right. For one thing, it's riding too low on its suspension for a truck with only two people in it."

"They're carrying something in the back," Lexi said.

Hawke nodded as Zeke pulled a handgun from a shoulder holster and slid a round into the chamber. "A drowning man will grab even a straw if it means saving his life, man. This truck is full of serpents, my new friend, and you know it."

"And that means the Dove and Zamkov are keeping a closer eye on us that we thought," Hawke said with a sigh.

"If you ask me," Lexi said, "we have our very own satellite, just for us."

Hawke weighed the thought. "Maybe."

Lexi took another look in the mirror. "Maybe it's the sniper."

"What sniper?" Franco asked.

"Not your concern," Lexi said.

"It's everyone's concern if he's out there someplace," Zeke said, staring up at the top of a ridge running parallel to the highway. "Son of a bitch could be up there right now, and my face is right in the crosshairs."

"Who are you talking about?" Franco said.

145

"We're being hunted, Manny," Zeke said. "One by one, someone is taking us out to lunch and leaving us with the bill."

Franco paled. "You think this man is up on the ridge now? How can he even know where we are?"

"We don't know," Lexi said coolly. The air came in through the vents and gently blew her hair up over her forehead. "But he's everywhere."

"Like he's working some sort of voodoo," the Texan said quietly.

"If he's working anything," Hawke said, "it's an international intel network connected to just about all the bells and whistles available – local spy contacts, real-time satellite data, phone and computer hacking and tracking. Whoever he is, there's someone mighty powerful pulling his strings."

Lexi said, "You're still thinking the Spider?"

"No. It has to be Faulkner."

Franco furrowed his brow. "When you say Faulkner, surely you're not talking about the President of the United States?"

"Got it on one, Franco," Lexi said.

The Mexican gasped. "This is unbelievable."

"Believe it," Zeke said. "And while you're thinking about it, take a moment to—."

The bullet punched a hole through the rear window, ripped through the car in a millisecond and tore right back out through the windshield. Another shot blew out their rear tire. Startled, Hawke leaned to the left and swerved the car off the road.

"Shit!"

Lexi's gun was already drawn and she spun around to look over the seats at the smashed rear window. "Looks like our friends have decided to introduce themselves at last."

Hawke struggled to control the car as it ploughed over the rocky ground on only three good tires and spewed up a thick column of dust in its wake. Dipping his head, he checked the side mirror, but a bullet ripped it off at the exact same second and send a cloud of glass shards exploding into the air. "Double shit!"

"They're gaining, Joe!" Lexi said,

Zeke twisted in his seat. "And one of them has an MP5!"

"And we're in the middle of nowhere!" Franco said.

"Not quite," Hawke replied. "There's a gas station a mile or two to the south."

"I know this road," Franco said. "That is three kilometres away if you are a bird and can fly over some very rough and hilly ground."

"We can make it in this," Hawke said.

"On three tires?"

A devilish smirk appeared on the Englishman's face. "There's no harm in trying, Manny."

CHAPTER TWENTY-ONE

The drive from the theatre to the Chapultepec amusement park was quiet and sullen. No one spoke much as Reaper cruised the SUV through the city's streets. The sun was rising over the mountains to the east, and slowly the chilangos were coming to life ready for one of the most important days of the year.

The Day of the Dead.

The holiday was a major celebration over two days across Mexico, when friends and family gathered together to pray for loved ones who had passed away. It was a time for joy in Mexican culture, not sadness, but Scarlet knew it would be a day of terror and dread if they didn't destroy the next supervirus vial in time.

Approaching the park, Scarlet stopped brooding and broke the silence. "What time does this place open, Alberto?"

The retired CNI agent looked across the SUV's back seat at her. She was sliding a fresh magazine into the grip of a Glock and waiting impatiently for some kind of answer.

"Nine a.m. every morning, but closed on Mondays."

"Today's a Friday," she said.

"True."

"So nine a.m. then."

"Also true."

She smacked the mag into the grip and pushed the gun into her shoulder holster. "Time, anyone?"

Camacho checked his watch. "Just after seven, babe."

"We have two hours to find the bomb," she said calmly. "After that, life gets much harder. The place will fill up with people, including kids and babies, but also a hell of a lot more security is going to come on shift."

"Two hours to find something the size of a small suitcase, hidden in an amusement park," Alberto said. "Again, I implore you to let me bring in back-up. There are people I trust, Cairo. People I *know*."

"Can't let you do it, Alby," she said. "If Zamkov or his little Dove bird find out, it's goodnight Lea and the Boy. Can't let that happen. We find it and we find it alone, and we find it fast. It's what we do."

Anxiety was plastered all over the older man's face, but he backed down. He had known Scarlet long enough to trust she could get the job done. "All right, then I will offer you a deal."

"No deals."

"We find the bomb by opening time, or I will have the park shut down."

"You can't do that," she said. "I thought I made this clear, Alby? You shut the park down and the Dove will know something's up. He'll report it to Zamkov and then our friends get executed. When I asked you to trust me, Alby, it was more like me telling you to trust me – got it?"

Alberto couldn't resist a defenceless smile. "You are one of a kind, Cairo Sloane. One of a kind."

The Frenchman's low, gravelly voice broke into the moment. "We are here, mes amis. Where do you want me to go now?"

Alberto turned to Scarlet. "Well? Obviously, you are running this operation. Where do we start?"

"We start with the areas that are going to be busiest during the day when the visitors arrive. Zamkov isn't going to waste his time planting a bomb somewhere out of the way. He has one device planted in the park and he wants the maximum bang for his buck."

"On the biggest rides, then," Alberto said.

Camacho nodded. "For sure – and here we are."

They approached some large, black, wrought iron gates. "Go in, Reap," Scarlet said.

"But there is a security gate," Alberto said. "We won't be able to pass without opening it, and the guards will not be at work yet."

"Fear not, Alby," Scarlet said. "I have a special key that opens the gates."

He looked at her sideways. "Oh yes? What is this key?"

Scarlet winked. "It's called my Reaper key."

At that exact moment, Alberto was pushed back into his seat as the Frenchman stamped on the accelerator. The SUV's three litre engine roared under the hood and seconds later they were ploughing through the gates. Sparks and grinding metal exploded into the air around them as they smashed through the barrier into the park, leaving two bent, twisted gates swinging back and forth behind them.

"That's the Reaper key," Scarlet said. "Opens basically anything."

They drove into the park, rounding a bend on the gravel road to see an enormous rollercoaster rising above them.

The introverted Russian monk stared up at it and whistled. "That is amazing."

"The Montaña Infinitum," Castillo said with pride. "It's a very large rollercoaster – the first in the whole world to have three vertical loops."

Camacho looked at Scarlet with a frown. "You hear what he just said?"

"Sure, he said it was the first to have three vertical loops."

"No, he said *stay away from it*, and so did I, got it?"

"You know me, Jacky, if there's a—."

"What is it?"

"Guy in a leather jacket and motorcycle helmet – over there."

"I see him," Castillo said. "A Serpiente, for sure – look at the markings on his jacket!"

"He's broken cover from over there in the bumper cars – and I don't like the look of that backpack," Scarlet said.

"You think the device is in it?" Nikolai asked.

"No way to tell. Where is he going?"

"It's the Casona del Teror – a haunted house."

Scarlet rolled her eyes. "Not again. What is it with pricks like this and haunted houses?"

"Que?" Castillo asked.

"Me and Joe Hawke once chased a scumbag called Marcus Deprez around a House of Horrors in Stockholm."

"And how did that end?" he asked.

"Roughly the same way it's going to end for this fool."

As the man vanished inside, Reaper screeched the car to a halt and they all piled out, ready for action.

"All right," Scarlet said. "I'm going in to flush him out. Jack and Reaper, you cover the exits. Kolya, you go over the bumper car ride with a fine toothcomb. He might have hidden the device in there. Alby, you're with me in case we need to get some info out of him."

"Got it."

With Camacho and Reaper racing around to the exits, Scarlet drew her gun and ran inside the Hall of Terror. A foot behind her, Castillo also drew his gun and followed her into the building.

The attraction was designed to look like some sort of apocalyptic nightmare, with graffiti all over walls of crumbling plaster and corpses hanging from meat hooks. Scarlet hated these places, but had seen it all before back in Sweden. She held her gun fast, swinging it from corner to corner as she made her way through the dark and gloomy ride.

During the day when the park was open, this place would be full of actors playing the role of noisy zombies, but right now a deathly silence clung to the slimy walls. Then, they heard a loud scream echo in the darkness, and the sound of someone mumbling the last rites in Spanish.

"He must have switched on the recording they play during the day," Castillo said. "I heard this exact same thing with my grandson when we visited recently..."

Another ear-piercing scream blasted out from a concealed speaker, and the man lunged in the darkness from inside what was supposed to be the door of a jail or asylum. Striking his fist into Castillo's face, the older man crumpled to the floor, knocked out cold by the blow.

Scarlet reacted in a second, rotating on her hips to the direction of the attacker and firing into the darkness. The muzzle flash lit the blackness around her and told her Castillo's assailant had already fled, then she heard the sound of him wrenching open a door ahead of her. A flash of bright morning daylight flooded into the narrow corridor and she just caught sight of the man's back as he vanished out the door.

"Dammit... sorry Alby, I'll be back."

She sprinted after the man, bursting out into the day just in time to see Camacho and Reaper running around the corner toward her. Camacho looked at her with an apologetic shrug. "We got held up fighting another couple

152

of Serpents. They rushed us from behind the candy floss stand."

"That's one to tell the grandkids," she said with a wink.

"They were both riding bikes," Reaper said. "Until we punched them off of their bikes."

"Where's our man?"

"There!" Camacho yelled. "He's getting on his bike!"

"Nice Ducati, too," Scarlet said. "Reap, Alby's out cold back in crazyland. Get him out and make sure he's okay."

"Consider it done."

"We're going after the other one – let's get their bikes!"

They ran to the Serpents' motorbikes – one was on its side next to the candy floss stand and the other was lying under the bumper car carousel. Scrambling over to them, they grabbed them and got them back up onto their wheels.

Scarlet straddled the Kawasaki Ninja and with the sun flashing on her tight leather trousers, she gave him a wink and turned the bike toward the fleeing man. "Last one there's a rotten egg, darling."

"Dammit, why is everything a game to her..."

Firing up the engine, Camacho skidded out after the fleeing man, skirting the rides and food carts as he gave lethal pursuit. Swerving around the corner of a Ferris wheel, he pulled up alongside Scarlet and saw the man up ahead, heading for one of the exits.

She looked over and winked. "You come here often?"

He shook his head and laughed. "No, it's my first time. You?"

"First time."

She revved the engine and roared away into the lead at the head of a spear of dust and exhaust fumes. Screaming with excitement, she twisted the throttle and increased velocity. For the first time since the battle back in Zamkov's Amazon jungle compound she felt truly alive, truly exhilarated.

Camacho called out behind her. "Hey! He's mine!"

"Early bird gets the worm, Jacky Boy."

Ahead of them, the gangster was weaving his bike in and out of a child's play area and heading toward an enormous rollercoaster. Seconds later, he ducked his head, roared underneath the vast structure and was out of sight.

Scarlet zoomed in after him, ducking her head to avoid a collision with the foundation rigging at the base of the ageing wooden rollercoaster. Her eyes got used to the darker environment and she saw she was in a labyrinth of chunky support columns, but not for long. The gangster shot out the other side and turned sharp, pulling up in a tight arc and racing his bike onto the platform where visitors waited for the rollercoaster car.

She never hesitated and she didn't think about what came next. She just turned her bike in sharp pursuit and following the reckless rider up onto the platform.

Camacho looked on with dismay and called up to her. "Oh no, surely not? You're not that crazy!"

"Sorry to disappoint you, Jacky Boy, but I most definitely am."

"He's going too fast, Cairo! He'll be killed! No one can go that fast."

"Hold my vodka, Jack!" Scarlet said, and raced up onto the rollercoaster.

CHAPTER TWENTY-TWO

Scarlet watched the man leaving the platform and turning onto the rollercoaster tracks. Without thinking, she turned the bike onto the tracks and gave chase. Unlike the larger Montaña Infinitum, the Montaña Rusa was much older and lacked the vertical loops, but was still a deadly ride on a motorcycle.

Racing forward, the wooden slats in between the two rails were more rickety than she had thought they would be and as she zoomed over it, the wheels bounced up and down on the shock absorbers. The entire bike rattled and shook, but there was no way she was going to stop and let this Serpent get away with the device.

Below her, Camacho had turned to the right and was driving along the ground in the direction of the rollercoaster's far end. Calling up to her, his voice was barely audible over the wild revving and roaring of their engines. "Are you out of your mind?"

"Without a doubt," she called back. "Why else would I be doing this?"

Camacho looked ahead and watched as the rider approached one of the rises, but instead of slowing down or looking for another way to escape his pursuer, he revved his bike, dropped down a gear and increased his speed.

"Dammit, no!" Camacho called out.

Scarlet liked her chances. Her bike was more powerful and the man had already demonstrated that she was the superior biker. Not only that, but she had watched a French motorcyclist do exactly the same thing on exactly

155

the same rollercoaster a few years ago. If he could make it, then so could she.

She watched with a thrill of excitement as he raced up the track and began to climb the first rise. She was in his wake, right on his tail. The track was flashing past, reflecting the rising sun and giving glimpses of the ground beneath it. She saw Camacho's anxious face but was going too fast to stop; she had to keep going.

Looking up above her head, the gangster was now at the top of the first rise and disappearing into the descent. She increased speed, climbing over a hundred feet above the rest of the amusement park on the narrow wooden track. Reaching the top, she looked down and saw he was already at the bottom of the first drop and revving up to make the next climb.

She tipped over the crest of the rise and sent the Ninja racing over into the drop. The motorbike's frame rattled hard once again as the suspension struggled to deal with the brutal combination of the wooden slats and the rapid descent, but she added more power and built more speed.

The other rider was already leaving the dip and reaching the top of the next rise just as she was at the base of it. As gravity slowed him down, she followed the curve of the tracks upwards. She twisted the throttle and gave the engine more juice for the climb, and for the second time she accelerated up another steep incline.

The sun was getting higher now, and as she climbed to a certain height on the rails it flashed in her eyes and startled her. The bike swerved, almost leaving the central slats and crashing through the wooden guiderails on her left. She shook it off and corrected the trajectory of the superbike just in time.

With the Ducati's exhaust fumes thick in the air, she could hear the gangster wildly revving his engine as he tried to outgun her. Looking ahead, she saw him leap his bike from the central track base to one of the outer rails. This immediately provided a smoother ride and gave him the speed he needed to complete a sharp bend to the right, but sticking to the rail was vital. If the tire slipped an inch either side, he would spin off the rollercoaster and crash to his death.

And so would she.

Making the same leap across to the side rail just as the track began to bend around for a sharp right-hand corner, Scarlet increased the speed of the bike. It was counterintuitive, just in the same way a naval fighter pilot pushed the throttles fully forward to maximum thrust at the moment of landing in case they miss the arrester hook and have to take off again. She knew that if her speed dropped too low she might lose balance on the bend and tip over.

The powerful racing engine roared beneath her. The wind whipped in her face and tugged at her hair, but she was doing it. She was powering the Kawasaki Ninja along a rollercoaster rail at high speed, over one hundred feet above the ground. Ahead, the rider was still the same distance away and heading for the final rise. One more drop after that and he would leave the rollercoaster.

She raced after him, hitting the top of the rise and bending around to the right once again. The gangster had already turned the bend and was now riding in the opposite direction to her as he began to head toward the final drop.

It was now or never. After this, it would be down to one of the others to catch him and she would have failed. Not in a month of Sundays, she thought. She was leading this team and it was down to her to take this goon out. It was risky, but she released her hand from one of the handlebars and reached for her gun.

Slowing for the bend, she turned into the final drop and aimed the weapon at the rider as he screeched down towards the ground. She fired and missed. Her round ricocheted off the rail and pinged off into the amusement park. It turned out riding a superbike one-handed on a rollercoaster, and firing on a man driving at least fifty miles per hour, was harder than she had thought.

She aimed again and fired.

And missed.

And now she was riding down the drop, gathering speed on the rickety wooden slates of the Montaña Rusa at a dangerous pace. The rider was heading up the final, gentle rise on his way to the end of the rollercoaster. Steadying her bike, and with the warm Mexican hair blowing on her neck, she fired.

The nine-mil round buried itself in the gangster's neck and ended the chase on the spot. He slumped forward over the handlebars and the bike wobbled wildly before losing control and flying off to the side. Ploughing through the wooden safety rail, it leaped into the air like a stunt bike, then tipped forward and dropped to the ground with all the aerodynamic grace of a refrigerator.

Scarlet breathed a sigh of relief, holstered the weapon and drove to the end of the rollercoaster, pulling off at the little wooden platform where she had joined the ride. She steered off the platform, killed the engine and parked up. Calmly flicking the kickstand out with her leather boot, she hopped off the bike and walked over to her friends who were all standing around the dead man.

A few yards away, the crumpled bike's engine was spluttering. She walked over to it and switched it off, then turned to her friends. "That was different."

Nursing a black eye, Castillo sighed with fatherly disapproval. "What next, Cairo – are you going to ride a unicycle on the Kingda Ka?"

"Don't put ideas into her head," Camacho said. "Please, just don't." Turning to Scarlet, his voice grew more serious again. "Did I not say to keep away from it?"

"Technically," Castillo said with the hint of a smile, "you said keep away from the Montaña Infinitum. She was on the Montaña Rusa."

Camacho threw his hands into the air. "God dammit! What is this, a conspiracy?"

"I got the job done," Scarlet said coolly.

"You could have gotten yourself killed," Camacho said. "Dammit, Cairo! That was the craziest thing I have ever seen you do."

He was trying to deliver a good, old-fashioned bollocking, she knew, but he backed down. They both knew what ran through her veins.

"Good job you weren't at my passing out party in the SAS." She shook her head. "I often think about that poor donkey."

Camacho went to speak but shut his mouth. Not only was he lost for words, but Alberto Castillo was now pulling an iPhone from the dead man's leather jacket. After a few moments, he located what he was looking for. With a shrug at Camacho, he said, "Cairo was right – we can use his phone's GPS to track his past movements. According to this, he was over in this location here through most of the night until we came into the park. When he saw us, he must have decided to move away from the device."

"So where is it?" Camacho asked.

"It's in one of the children's rides – a carousel in the center of the park."

"Mon Dieu," Reaper said with disgust. "Infecting kids first. These people really are scum."

"We can save the hate for later," Scarlet said. "Let's get over there and destroy it before it goes off. In the meantime, we need to know where the other devices are."

They hurried across the park and reached the carousel. It was a beautifully ornate ride for young children, with wooden horses painted and polished to perfection below deftly carved latticework festooned with colourful bulbs.

"I remember these from when I was a kid," Scarlet said, tracing her hand over one of the horse's necks.

"But this one has a difference," Castillo said. "This one is hiding Armageddon itself somewhere inside it."

The ride was small and hiding places were limited. Nikolai found the case hidden inside the gears at the center of the carousel. It was identical to the one they had found and destroyed in the theatre.

Thinking of the children who would have been playing on this ride in less than an hour, Scarlet looked down at it with contempt. "Bring it over to the car park," she said. "I'll blow the damn thing up out there. No need for the fire department this time – it'll just burn out on the tarmac. In the meantime, go through this clown's phone like a dose of salts."

"You mean like MI6 would?" Castillo said.

"No, even worse than that," she said. "Like the taxman would."

He gave a reluctant titter. "Leave it with me."

They returned to the empty parking lot where Camacho disconnected the cartridges, then Scarlet walked the case over to the center of asphalt expanse. Going back to the SUV, she aimed at the case and fired on it, blowing it into an enormous fireball. The case blew at least three hundred feet in the air and the cloud of smoke and fire and debris blasted out in a radius nearly as big.

"Another one bites the dust," she said. "Alby, what have got from the phone?"

He hesitated. "It's not good. It looks like some sort of schematic for… oh my God!"

"What is it?" Scarlet said.

"It's inside Chapultepec Castle!"

"How far, Alby?"

"Not far at all, thank god!" He checked his watch. "We can be there in less than ten minutes if we cut through the Bosque de Chapultepec."

"What's that?"

"A large park to the west of the castle.. but it gets worse."

Scarlet's voice grew lower and more serious. "Why does it get worse, my old friend?"

"See for yourself."

She took the phone from him and stared at the screen. "What am I looking at?"

"At the bottom of the schematics is a blown-up section," he said glumly.

Her eyes moved down to the bottom of the print. "Holy shit."

"What is it?" Camacho said.

"It looks like not all of the devices have the same timer lengths, Jack. According to this, the one in the castle is going to explode in less than an hour."

CHAPTER TWENTY-THREE

Time was passing in a blur, and by the time they reached Chapultepec Castle, it was after nine in the morning and visitors were already lining up, waiting to pay to come in. Taking one look at the long line of tourists waiting to gain entry, Castillo sighed and scratched his balding head. "We can't wait in this line – it'll just take too long."

"Maybe we could find another way in?" Camacho said. "There has to be a service entrance we could use to break into the place."

Scarlet looked up at the castle, sitting at the top of the hill in the sunshine. "Scaling the castle walls is a bit passé, isn't it?"

"And we don't even have a grappling hook," Reaper said.

The Russian monk was silent as usual, and instead was flicking through something on his phone. As he worked, he pulled up his hood. Born and bred in Moscow, he was not used to the intense UV of the Mexican sun. With his head safely protected by the shade of the hood, he continued to swipe his thumb on the screen.

"And we're not shooting our way in either," Castillo said. "There has already been quite enough of that today."

Without speaking, Nikolai turned and walked to the line of people, passed it and headed inside the castle.

"What are you doing, Kolya?" Camacho asked, then lowering his voice. "Dammit, I wish that guy would tell us what he was thinking sometimes."

The monk turned and waved his phone. "I'm going to pick up our tickets – I just bought them online with their Skip-The-Line Admission facility. It's very good."

Scarlet cocked her head and put her hands on her hips, a smile spreading on her face. Nikolai was easily the most serious person on the team, and probably the sharpest. His insider knowledge of the Athanatoi was invaluable to ECHO, but he was more than that now. He had become a valued team member in his own right, and fought bravely, but no one had yet seen any sign of a sense of humor.

Until now.

"Nice work, Kolya," she said.

The Russian was fighting a smile from his lips. He had a reputation to maintain, after all.

Camacho shrugged and said, "Hey, sometimes the simplest ideas are the best."

They followed Nikolai into the castle and after showing the online receipts on the Russian's phone, they followed the directions on the schematics. Scarlet sped up the pace, keen to get ahead of the curve. If the intel they had gathered from the phone was true, this was a chance to take another of the vials out of the game, and with the dawn now behind them, time was running out fast. Behind her, Reaper, Camacho, Nikolai and Castillo struggled to keep up. When they reached the top of the steps at the castle entrance, Camacho blew out a breath and patted his stomach.

"I still got it."

Scarlet glanced over at him. As her eyes crawled down to his stomach, she arched an eyebrow. "What, a gut?"

"I object to that terminology," he said with a grin. "I meant I still have my mojo, of course."

She turned on her heel and aimed for the main entrance. "You blush when you're embarrassed, sweetie."

Camacho was suddenly aware of Reaper and Castillo staring at him. "It's from the run, guys... really."

Reaper laughed and landed a heavy hand down on Camacho's shoulder. "Don't worry, I believe you. It was a long run. At least thirty seconds."

As they walked into the shadows of the giant portico, Camacho protested. "I'm just a bit out of shape."

"Yeah, because of the gut," Scarlet said. "Now haul it over here and help me find this damn supervirus."

Inside, they were able to walk quickly and made good progress; it was still early and most of the rooms and corridors in the vast building were still largely empty of tourists.

"This place is kinda spooky," Camacho said.

"It'll be even spookier if we're rushed by a load of Serpents," Scarlet said. "And remember what the messages on Lopez's phone said – they've got people guarding the device here in the castle."

"They could be hiding among the tourists," said Nikolai.

Castillo snorted. "Not many tourists have snake tattoos on their faces, necks and arms, my friend. Just look out for that."

"I'll bear that in mind," the Russian said, casting a suspicious glance around the small handful of men and women ambling along the corridor just ahead of them. Passing them, Scarlet led the team down another long, broad corridor lined with works of art and sculptures from across the centuries.

"Tell me if I'm wrong, Alby," Scarlet said, "But we must be nearly at the location on the schematics, right?"

He nodded and loosened his tie. "Yes... you people walk *fast*... ah – here we are. If we go through this room, we should get to some stairs."

They stepped into a large special exhibition room decorated with Aztec pottery and followed Castillo to a fire exit on the far side. He smacked the panic bar down and flung the door open to reveal a small stairwell. "Down these steps," he said hurriedly. "They should take us direct to the basement."

"Down usually does," said Camacho, a twinkle in his eye.

At the bottom of the steps they reached another tiled corridor. There were no tourists down here, and their shoes and boots tapped quietly on the smooth tiled floor as they hurried forward.

"We're still not on the basement level," Castillo said. "Over here…"

Up ahead, the corridor curved around to the left and revealed another colonial marble stairwell behind a set of closed glass doors. Approaching them, they saw the doors were locked.

Camacho stepped forward. "Allow me."

The force of his boot impacting on the flimsy interior lock blasted the two doors apart and blew a cloud of dry, powdery wood dust out into the stairwell. Taking the stairs leading down to the next floor, the emergency lights flickered on and off a few times before finally coming on full power and lighting the stairs in a pale green glow.

"We're looking for any sort of access to the basement level," she said. "And this is where the schematics run out."

Reaper said, "And this time there's no Alex or Ryan to hack the government's website and pull up some more, either."

"Pfft," Camacho said. "That just takes the fun out of it."

ROB JONES

"Maybe, but it also takes most of the time out of it, too."

They reached the bottom of the stairwell and were confronted with more double doors, also locked. This time, Nikolai broke them down, earning a vague look of approval from Reaper. They pushed through them, emerging into a vast storage area deep underground. Here, the castle's authorities stored the countless pieces of archaeological treasure that were not on display.

"Any clues?" Camacho said.

"Over there," Reaper said. "It looks like an air-conditioner unit. My money is on us finding what we're looking for right there."

"Good call, Reap."

They walked over, and Scarlet saw it first – two black boots twisted around at a strange angle. She took another step forward and saw the rest of the problem. A dead man was lying on the ground behind the AC unit. She saw a bullet hole in the center of his forehead and a look of terror on his face. Reaching down, she put the back of her hand on his throat.

"Still warm," she said quietly. "I'd say he was alive less than half an hour ago."

"Dammit," Camacho said. "Maybe the killer's still down here, guarding the device."

"A possibility." Scarlet got to her feet and reached for her gun. "But unlikely. My guess is he broke in here, killed this guard, took his key-card, deployed the device and got the hell out of Dodge as fast as he could."

"Allons-y," Reaper said. "We must find the device."

With the Frenchman's gravely words still hanging in the intense quiet of the storage area, Scarlet was already on it. Where would someone hide something like one of

166

Zamkov's vial bombs? They were small and light and could be tucked away inside of just about anything.

"There," Reaper said. "Behind the aircon unit, just as I... run!"

Scarlet felt adrenaline flash through her veins. Her pale skin prickled. Reaper rarely raised his voice in panic, and now he was turning and grabbing hold of her. The next thing she knew, he had rugby tackled her behind the nearest storage shelf and Camacho, Nikolai and Castillo were scattering behind whatever cover was closest.

She had no time to speak, no time to think. Before another thought formed in her mind, a deep, raw explosion ripped out of the corner like an enraged, wild animal and tore through the basement. Inside the enclosed area, the blast was intense, shredding through the shelving units and obliterating pieces of pottery and jade ornaments.

With the Frenchman still bear-hugging her and using his body as a shield to protect her, she cradled her head in her hands and cried out. "Shit!"

The deep, bass roar was still coming, making the entire room shake. Then came the fire and smoke and shrapnel and fierce, skin-scorching heat.

"Alberto!" Camacho yelled.

She looked up, straining to see through the gap in Reaper's arms. Nikolai was crashing to the floor behind a storage unit on the other side of the basement, Camacho was nowhere in sight and Castillo had moved too slowly and had been blasted by the bomb.

Reaper rolled over and they separated. "I must go to him," he said.

"No, this is my team and he's my friend. You wait here."

"Cairo!"

She was up and sprinting across to the Mexican. She grabbed him by his arms and began to pull him to the safety of the shelving units near Camacho. The American had now broken cover and was running over to her. "Are you crazy?" he yelled, his face covered in soot from the explosion.

"Was the damn virus in that bomb?" Scarlet called out.

"No." Reaper's voice, lost in the smoke. "It was just explosives, I saw it. It was a booby-trap."

Scarlet started to speak when a second detonation ripped through the basement.

"No!" she screamed, and the last thing she registered was the force of the detonation lifting Camacho off his feet, blowing him through the air as if he weighed nothing at all.

CHAPTER TWENTY-FOUR

Camacho crawled out of the rubble, profoundly aware of a sharp, shooting pain in his right hand and arm. At first, he feared the worst and thought he had broken something. Squeezing his hand open and closed a few times, he saw he'd gotten away with it and just sprained his wrist when the explosion had smashed him into the wall. Straining his eyes in the smoke-filled room, he prayed the others had been so lucky.

He saw Scarlet first; she was lying face-down in a pile of debris. He crawled over to her, once again fearing the worst. She had been closest to the IED, taking the brunt of the explosion and might have a serious blast injury. Worse, the bomb hadn't finished its work. As he reached her, still lying motionless in the rubble, one of the display cabinets that had stayed standing now creaked and groaned and lurched forward.

The bomb had torn a good chunk of the cabinet's base clean away, converting it to matchwood and dispersing it all over the storage room's floor. The unstable cabinet, full of heavy, jade Aztec death masks, was now toppling over and threatening to crush her where she lay. Images of the ECHO team standing around her grave on Elysium flicked through his mind like a speeded-up film reel, a broken Joe Hawke throwing flowers down on the coffin.

Then she moved. Just her arm, and only the slightest of movements.

Camacho coughed the smoke and dust from his lungs and scanned the chaos as he moved closer to her. He heard Reaper groaning as he got to his feet, then a wild string of profanities in Scarlet's cut-glass accent. *Thank god*, he muttered, reaching her.

The cabinet had tipped another ten degrees away from the wall. The death masks had been attached to the rear panel, but the IED had blown some of them loose, and now they started to tumble out of the cabinet and crash down on top of her.

"Cairo!" He hefted her over his shoulders in a hasty fireman's lift and staggered to where he knew the door was. Halfway across the room he saw Nikolai and Castillo had both gotten to their feet and were trying to gather their thoughts.

As they approached him, Castillo saw it first. "My god, is she all right?"

"She's cursing so, yeah, I think so," Camacho said. "But it looks like she might have some burns on her hands."

"Get my phone!" she whispered in Camacho's ear. "The explosion knocked it over there."

He walked over to the phone, crouched with her still on his shoulders, picked up the phone and slid it in his pocket. When they made it to the door, he slipped her off his shoulders and down onto the corridor's tiled floor. They three of them gathered around her, and Camacho cradled her head in his hands. "Cairo? Can you hear me?"

"Thanks to the very fucking loud whining in my ears, not very well."

Camacho breathed a sigh of relief. Smart-ass humor meant she was probably going to be okay, but she clearly had a concussion. "That bastard Loza is paying for this, with interest."

"Damn straight," Reaper said. "This whole thing was a set-up."

"They're more professional that I thought they would be," Castillo said. "The logistics of coming all the way out here, bribing security guards and setting an IED so they can throw us off the scent and waste our time, are… impressive, to say the least."

"We can talk about that later," Camacho said. "Right now, we have to get out of here before this place gets busy. An IED going off in one of the city's museums at three in the morning is not going to go unnoticed. We're going to be looking at hundreds of police and anti-terror squads in a matter of minutes."

They shouldered their bags, staggered out of a second set of fire doors in a cloud of smoke and found themselves at the bottom of another stairwell on the opposite side of the building from where they had entered the storage room. After carefully sitting a dazed Scarlet on the steps, Reaper slumped against the steel banister rail while Nikolai wiped the soot from his face. Castillo paced the small area at the bottom of the stairs and Camacho stared down at the woman he loved, all battered, and coughing.

"It was a trap, god *dammit!*" he cursed. "We should have known better."

"Yes, we should have." Scarlet's tone was ice cold, but still slightly slurred.

Nikolai spun around and stared down the staircase. "There – I saw someone!"

"It's a Serpent," the dazed Castillo said, craning his neck to see down through the narrow gap. "He must have waited around to watch us die. To make sure we were dead."

"And he's got one of the Dove's cases with him," Nikolai said. "He hasn't planted his device yet."

"But we're already on the basement level," Camacho said. "What the hell is down the bottom of these stairs?"

171

Castillo explained, "There is a large network of tunnels beneath the castle, but they go much further. They were built originally as escape routes in case the castle was ever besieged, and today they are of course off-limits to the public They are very dangerous."

"You said they go much further," Camacho said. "How far, exactly?"

Castillo rolled a hand to show he was uncertain. "Unfortunately my friend, I cannot be sure. As I say, it is prohibited to come down here and I for one have certainly never ventured into this place, but I have read they go east all the way into the city center."

Scarlet got to her feet, swooned a little and grabbed hold of the rail. "Jesus, I haven't felt this bad since I downed that bottle of Pernod at Richard Branson's place."

Camacho stared at her with astonishment. "And when the hell did that happen?"

"If only I could remember, darling. He still hasn't forgiven me for what I did to the pool. Anyway, shouldn't we be getting after the nasty little scumbag who just tried to kill us?"

"That's my girl!" Camacho said, and with Reaper in the lead, they made their way down the stone steps. Halfway down they heard a gunshot, but it wasn't aimed in their direction. When they reached the bottom, they saw what had happened; the Serpent had blown the padlock off a heavy steel door to facilitate entry into the tunnel system Castillo had talked about.

Staring into the black beyond the door, Reaper turned back to face them. With his famous Gallic shrug, he pulled his gun and grinned. "Pour un sou, pour une livre, n'est-ce pas?"

172

Scarlet returned the smile. "In for a penny, in for a pound? I accept the challenge, old friend."

With nothing to lose, the battered team ran through the tunnels, lighting their way with the small flashlights on their phones and without a care for their own safety. Scarlet felt the same sense of exhilaration she had experienced back in the amusement park. It rippled through her and made the pain of her mildly burnt hands recede into the back of her mind.

This was life, she thought. A rush of cold air whipped through the tunnel and washed over her, blowing her hair back off her shoulders and energising her, validating the sense of adventure she felt as she sprinted through the narrow channel carved in the bedrock below the castle.

"Keep up, Jack!"

"I'm doing my best."

"I don't want you to miss any of this. I can still hear him just ahead of us. His boots scuffing against the gravel in the tunnel floor. He's not far away now, and when we catch up with him, man am I going to... Woah!"

She screeched to a halt, inches away from a crumbling rock ledge which gave way to a deep black abyss. Reaper, Camacho and Nikolai were next to her now, and then a huffing and puffing Alberto Castillo stumbled onto the ledge. Cursing in Spanish, he stared down into the darkness and made the sign of the cross.

Scarlet felt her skin crawl. "What is this place, Alby?"

"I have..." he swept his eyes from side to side but saw nothing except black. "I have no idea."

Zeke reached into his bag and pulled out some rope. "I don't want to say it, but I think we're going to need this."

"My God," Camacho uttered, taking a step back.

Nikolai shuddered. "This is not the work of God, my friends."

173

Reaper passed a hand over his face, eyes wide with uncertainty. "And if you gaze long into an abyss, the abyss also gazes into you."

The others turned to him and he shrugged. "Friedrich Nietzsche."

"He's very well read, you realize," Scarlet said. "Especially poetry."

Camacho tried to laugh, but something stopped him. "I don't know what the hell this place is, but I want to know where our little friend went. He still has the supervirus device in his bag and…"

When the rock ledge crumbled and broke away beneath his feet, Camacho never even had time to scream or cry for help. Flicking his hands out to try and save himself, he found nothing but the damp, cloying wetness of the cavern's air as he felt himself tumbling backwards into the abyss.

CHAPTER TWENTY-FIVE

Hawke's day had started badly and was getting worse by the second. The nightmare in the Amazon jungle was barely behind him and now he was being hunted across the Mexican scrub by a small army of El Jefe's gangsters.

He checked the mirror and saw they were closing in. Their vehicle was a rugged all-terrain 4x4 and taking the off-road punishment much better than Franco's comfortable three-wheeled saloon. Ahead, he saw an incline leading down into a dry riverbed and steered toward it.

Pressing down on the throttle he pumped enough gas into the engine to increase the speed up to seventy miles per hour, then eighty. With a cloud of dry dust billowing out behind them, they struck the base of the valley and levelled out on the broad riverbed with a hefty whack.

The car bounced up and down on its suspension, and Hawke didn't have the heart to tell Franco that the front shocks were wrecked. The gangsters raced down the slope behind them and he smashed his boot down on the throttle again, surging the car forward. The bone-dry undulating ribs of the riverbed rumbled beneath the car as he raced across to the other side and steered up the opposite bank.

"They're still on our tail, Joe."

He glanced at Lexi and saw not fear but the ghost of a smile. She was enjoying the thrill of the chase, even though this time she was the prey. He shook his head, navigating the car off the riverbank and onto another stretch of flat scrub. Ploughing through a clump of mesquite bushes and only narrowly avoiding a Joshua Tree, he laughed.

"What is it?" she asked.

"You're insane, Lex."

"Huh?"

"Admit it, you're having fun."

"Maybe."

A terrified Franco looked at her with horror. "You think this is fun? You know what a man like El Jefe will do to us if these men catch us?"

She pushed her sunglasses on her forehead as she waved the thought away and wiggled her steel fingernails in his face. "You know what it feels like to have your fingernails pulled out one by one by the Chinese State's most experienced torturer?"

Franco sat back in his seat, his eyes fixed on the prosthetic fingernails. As Hawke spun the car to avoid another giant cactus, the sunlight streamed into the car and shone on the metal fingertips.

"No, I don't. I'm sorry... I didn't realize you were a victim of torture."

"I'm no victim, Manny," she said, turning and sliding her sunglasses back down over her eyes. "Besides, you should have seen the other guy."

Hawke gave a low laugh, but what he felt was far from humor. At the cruel hands of the Zodiac's Pig, Lexi Zhang had sustained hours of the most brutal torture a human could endure, and not once had she complained about it or let it get to her. Here she was now, making light of it. He had always admired her strength of character, and once they had even been lovers, but now he felt something else, something deeper, almost brotherly.

A fusillade of bullets raking across the back of the trunk and blowing out the lights brought him back to the

176

moment. He swerved to get out of the line of fire, but the gas station was still at least a mile away, and that mile cut through nothing but featureless desert. He hammered the throttle and drove flat out across the sun-baked wilderness, skidding and swerving to avoid the gangsters' gunfire.

"We're almost there, Joe," Zeke said. "And I might add, thank fuckerola for that."

The gangsters hit the gas and caught up with them. Pulling alongside on Hawke's side of the car, they slammed into them and sent it skidding wildly to the left where it careered down another slope.

Hawke fought hard to control the car as it skidded on the gravel and scree. Dust billowed into the cab through the open windows and aircon vents. Franco, who was directly behind Hawke, aimed his gun through his window and fired on the gangsters. They were elevated above them now, up on the rise where the ECHO team had been before being pushed off, and his bullets all missed.

The car slid on the scree and Hawke knew what happened next. "We're going over, everyone hold on!"

"Going over?" The terror in Franco's voice was clear for all to hear. "If we land on the roof, we will be helpless! Like a turtle on its back! The Serpents will take us prisoner and drive us to El Jefe! They will cut out our tongues and feed us to the vultures."

It all happened in seconds. As they raced sideways along the slope, the car started to tip over on its side. "We're not going to end up on our roof," Hawke said. "Because I'm going to make sure we do a full roll."

"Why does this fill me with dread?" Franco asked.

"Because you're not used to it," Zeke cried out. "I'll get you through it, Manny, but I draw the line at holding your hand."

Before Franco could reply, the car tipped on its side and then immediately rolled onto its roof. Hawke had steered into the manoeuvre to make sure there was enough momentum to go all the way over again, and it did. With another heavy bang and the crunching of crumpled metal on loose gravel, the car tipped onto its other side and finally back onto its wheels.

Desert dust filled the cabin again and the engine howled like a dying beast. Behind them up on the ridge, the Serpents had turned to pursue them down the slope. Hawke dipped his head and looked past Lexi at the 4x4.

"Fools are trying to come straight down," he said.

"Huh?" Zeke asked.

"The reason we tipped is because I came down at an angle. It's too steep to drive straight down. The brakes can't handle it and they won't be able to stop in time before they hit the bottom and those rocks. They'll be as flat as pancakes in a few seconds."

Relief flooded over Franco. "Then it's safe to say El Jefe's going to want another 4x4 by the end of the day."

"El Jefe's going to need an undertaker by the end of the day," Lexi said. "And in the meantime, let me help these goons on their way."

She leaned out of the window, the hot air flicking her hair back from her face as she raised her gun and fired once again on the Serpents. Unlike the thugs pursuing them, she knew how to handle a sidearm properly, and this time her bullets blew out their front left tire.

Zeke whooped and gave Franco a high-five as the 4x4 swerved all over the dusty slope and slammed into the rocks at the bottom. The impact of the crash smashed the entire engine compartment into the cabin, killing everyone on board in an instant.

The 4x4 looked like it had been through a car crusher. Lexi fired on the fuel tank, igniting the gas and consuming the wreck in a savage fireball. Smoke bloomed up into the hot, blue sky, and Lexi slipped down into her seat.

"You can forget about them now, Joe."

Hawke pulled off the scrub, crossed both lanes of the deserted highway and pulled up onto the gas station's forecourt. "Thanks, Lex. I can always rely on you for some classic, old-school overkill."

She leaned over and kissed his cheek. "You're welcome."

The battered saloon crawled to a stop in the parking lot in between the gas pumps and a giant Kenworth semi-trailer rig full of luxury cars. Hawke killed the engine. "Sorry, Manny, but I hope you're insured."

Franco shrugged. "Don't worry, it's a work vehicle."

Hawke kicked open the door and ran his hands through his hair. The deep sigh of relief was palpable. "That was close."

The others climbed out of the car and stretched their legs. "I need a coke," Franco said.

"Do they sell whisky in these places?" Lexi asked.

"I don't think so," Franco said.

Behind them, the Texan was slowly scanning the ridge to the south with a small monocular. "Er... don't relax yet guys."

Hawke shot a look at him. "What's up, Zeke?"

"Up there on the ridge where the 4x4 forced us off the road, I can see two more pick-ups, and they look like they've got bikes in the back."

"Bikes?" Lexi said. "What do you mean?"

"Little pushbikes with baskets and pink bows tied to the handlebars, Lex – what the hell do you think I mean? I mean motorcycles!"

He tossed her the monocular, and Lexi caught it and looked up at the ridge.

"Oh *shit*."

"Fuck a hole in it!" Zeke sighed and kicked a stone across the highway. "If we thought a car full of those assholes was bad, how the hell are we going to handle two trucks full of them, and more on bikes?"

"And my car is wrecked!" Franco said.

Lexi checked her magazine and smacked it back into the grip. "I don't know about you guys but I'm almost out."

"Me too," Zeke said.

Franco slipped his gun back into his holster. "I still have almost a full magazine."

"And me," Hawke said. "But it's not enough. We need to get out of here, and fast."

"And what do you suggest?" said the CNI agent. "That we stick out our thumbs and wait to hitch a ride?"

The Londoner turned and looked up at the answer, but the others reacted with horror.

"Oh, no," Franco said. "That is insane!"

"Have to say, chief," Zeke said. "I might have to agree with Manny on this one."

Hawke took a step back, looked at the pickups racing down to the gas station and then back over to his idea. "I really don't see why this can't work."

"Guys, whatever we do, we need to do it fast," Zeke said. "Those guys are gaining on us fast and they can't be more than a few minutes out."

Hawke looked at his old friend. "What do you think, Lex?"

"Honestly?"

He nodded.

"I think it's the most insane idea I ever heard in my life."

"Great," Hawks said, clapping his hands together. "Then let's get on with it."

CHAPTER TWENTY-SIX

For Jack Camacho, time in the abyss had slowed almost to a standstill. He felt his boots crunch against the loose gravel of the ledge as it gave away beneath them. He felt the sweaty, stale air on the nape of his neck. He felt the momentum of the fall turn his stomach. He turned and saw the gaping black void and threw his arms out, desperately reaching for the top of the pit but missing.

"Kolya!" Reaper yelled.

Nikolai was closest to the pit and now the Frenchman tossed him the rope. He caught it in one hand and without missing a beat he hurled the rope down at Camacho. He whipped out his hands and grasped the lifeline with everything he had.

For a few seconds, he carried on falling and his hands slipped down the knotted nylon rope at high speed. He cried out in pain as the friction burn bit into his hands, but then he slowed his fall and brought his legs up. Slamming his boots into the wall of the pit, he breathed a sigh of relief as he realized he was safe.

"That was too close," Nikolai said, heaving on the rope. "Let's get you back up here."

Camacho gave a nervous laugh. "I'll buy that for a dollar."

Scarlet had said nothing, but for a solid second she honestly thought she'd lost him. If it weren't for Reaper's and Nikolai's lightning reactions, Camacho would be a dead man. As the Russian pulled her lover up over the edge of the pit, she turned to him. "Jack, are you all right?"

"I think so."

"Then I have something to say to you, something important."

"What?"

She leaned into him, parting her lips and standing on tiptoes until she was level with his ear. "Do try and refrain from doing fucking stupid things like that in future. Clear?"

"Sure."

"Good, because having to put you in a set of baby reins is really going to cramp my style."

He nodded. "And I want you to know I love you, too."

She kissed his unshaven cheek. "Yeah, I know."

"If that was me," Nikolai said deadpan, "I think I would need a change of underwear."

Scarlet and Camacho laughed, and then the others joined in – it was relief. There were close calls and then there was what just happened inside this cavern. The old CIA man got to his feet and dusted down his jeans and jacket. For an old-timer, he was still pretty fit and strong, Scarlet thought, but like everyone else on the team, he couldn't go on forever.

"You sure you're okay?" she asked, touching his elbow.

"Sure, why – were you worried?"

"Fuck no, I just realised my phone is still in your pocket."

Camacho shook his head and handed her the phone. Then, he kissed her on the mouth and gave her a hug. As Nikolai pretended to vomit, he leaned into her ear and whispered. "Yeah, right."

"You know what I just realized?" Scarlet said.

He looked into her eyes. "What?"

She turned to Castillo and pointed her gun at the pit. "That is a major health and safety breach. I expected more from the castle authorities."

Castillo leaned over the hole and sucked his teeth. "But what the hell is it?"

"That can wait for now," Scarlet said. "More pressing is how our man got across this abyss."

"Please," Nikolai said. "If we call it a ravine, I think it will be much easier to cross."

They all agreed, and began to make their way along the ledge, this time staying much closer to the cavern wall on their right. The flashlight beams were strong enough to light up the path several yards ahead of them, and after a short walk they soon found what they were looking for.

"A rock bridge," Reaper said. "Amazing."

Camacho pointed. "And there's the asshole's footprints."

Scarlet blinked in the gloom as she angled her beam along the narrow structure spanning the two sides of the ravine. It looked unsafe and badly deteriorated by a mix of water and wind erosion, possibly over millennia, but she took her role as leader seriously. "Ladies, first, I guess."

Stepping onto the ancient causeway, she followed the Serpent's footprints and led her team safely to the other side where they stepped through a stone archway and saw another tunnel carved into the bedrock. A low, distant rumble shook clouds of dust and gravel from the rock ledges above their heads.

"What the hell was that?"

"It lasted for exactly twenty seconds," Camacho said.

"Maybe it was one of hell's furnaces," said Nikolai.

"Either that," Castillo said, "Or a train running along the Mexico City subway network."

Scarlet looked at both men. "I like your explanation better, Alby. Keep talking."

"We descended the other staircase until we reached about the same depth as many of the subway tunnels, and this area is a particularly busy part of the network."

Camacho smacked the rock wall with his fist. "Damn! That must be how that son of a bitch got into the castle to plant the bombs in the first place."

"I think so," Reaper said. "Which also explains how fast he was able to evade us after the bombs."

Castillo took out his wallet and pulled out a map of the subway.

"You don't have that on your phone?" Scarlet asked. "You're still in the stone age."

"And just as well," he said. "You think there is a signal down here?"

Scarlet accepted the rebuke as the Mexican pored over the folded map. "I think we must be about here."

As Scarlet stared at the map, Camacho and Reaper and Nikolai also gathered around her and peered down at it. "Where?"

"Around here, I would say, in this part of the tunnel system that runs to the west of Chapultepec Subway Station."

"He's going to stash the device on one of the trains and make a break for it," Scarlet said.

Reaper nodded. "Makes sense. He has to get rid of it before we find it, and that is a high-profile target."

"Yes, it makes sense!" Castillo said. "This is one of the busiest lines in the entire network, and today more than ever because of the festival. Thousands of people use the line every hour – maybe tens of thousands! They will all be infected, but we have no way of knowing when it's timed to go off."

"The morning rush hour would be a good time," Nikolai said.

"Then it just turned into our rush hour, too," Scarlet said.

*

Racing through the subterranean world beneath Chapultepec, Scarlet Sloane didn't care if she never saw another tunnel again for as long as she lived. The air was damp and foul, and the gravel path beneath her feet was rocky and dangerous. Worse, none of them had any idea if there was another abyss lurking ahead. Looking forward, at last, there was light at the end of this particular tunnel. When they drew closer, they saw it was coming from a grate in the roof of the tunnel, and it took all of Reaper's not insignificant upper body strength to push the steel grate out of the way.

Climbing up, they found themselves in what turned out to be a janitor's cupboard deep in the furthest reaches of Chapultepec subway station. In the gloom of the cupboard, they heard a train approaching. Scarlet checked along the platform through the horizontal ventilation slates in the door. "I see him. He's standing with the case in his arms at the other end of the platform, waiting for the next train."

"We have to stop him!" Castillo said.

"Agreed, but let's keep things under control," she said. "No civilian casualties, at least not caused by us."

They nodded, readied their weapons and stepped out of the cupboard just as the train pulled up at the station. Slowly, the platform filled up with people pouring out of the train, many of them already dressed up for the day's festivities. Scarlet weaved through the crowd, full of faces painted up like skulls and zombies, and drew closer to the man with the case.

He moved to step onto the busy train and turned. Seeing Scarlet, he calmly pulled a silenced pistol from his jacket, aimed it at her and fired. The suppressed weapon made a low, airy darting sound in the noisy platform, but the people around the man saw and heard what happened and screamed in response.

Scarlet dived out of the way. "He's firing!"

The team were already on the deck, guns drawn and desperately trying to keep track of the man in the crowd of skeletons and zombies. The train started to close its doors and pull away.

"The driver's trying to save everyone on board," Castillo said.

"Fuck it all!" Scarlet said, getting to her feet and pulling her gun. "Where is he?"

"There!" Camacho said. "He's getting on the train."

She saw a flash of black leather as the man zipped onto the last carriage. "Let's go."

They dived on board just as the doors closed and Castillo tried to pacify the travelers. "It's all right – I am a former CNI agent and we are in pursuit of a wanted man."

It brought some relief, but not much. The skeletons and zombies clung to their bags and belongings, and stared wide-eyed with fear at the small crew of armed people working their way down to the end of the carriage.

"There's only one more to go," Scarlet said. "He's caught like a rat in a trap."

When they saw him at the end of the final carriage, a look of grim surprise crossed Castillo's face. "I know this man, Cairo."

"He's not a man. He's a rodent."

"Fine, but I still know him. He's a small-time drugs runner for Vicente Alonso. His name is Rodolfo Ordaz."

"You must introduce me to him if we're ever at a party together…"

The pane of safety glass in the door between them shattered but held. He had fired on them from the other carriage. Scarlet darted to the side of the door, knowing a second shot would break the glass and strike her. The others followed her into position as she smashed out the glass with the grip of her gun. The Serpent was trying to open the door at the other end of the carriage.

No words now, just a cool shot blowing the back of the man's head out and spraying the door with blood and brain matter. It was grim. Many of the passengers were screaming and crying at the horror. A woman vomited. She couldn't blame them; not everyone had gone through SAS training and spent years working for ECHO. What was normal for her was a nightmare for a normie. She knew that. She knew she had become badly desensitized to all of this.

"The door!" Nikolai yelled. "He got it open and he's falling out."

She saw it now. The Serpent had managed to unlock the door before she had killed him, and now as the train rounded a bend in the tunnel, it was swinging open. His dead body tumbled out of the back of the train and crashed onto the rails. The case was tipping over the edge of the open door.

"We can't leave it, Cairo!" Reaper said. "It could go off at any time."

She already knew it, and was pounding down the carriage with her gun raised ahead of her. Camacho slid to a stop and scooped up the case. Working with steady fingers, he disconnected the cartridges. "All clear. We can blow it now."

She booted the case out onto the rails just as the train was reaching the end of the bend. The corpse was rapidly slipping out of sight, and so was the case. She had one chance this time, not two or three. Only dimly aware of the sobbing and crying around her, she fired on the case and detonated the C4.

The explosion was savage, instantly filling the tunnel behind the subway train with a bright yellow fireball that chased after them like the devil himself. Smoke flashed up over the curved, tiled roof above the flames, twisting into foul, acrid tendrils that seemed almost to reach out for her as the train raced away from the devastation.

But she was safe.

They all were.

She had taken out the Serpent and burnt the supervirus in two shots. She had saved Mexico and the rest of the world for the third time since midnight, but the pressure was taking its toll. For a fleeting moment, she felt like crying, and turned away from Camacho and the others as she closed the rear door. In reality, she was wiping away a tear.

"You did it, Cairo." Castillo wrapped an arm around her shoulder and gave her a fatherly shake. "You did it again!"

"I think the subway system might need a bit of TLC though."

"You killed the supervirus, Cairo," Camacho said. "Come here."

Castillo saw he was no longer wanted, and stepped away to explain to the passengers what had just happened. Without another word passing between them, and with the sound of dozens of relieved people whooping and applauding her, Camacho put his arms around her, gave her a deep, strong hug and kissed her.

"Good work, babe."

Castillo wandered over to them just as the train was pulling into Chabacano subway station. "This place will be crawling with cops and counter-terror units after what happened back in the Chapultepec tunnel."

"And we can't risk getting arrested," Nikolai said. "Not with the fourth device still out there somewhere."

"I can use my influence to get us through the police cordon," Castillo said. "I was a very senior agent at the CNI at the end of my career."

Reaper took a deep breath. "Where did this Ordaz live?"

After a brief check on his phone, Castillo gave the reply. "A small house in Michoacana."

Scarlet didn't recognize the district. "Distance from here?"

"A thirty minute drive."

She nodded. "Okay. We're going to need a vehicle."

"This is no problem," Castillo said. "A good friend of mine lives not far from here. I'll phone him and get him to bring a car."

"Is he CNI?"

"Yes, still active."

"Then get him to *leave* a car here," she said. "Sorry, but we trust no one."

"We can trust him, but fine. It's your mission."

"Then c'mon," Scarlet said. "Let's get to Ordaz's place – maybe there's something there that leads us to the fourth device. It's already after lunch and time is running out fast."

CHAPTER TWENTY-SEVEN

As Hawke led the ECHO team over to the massive semi-trailer truck parked up beside the gas pumps, Franco made a final plea against the madness. "I must object! This is suicide!"

Lexi turned around and walked backwards as she spoke to him. "Why?"

"Because it must weigh a hundred tons, that's why!" Franco said.

Hawke cocked his head as he counted the wheels. The trailer was full of luxury supercars – Ferraris, Lamborghinis, even a Bugatti Veyron, all sparkling in the hot sun. The load was full, and the tag axle was deployed. "More like eighty, I'd say."

The Mexican threw his arms in the air in despair. "Oh, then that's okay."

"It might take a while to get to speed," Zeke said.

"Might?" Lexi said. "With a trailer full of cars, you're looking at nought to sixty in maybe…"

"Two or three minutes!" Franco said, laughing at his own joke.

Lexi raised an eyebrow. "Two or three *miles*, amigo."

"Then what good is it? How can we escape from them in it?"

"We're not planning on escaping from them," Lexi said. "We need a ride to the Buena Vista Ranch, remember?"

"Plus," Hawke said. "We need somewhere to shoot at them from."

191

Hawke's boots crunched on the gravel as he walked over to the truck's cab. Tapping the dusty steel door with his hand, he turned to the anxious Mexican agent. "Don't worry about it. What she lacks in speed, she makes up for in grace and elegance."

"It's insanity," Franco said.

Hawke climbed up into the cab and pushed an old, oily toolbox off the passenger seat to free up some space. "It's our best shot."

"And it's time to go, boys and girls," Zeke said, pointing beyond the rear of the truck's trailer at the hills. "Either that's a dust storm, or our friends are back with a vengeance. Two Hiluxes."

The Englishman turned the ignition and the colossal W900 sixteen litre engine roared to life with an angry rumble, shaking the cab. "All aboard!"

Hawke checked the mirror on the side of the cab. Glancing down the long, dirty trailer he saw the two pickups just about to hit the highway. Behind them, a desert squall played with the thick column of black smoke twisting up from the wrecked 4x4.

"Hold on, everyone."

He pushed down on the clutch and took in the three gear levers with interest. "Well, that's different."

Franco was horrified. "You never drove one of these before?"

"Out of my way," Lexi said. "I can do it."

They heard screams of anger, and then through the windshield they saw a man in jeans and a greasy brown shirt waving his hands in the air, running toward the rig.

"You think he's telling us the gas station ran out of toilet paper?" Zeke asked.

"No," Franco said with disgust. "He is saying we are thieves, and begging us not to steal his truck."

192

"Which under the circumstances seems fair enough," Hawke said. "Care to get us out of here before he catches up with us, Lex?"

"Sure thing."

Hawke released the clutch, shifted out of the way and slammed down on the passenger seat, pulling a gun from his holster. "You never cease to amaze me, Lex. Where the hell did you learn to drive one of these?"

"Not one of these, exactly." She pushed down on the clutch, selected first gear and pulled out of the parking lot. "But we have trucks like this in the Chinese military, you know. We don't drive around with horses and carts."

"I'm still amazed."

"It's simple," she said.

"Three gear sticks can never be simple," Zeke said, joining Hawke now by pulling his gun from his holster.

Lexi shrugged. "You have six low-range gears, very low torque, and then higher gears for higher speeds. This stick here is just the high-low selector which allows you to shift from low to high, and the one over there on Joe's side of the cab activates an air cylinder to shift into an even higher range, gears twelve to eighteen."

"Like the lady said," Hawke said. "Simple."

Lexi tipped her head and checked the mirror. "Our friends are nearly on our asses, and that's the good news."

"What's the bad news?" Nikolai asked.

"The motorbikes in the back of the trucks are driving down ramps and also coming after us."

"Excellent," Hawke said, pulling the door handle and kicking it wide open.

"And where the hell are you going?" Franco said.

"I feel like some fresh air, Franco. Care to join me?"

"As I said, this is insanity… but what the hell? If I'm to go out of this world, then I may as well make the journey in style."

"Attaboy." Hawke gripped the rim running around the open doorway and swung his legs up onto the seat. Leaning back, he saw three of the six riders racing up on the passenger side, each of them was armed with handguns, but for now the guns were holstered and all hands were on the handlebars.

"Looks like they're going to try and get on board," Hawke called back into the cab. "It's our job to make sure that doesn't happen. Cool?"

Zeke gave a mock salute.

Franco simply shook his head and tried to disguise the look of sheer terror on his face.

"Then, off we go."

Hawke hauled himself up onto the roof of the Kenworth, grabbing hold of the airhorns to help him make the last few feet. Carefully standing up straight, he leaned on one of the enormous chrome exhaust stacks until he got his balance, then leaped onto the upper part of the cab roof above the driver's sleeping compartment.

Zeke was already climbing onto the roof behind him as he stepped over the steel dovetail and jumped down onto the trailer behind the truck, landing with a heavy smack on the hood of a Ferrari California. He stepped off the hood just as Zeke crashed down in the same place. As Franco made the jump, Hawke was checking how the cars were secured to the trailer. Each one was tethered down with fairly substantial tire straps, but they were no match for his Glock.

He turned to his small army – a former Tank commander and a Mexican CNI agent.

"All good?"

Two nods.

"Good, then let's get this party started."

"What are we going to do?" Franco asked.

"We're going upgrade the Serpents' transportation."

Franco's jaw dropped. "You can't be serious?"

Zeke leaned forward and looked at Hawke. "He is being serious. That is his serious face."

Hawke was already moving down the top tier of the tandem rig, gun stuffed in his belt, carefully walking along the side of the trailer. He clung to the rail with his hands as he edged the toes of his boots slowly along until he reached the middle. As he released one of his hands to reach down and draw his weapon, one of the biker's fired at the rear tires and blew one of them out.

The rear-end of the trailer swerved violently over to the side, knocking Hawke from his position. He tumbled through the air on a direct course for the road speeding beneath the truck, but just managed to grab hold of the side of the trailer's lower tier. He clenched his fingers tight on the metal rim as his boots scratched and scraped along the asphalt below.

With the blown-out tire right in his face, he tucked his face down into his chest to avoid getting pieces of the shredded rubber flying out and going in his eyes. He had to get back up before the biker fired again and took him out; to say he was an easy target was the understatement of the year. The hot desert air whipped at his shirt and hair as he reached out and grabbed the taut tire strap of the Bugatti Veyron.

Pulling himself back up, he made his way along the rig once again. When he reached the end of the trailer, one of the riders racing up the side of the truck hit the brakes and pulled level with him. Drawing his gun, the rider fired on him. Hawke was dangerously exposed – all three of them were – but he acted fast.

Shooting the window of a brand new Porsche Boxster and blasting it to pieces, he dived inside and landed on a sea of smashed glass. He heard more shots. Turning around inside the Porsche, he fired on the rider, giving Zeke and Franco time to scramble over the hood of a Mercedes AMG behind the Boxster.

He fired again, striking the rider in the hip. The man on the motorcycle instantly dropped his gun and instinctively reached for his wound, releasing the handlebars. The bike responded even faster, swerving all over the hot asphalt before leaving the road and dumping its rider into the desert at high-speed.

Hitting the ground at that speed and having a bullet in your hip meant there was no way back, and Hawke wrote him off, but then another rider zoomed up and started firing on them. He returned fire from the Porsche as Zeke and Franco blew out the windows of the AMG and climbed inside its cab to get out of the line of fire. Hawke knew a direct hit on the gas tanks would mean instant cremation, but right now it was safer than being a sitting duck on the back of the trailer.

And now it was time to give these scumbags something to think about.

He released the handbrake, pushed down on the clutch and took the car out of first gear and into neutral. Opening the passenger door, he slipped out of the car and shot through the tire straps. Dodging bullets, he ducked down low and moved to the rear of the Boxster and pushed against it with all his might.

Judging from the looks on his friends' faces back in the Merc, watching the Boxster roll forward off the top of the ramp and smash down backwards onto the asphalt was a sight to behold.

But the main show was still to begin.

CHAPTER TWENTY-EIGHT

The Porsche was still rolling back in the center of the road, and the two pickup trucks were rapidly approaching it. Keeping low behind the AMG, Hawke took aim and fired on the car, aiming at the gas tank. He knew enough about rear-engine cars to know the tank was located just in between the bulkhead and the partition at the front of the vehicle behind the trunk.

And when it went up, boy did it go up.

The explosion ripped the German sportscar to pieces, blasting pieces of bent shrapnel upwards and outwards with terrifying force. Several of them embedded themselves in the side panels of the pickup trucks as they swerved either side of the explosion, leaving the burning, gutted Porsche in their wake.

Only one of them made it, skidding off the desert and ploughing through a young cactus before swerving back onto the road and resuming pursuit of the Kenworth. The other wasn't so lucky. A piece of shrapnel from the annihilated Boxster ripped through its front tire and tore the rubber to shreds. The force of the wheel's high-speed rotation flung the blasted rubber strips out into the desert air like a centrifuge and dumped the truck down onto the magnesium alloy rim.

Sparks sprayed outwards and up the side of the pickup as the driver struggled to control the vehicle, but they were going too fast. The front axle snapped like a twig and sent the truck flipping forwards, grinding its front grille into the asphalt. It rolled longways, nose to tail, like a domino going over, time and time again until finally coming to a smoking, steaming halt just off the south side of the road in the desert.

Franco whooped and gave Zeke a high five. "Great work, Hawke!"

"What now?" the Texan shouted. "The others are surrounding us."

"We need to get rid of Mission Control."

"What do you have in mind this time?" Franco asked nervously

"I'm going to take the Performante for a spin."

"Oh *god*... I was afraid of something like this."

Shielding his eyes, he shot out the driver's window and climbed inside where he was pleasantly surprised to see the keys in the ignition. He guessed that was the safest place for them until they reached the garage, and now he put his foot on the brake and hit the start button.

The engine growled like a thirsty tiger, and after strapping himself in, he revved the powerful engine. He took the parking brake off, put the car into reverse using the lever on the center console and used the paddle on the steering column to select first. He revved some more, holding down the footbrake, carefully gauging the launch control until finally releasing the brake and racing off the back of the trailer.

The Lamborghini's position on the lower tier meant a much lower drop to the asphalt, but the low-slung car still crashed down onto the road with an unforgiving scraping noise and an impressive shower of sparks.

Hawke never flinched and instantly floored the accelerator pedal. The car responded wildly, pushing him back in his seat as the terrific acceleration launched the half million-dollar vehicle down the road toward the pickup. He had no intention of playing chicken, but the driver of the Toyota clearly misjudged him. The gangster swerved off the road and ploughed into the desert.

Hawke slowed the Lambo and pulled around in a tight circle until he was facing the action once again. The Hilux was at the head of a long column of dust spewing up into the air as it turned and headed back to the highway. In the distance, Hawke saw the Kenworth maintaining a good speed and slowly receding into the distance.

"C'mon, you bastards," he muttered. "Come to daddy."

The gangsters didn't take the bait, and when they pulled back up onto the road they turned right and headed off in the direction of the truck.

"Dammit." Hawke smacked the steering wheel but got back to business. Ripping up through the gears, he was soon gaining on the Hilux and close enough now to see one of the riders pulling closer to the trailer. Zeke and Franco fired on him and he swerved away from the rig in response.

Hawke easily caught up with them and pulled alongside. The pickup handled the rough desert terrain easily enough, but the Italian supercar was suffering, and he knew he didn't have much longer to make his point. Firing out of the window, he emptied the last of his mag into the driver through his door.

The man slumped down over the wheel, causing the pickup to spin off down a ravine to the north, rapidly disappearing in a cloud of desert dust and burning oil. Looking ahead, Hawke saw the last few bikers still circling the rig and accelerated towards the action. Zeke and Franco were keeping them at bay and without the last Hilux the goons had lost their backup, but they were still dangerous.

Pulling up alongside the front end of the rig, Hawke climbed out through the window and pulled himself up onto the lower tier of the trailer. Kicking the steering wheel as he heaved his legs out of the car, the Performante spun away into the desert at the tip of a long line of dust.

With Franco firing his last few rounds at the remaining two bikers, Zeke helped pull Hawke up onto the rig. "Good work, man!"

"Thanks, but it's not over yet. We still have two left. Where are they now?"

"One's around the front and one at the rear."

Gripping hold of one of the trailer's vertical support struts, Hawke leaned out at full arm's length and saw one of the bikers pulling to the cab at the front. Lexi swerved to hit him, but he was faster. He flashed away like a firefly then zoomed back over to the other side. Seconds later, he was climbing up onto his saddle and jumping onto the front fender of the Kenworth.

"Crap, Lex is in trouble," Zeke said.

"That wasn't my reading of the situation," Hawke said. "The biker's the one in trouble."

The biker behind fired on them but missed. "And what about that asshole?" Zeke said.

Hawke considered his fate. "Looks like the Sian's not long for this world, either," he said, loosening the car's tire straps.

"Huh?"

"Question." Hawke pulled the hammer back and looked down the sights. "How do you blow half a million dollars in half a second?"

"Tell me."

Hawke rolled the Sian off the back of the rig. It smashed into the asphalt speeding along beneath it.

landing with a metal-scraping bounce and a shower of orange sparks right in the biker's path.

Zeke couldn't believe his eyes. "If you pull this off, I'll buy you a beer."

Hawke waited half a second, then, aiming at the Lamborghini's fuel tank, he squeezed the Glock and punched a single 9mm Luger full metal jacket through the Italian supercar's aluminum and synthetic bodywork. The high-octane rated fuel caught a spark from the impact and detonated, instantly turning the car into a massive fireball and blasting it into a thousand pieces.

"Holy shit, Hawke!"

The biker swerved to avoid the burning Lamborghini, but the force of the explosion had ripped the supercar into a thousand shred and shards. Then shrapnel tore away from the fierce fireball and ripped through the rider, killing him before he fell from his bike. As the Lambo's burning, blackened chassis rolled out across the road, the empty dirt bike swerved off the road and into the brush, its headlight flickering through the mesquite bushes and Joshua trees before it finally lost speed and tipped over.

Hawke holstered his weapon and turned to the Texan. "Thanks. I'll take a chilled Budweiser."

"Dammit, man! You are dangerous. You'll take *two* Buds."

The truck swerved again, and when they turned to run along the trailer toward the cab, they saw Franco already making his way over the roof. Hawke and Zeke made their way up over the cab's roof where they found the last biker climbing up the side of the cab and trying to open the driver's door. The Mexican CNI agent was desperately clinging onto the exhaust stack as he tried to kick the rider in the face, but the gangster was already halfway in the cab.

Lexi waited until the door was almost fully open, then pivoted on her backside and darted her left leg out of the window, planting the heel of her boot squarely into the biker's face. He grunted in pain as the door swung open, leaving him dangling out over the speeding asphalt.

His legs kicked in the air, but he managed to climb back up onto the hood, blood pouring out of his smashed nose and lips. He swore at Lexi in Spanish, pointing at her and vowing revenge, but the Chinese assassin's reply was cool and measured. Hawke already knew what was coming.

"Manny, Zeke – hold on to something fast."

The men grabbed hold of the exhaust stacks as Lexi brought her leg back into the cab and hit the air brakes, rapidly slowing the truck and forcing the biker to fall over the front edge of the truck's massive hood.

"Oh dear," Hawke muttered.

Lexi accelerated again as the gangster gripped onto the grille mesh, then screamed in pain as the hot metal burnt into his hands. Instinct impelled him to release his grip, and he fell onto the bumper bar before hitting the road. The eighty-ton truck ate him up like a snack, no one on board even feeling the bump as they ploughed over the top of him.

"I just feel sorry for whoever has to clear that up," Lexi called up to them.

"Never feel sorry for vultures," Franco said with a frown. "In a few days there will be nothing left of him but a pile of broken bleached bones."

Hawke shrugged. "It couldn't have happened to a nicer guy."

"Agreed," Lexi said. "Now, if everyone wants to catch some shuteye, we'll be at the Buena Vista Ranch in less than an hour."

*

With the Antarctic storm raging outside her window, Valentina Kiriyenko looked at the razor blade for a long time. She had placed it on the smooth glass top of her dressing table more than an hour ago and not touched it since. The smooth high carbon steel reflected the light above her head dully. The blade was naked. There was no protective cover. It just sat there on the table. Glass and steel.

But it meant much more to her than just glass and steel. To the woman sitting at the table, the tiny razor blade meant the difference between life and death. It offered her the chance to know the truth or keep living a lie, and all she had to do to know the truth was take the blade and...

She closed her eyes and muttered a prayer to god. She knew the entire Bible by heart. That, it struck her now, was odd. Was that even possible? And how come she spoke so many languages? She had no memory of going to a language school. She spoke Russian, and some English and a smattering of French. How did she know Japanese and Arabic?

When she opened her eyes, she was shocked to see she had picked up the razor blade and was gripping it in her fingers. She turned it slowly, careful not to cut herself and draw blood – but that was odd, too. She had a strong memory of falling from her bike and cutting her knee open when she was a small child, and yet there was no scar on her knee.

She hated that scar. She wore long skirts to cover it, and preferred leggings or jeans for the exact same reason. Why was there no scar on her knee? Had her darling sweetheart Niki invented some high-tech AI technique that changed the world of cosmetic surgery? Yes, that must be it – but then, why did she have no memory of that, either?

She was breathing too fast. She took some long, deep breaths and slowed her heart. The grim thought of some unknown illness crossed her mind. Is that why her memory was failing her?

You know it's not that, Valya. Take the blade. Do it.

Yes, if she just took the razor blade and…

She felt the tears streaming down her cheeks. What the hell was she even doing in this place? Surrounded by thousands of square miles of ice and snow, it was bleak and horrible, and this was the summer. By winter it would be a thousand times worse. Much worse than the darkest, coldest Siberian winter. She felt her heart quicken, and then she felt dizzy. Was she having a panic attack?

One simple cut, end it now or know the truth forever.

No, she tossed the blade down on the desk and wiped the thought from her mind. Niki loved her, and they would get married. She would have his child and they would live in his brave new world together.

Man and wife and son.

CHAPTER TWENTY-NINE

Cougar had been tracking one of the ECHO teams since she landed at Santa Lucia Air Force Base in Zumpango, just north of the city. For a short time, they had lost track of both teams, but then Pegasus activated his double agent in Titanfort's massive Manhattan spy-hub, and they soon located their targets again.

The intel from the undercover agent was clear: within a few minutes of ECHO entering Mexico, two of the team had been kidnapped by a gang working for a third party, most likely the Brazilian hitman known as the Dove. In response, the team had divided in two, with one pursuing the kidnappers of their friends while the other was tracking down an unknown threat, mostly probably terrorist bombs.

Cougar had no problem deciding which team to pursue; she never diverged from her plan and that meant the next target on her list was *always* the next target. Now, as she sat outside Chabacano subway station in the GMC Sierra, she waited patiently for the team to step out into the day. Checking her phone, she followed the GPS signal on former Agent Castillo's phone as it trundled along Line 1 of the city's subway.

Not knowing where they intended to get off the subway, she had followed them along the line all the way since Chapultepec Station. She knew from scanning the radio that some sort of explosion had occurred at the station. All of Mexico City was going crazy over it, and speculation was rife that terrorists had bombed the station to strike fear into the city's population on such a sacred day. Here at Chabacano, there were cops everywhere trying to work out what had gone down.

But she didn't care what had happened. She knew from watching the GPS tracker that at least Castillo had survived the blast. If the others had died in it, she could cross them off her list and save some time. If not, then the mission continued, and in the meantime, she simply had to wait and see if they exited the subway network at Chabacano or went to the next station.

Either way, it would almost certainly be the last train ride for one of them.

*

As Scarlet walked up the steps inside Chabacano subway station, the afternoon was getting older, and time was rapidly running out. The heat of the city was rising, and thousands of people were already out on the streets for the Day of the Dead celebrations.

Castillo had been as good as his word at the station's entrance. As they had expected, the entire station was teeming with law enforcement officials. When one of them saw Castillo's former credentials and waved them through, he had told them every station on the entire network was now closed and all passengers were being interviewed regarding the explosion in the tunnel.

Moving toward the exit, Castillo pointed at the little station sign. "The name means *apricot* in my language," he said.

"Thanks for that," Scarlet said.

"You know, they filmed part of the Total Recall movie here back in 1990," Camacho said.

"And thanks for that, too."

"Hey, I love that movie."

"Moi aussi," Reaper said. "But it reminds me how old I am."

"You and me both, Reap," Scarlet said with a wry smile. "But don't tell the boy I said that."

"We have to rescue him first," Camacho said. "And, *damn*, it's busy in here."

Scarlet raised an eyebrow. "Maybe they're all here to see where Total Recall was filmed?"

"Yeah, right."

They made their way outside into the hot, busy day and weaved their way through the crowd to the road. Castillo's trusted friend in the CNI had texted him the location of the vehicle, and when they turned the corner of Juan de Dios Arias, they saw a white Chrysler Touring parked up on the side of the road.

Castillo laughed. "His wife's car."

Scarlet caught Camacho's eye, and when he started to speak, she put her finger to her lips. *No sense in worrying Castillo unnecessarily*, she thought. "This is great, Alby. Thanks."

"It's almost new, so please, can we make sure it gets back to Silvia without any problems?"

"I'm sure it'll be just fine," she said, again glancing at the American. "Come on, time's getting on."

They climbed into the car with Castillo at the wheel, and slammed the doors shut. He fired up the powerful engine and pulled the car away, passing the station and turning onto the main road running north to Transito. None of them noticed the GMC Sierra pull out behind them and tuck in three cars back.

*

Cougar had gotten the answer to her question when she saw finally Scarlet Sloane, Jack Camacho, Vincent Reno, Nikolai Petrov and Alberto Castillo. They had stepped out of Chabacano Station and walked along the street towards a new white Chrysler.

They looked stressed and busy. Five people in pursuit of an enemy.

And she was in pursuit of them.

They knew it, too, but right now they would be distracted by what they considered to be the greater threat. None of them would be thinking too hard about the sniper who had already taken three of them down. By the end of the day, that number would be four. Then they would all be thinking about the sniper again.

She looked inside her box of specially engraved bullets and carefully located the one she would be loading into her CheyTac M200 Intervention. The gun was the most powerful sniper rifle in production today, and she knew it so well, it was more like an extension of her body than a separate firearm.

The round was .408 bottlenecked cartridge, solid with a non-lead core. Outside on the smooth, shining jacket was the name of her fourth target. She looked down at the name with no emotion at all. It meant nothing to her. How could it? No one who did a job like hers could ever feel anything toward her targets. It would compromise the mission and ruin her career, and as this was her last ever mission, she wanted to go out with a perfect score.

That time was fast approaching, but now she pulled out, cruising well behind the Chrysler. She had studied all of the targets on the contract, but now she thought about her next victim's strengths and weaknesses; how they moved and fought. Right-handed or left-handed? Right.

Her mind wandered to their family life. Yes, they had family. Yes, they would be at a funeral next week.

No, she didn't care.

It wasn't personal. She wasn't a bad person. She was a professional assassin working for a democratically elected government and she was very good at what she did. Anyone she had been ordered to take out had been deemed a threat to the vital national interest of the United States of America. In doing what she did, she was protecting her country.

Yeah, right, she said.

A country that's letting my kid slowly die.

She closed the box and pushed herself back into the seat. None of this shit matters, Jess. Stay focussed on the mission. Take out the next target on the list, then move onto the fifth. Keep going and don't stop until they're all gone. Then take the cash, get Matty his operation and meet Justin in Los Cabos.

Los Cabos.

She had read it was one of the most dangerous places in Mexico for murders. With a wry smile, she thought, *better not break into my new villa, assholes*. If anyone did, it was unlikely they would ever walk out again. No, anyone threatened her family, they'd be going out in a box with a smoking-hot double tap to the forehead and one in the chest.

And that wasn't just hot air when Agent Cougar said it.

Following the ECHO team as they made their way north through the sprawling city, she brought her mind back to the mission. Checked the mirrors, stayed out of sight. Counted down the days to when this was all over.

*

210

Scarlet was feeling tired. She had been on her feet since landing in the city at midnight, and that meant over twelve hours of non-stop running and adrenaline. She pushed back in the comfortable leather seat and let Castillo take the strain of the traffic for a few minutes.

Trying to purge the tension from her neck and shoulders, she glanced lazily out of the tinted window and watched the graffitied commercial units of Transito turn into the ancient city's historic center. Here, the mindless vandalism of a few moments ago was replaced with the sparkling sight of smart roads lined with jacaranda trees covered in vivid purple blossom and lines of bright green cypresses studding the sidewalks outside expensive boutiques.

She watched it all flash by, only dreamily noticing it all. Maybe that silly sod Bale was right after all and she really was too old for all this. An afternoon spent shopping and sipping coffees under the shade of these trees was starting to seem a damn-sight more appealing than hunting down the scum of the world and burning bio-engineered pathogens to death.

Bale.

Remembering his constant sniping at her age had brought both him and Lea back into the front of her mind. Their kidnapping outside the airport seemed like a hundred years ago, and yet they had only been gone a few hours. Had Hawke found them yet? She checked her phone but there were no messages. Well, no news is good news, as Hawke often said to her.

"Anything?"

She looked over her shoulder and saw Reaper looking at her with an expectant look on his rugged, unshaven face. Camacho and Nikolai were also looking. She smiled, seeing how even the expansive back seat of the Chrysler was barely big enough to accommodate three men of their size.

"No, nothing."

Reaper nodded, turning to watch the zombies and skeletons moving along the sidewalks in their hundreds. "This a good thing."

"I think so too," Nikolai said.

"Joe's hot on their trail, Cairo," Camacho said at last. "Let him get on with it, the way we're getting on with this."

She agreed and slipped her phone away. "How far, Alby?"

The Mexican was following satnav instructions on his phone. "Not far. We're driving into Morelos now, and then we're in Michoacana."

Minutes later, he signalled to turn into a small residential road and pulled the car up on the sidewalk. Scarlet took in a view of yet more graffitied houses and apartments, a pickup truck stacked up on bricks and an old closed butcher's shop with half a dozen car tires slung out of the front of it to stop people parking there.

"Delightful."

"Hey, these people have no money," Castillo said. "And when I say no money, I don't mean like when you can't afford an extra Netflix subscription. I mean *no money*."

"Sorry, Alby," she said. "I'm just tired. This damn mission is really getting to me."

"It's not over yet, Cairo," Camacho said from the back. She heard him loading his sidearm. "When this is over, we have to rescue Kamala and then get up to Tartarus."

Scarlet said nothing, but she knew the enormity of this mission well enough. She looked up at the apartments above the butcher's shop. "Which floor, Alby?"

"The top floor."

She opened the door and a blast of warm air rushed into the car. "Then let's get this done – we're looking for anything or anyone who can lead us to the last supervirus vial. And Jack's right. We're nowhere near the end of the road yet."

CHAPTER THIRTY

Still dark outside but as hot as hell, Mason glanced at his watch. Five a.m. on a steamy Hong Kong morning and thanks to a long night working with Maggie Lai, their target had already been acquired. Standing on Maggie's balcony, he watched a man loading up a van down in the street below her apartment. Opposite him, a shopkeeper was already up and preparing for anther busy day of trading.

If, he thought grimly, the Raiders team were able to take Barbosa out of the equation and destroy his batch of Zamkov's supervirus.

"Coffee?"

He turned and saw Zara.

"You look like shit," he said.

"Gee, *thanks*." She handed him a cup. "You don't look so good yourself, Jed."

"It's been a rough night," he conceded. "And thanks for the coffee."

"Don't thank me, thank Maggie. She's making breakfast if you want some."

"What's on the menu?"

"Salted egg lava toast," she said. "She made it just for you."

"And here I was thinking we'd hit it off. Turns out she hates me."

She laughed. "Smells great, as a matter of fact, you cynical bastard."

"Sorry, it's the soldier in me. I just can't shake it off." He sipped the coffee and took a deep breath. "As matter of fact, I like lava toast. I spent some time training out here with the Gurkhas back in the nineties and I got to know the place really well. It was a fun time."

"The nineties, huh?" she said with a smirk. "I wouldn't know about that, Pops; I was still in junior high."

"Yeah, yeah, I get it. I'm an old grandad. How are the others? Anyone manage to get any sleep?"

"Caleb's still sleeping now, but Ella's up and watching the news."

"And Milo?"

"Milo is in a sulk because Maggie said it's too early to put the aircon unit on."

"Great, all present and correct, then."

A moment of silence passed on the balcony. They smelt Maggie's breakfast drifting over to them, then heard her shouting at her nieces and nephews.

"Guess it's still a school day," Mason said. "Even with this nightmare on our shoulders."

She nodded. "What time are we going to take Barbosa down?"

He checked his watch again. "Maggie's contact says Barbosa is still in the hotel. We're going to hit him there before he has a chance to leave, but there's a chance the hotel itself is Hong Kong's ground zero for the release of the pathogen."

She finished her coffee. "Then I guess it's time to go, before the son of a bitch gets out of his fart sack."

"Yes," Mason said with a grin. "You guess right."

*

Just after ten at night and Paris was electric. Vibrant, neon-lit streets hummed with an urgency that fired Danny Plane's neurons like nothing else. As Mack cruised the

SUV through the buzzing traffic, the young former SAS trooper thanked God, not for the first time, that he was part of Bravo Troop.

And still alive.

After leaving the SAS, the young soldier's life had quickly spiralled out of control in a big way. Like others he had known in the regiment, adjusting to civvy life was no walk in the park, and he soon found himself with nowhere to go and nothing to do. Nothing offered the same excitement, triggered the same wild rush. Years in the world's most highly trained Special Ops force had left him a changed man, a man without a place in normal life.

Some former SAS soldiers wrote books, others set up adventure training course, but none of those things were him. Crime was the most likely avenue, but first he found refuge on a Thai beach with a woman from Bangkok. Achara was also on the run, but from a violent and aggressive husband. Turned out Danny could lend a hand, and after using his combat skills to liberate her from the nasty drunk, they got together. Months of tropical, beer-drenched bliss ended when she told him it wasn't working out. His night terrors were too much for her.

He understood.

They went their separate ways, and he started hitting the bottle again. Drinking in the bars of Ko Samui and wondering just what the hell was the point in anything when his former CO, a man named Clive Hudson, called him up and offered him a new job.

And a new life.

He accepted and flew back to England. The next thing he knew, he was on his way to Paris to take out a bag of scum called Francisco Rodrigues. Why couldn't this have happened three years ago, he wondered? Life, it seemed, had a funny way of giving you what you wanted, but rarely when you wanted it. No matter, he had it now and he wasn't going to blow it. He was the best and he knew it, and now it was time to prove it.

"So Kyra, any luck on finding out whose address this is?" Hudson asked.

"Sure," the young American said. "It belongs to a man named Jean Cotillard, and according to my research, he's a senior officer for the *Préfecture de police de Paris*, the Paris Police Prefecture."

"This is not good, Hud," Mack said. "If we're looking at corrupt coppers, then this is not good at all."

"Just what I was thinking," Hudson said. "We could be in a lot more trouble than we thought."

"True story," Kyra said. "Means we should be very wary of police CCTV for one thing."

Danny craned his neck up and looked through the window at a camera fixed to the side of a department store. "You think they're already watching us?"

"Yeah, yeah, sure," Kyra said. "Surprised you didn't consider that already, moron."

"Hey! Watch your mouth," Danny said. "I *did* already consider it."

"Jeez, there's no need to be rude." She lowered her voice. "What are you, like Wooster to his Jeeves?"

"Eh?" Danny said.

"Kyra calls me Jeeves," Hudson said. "But usually only behind my back."

Danny feigned offense. "I'm not being funny, but if you think he's Jeeves and I'm Wooster then you demonstrate a sad and depressing lack of understanding of the British class system. Geezer up front was a freaking major in the SAS, darlin'. I'm just a proper little gutter rat from Camden Town."

"Talk to the jewellery," she said, raising her palm in his face. "Cause the ears ain't listening, Gutter Rat."

Mack chortled. "Aye, it's good to be back with the Brady Bunch, and no mistake."

"Yeah," Kyra said. "But Trooper Gutter Rat here is Cindy, right?"

Danny's face lit up. "Does that mean I get to wear pigtails?"

She shrugged. "If it floats your boat, sure."

"Talk about Memory Lane," he said wistfully. "Throw in the red minidress and I'm right back on my initiation into the SAS."

Hudson laughed. "So that's where my dress went."

Mack chuckled again, but then grew more serious. "According to the satnav, we're almost there, boss."

"I know we are, Mack," Hudson nodded. "I'm familiar with this district."

They pulled up and emerged from the car into the Parisian night. The aroma of Mack's cigar seemed to warm the chill of the autumn breeze as they made their way into the block that housed Cotillard's apartment.

Inside the lobby, Hudson took one look at the bird cage elevator and said, "Bugger that – I think I'll take the stairs."

"Aye, good call," Mack said. "You stand no chance at all trapped in one of those things with some rotten bawbag shootin' at you."

They walked quickly up the traditional Parisian spiral staircase until they reached the apartment. Out of sight of the door, Hudson pulled his gun. "All right, this is it. Mack, be an angel and knock on the door."

"With pleasure, boss."

Mack drew his gun and smashed the door in with his riot boot. The wooden door smacked into the hallway wall and started to rebound, but the team were already inside the apartment before it got halfway back to closing.

"Nobody fuckin' move!" Mack yelled, gun held firmly in front of him in a two-handed grip. Sweeping the weapon from side to side, the Scot led the team as they cleared the apartment room by room. It wasn't until they reached the kitchen that the action began.

Tied to a chair in the center of the room was a man in his sixties. His mouth was taped up but his eyes were terrified. Then they heard a crashing noise in the hall, and the bound man desperately moved his eyes to indicate behind them.

Hudson turned and saw two men, one in a roll-neck and the other in an ankle-length raincoat. Both had hidden in the living room when Mack smashed the door in and were now trying to escape through the front door.

"Put your hands up!" Hudson yelled.

"Fuckers!" said Danny.

Both men bolted. One ran into the living room and tried to open a window looking out onto a balcony, and the other turned and tried to make the front door. The man in the roll-neck had already got the window open and was halfway out of it when Danny burst into the room.

The young man from Camden Town holstered his weapon and threw himself into a diving roll across the carpet. Mr Roll Neck was close enough to take down without having to discharge his weapon, which in an apartment block like this was a bad idea.

Coming out of the roll, he grabbed hold of the other man's leg, pulling him back inside the living room, delivering a sharp punch to his face, splitting open both his lips. He punched him again, crunching his nose into pulp with a knuckle-bruising smack, smacking him out cold.

With the man down, he stepped into the hall and saw Kyra untying Cotillard in the kitchen. Hudson was firing questions at him in French, and to his right, Mack was chasing the man in the raincoat as he fled toward the apartment door. The Scot grabbed the telephone table and hurled it at him, striking him on the back, knocking him down onto the parquet flooring, giving him enough time to pad over and grab the back of his coat.

"Who are you working for, boy?"

He babbled in French, turned and spat at the Scot.

Mack's reaction was instantaneous, gripping the side of the man's head and smashing it down into the hardwood tiles. Wiping the spit from his face, he slipped his hand around to the man's throat and squeezed hard, pushing his fingertips deep into the soft flesh of his unshaven neck.

"I said, who are you fuckin' workin' for?" he shouted. "Don't make me ask again."

"My boss is called Mr Fuck You."

Another punch, breaking his lips open and flattening his nose. "I can go all night, ya wee bastard – can you?"

He punched him again, and again, causing him to pass out and Mack tossed his broken, limp body down onto the carpet.

"I hope Monsieur Cotillard has some freaking Scotchgard on that fuckin' carpet," Danny said.

Mack straightened up to his full height and wiped the man's blood from his hands. "He wouldnae speak."

Kyra's head appeared in the kitchen door. "Hud's getting something out of Cotillard."

They moved to the kitchen, where the former SAS officer was still crouching in front of the Parisian. Free from the duct tape, he was dabbing at a wound on his forehead with a cloth from the kitchen side. "They beat me, and told me they would kidnap my granddaughter if I didn't cooperate."

"They're working for a man named Rodrigues, am I right?" Hudson said.

The man looked up at him, blinking in the harsh overhead light. "Oui… but how did you know? Who are you people?"

"We're from out of town," Kyra said.

"Why did Rodrigues's thugs attack you?" Hudson asked.

The man hesitated, still dazed by his beating. "They took my security clearance, I'm so sorry."

"Security clearance for what, Monsieur Cotillard?"

The man started to cry. "I'm in charge of security for…"

"For what?"

"La dame de fer," he muttered quietly, and began to sob.

"What the hell?"

"It means the Iron Lady," Hudson said.

Danny frowned. "Eh? What's Margaret Bloody Thatcher got to do with it?"

"It's what the French call the Eiffel Tower."

Cotillard said, "I think they plan to use the tower for some sort of terrorist outrage, but what could I do? They said they would murder little Celeste."

"This is bad," Kyra said.

"No, it's good," Hudson said, fixing his eyes on Cotillard's bruised face. "Looks like you don't want the authorities to know about this anymore than we do, am I right, Jean?"

He shook his head. "For giving them the security clearance, I will be fired in disgrace and lose my pension, probably even go to jail."

"So what would you say to helping us out and stopping the scum that did this to you and your family?"

His face brightened. "I would say, you can count me in."

"Can you get us into the Eiffel Tower with the minimum of fuss?"

"I think so."

"Then we're out of here," Hudson said. "C'mon everyone – time is running out fast."

CHAPTER THIRTY-ONE

As they snaked up Rodolfo Ordaz's litter-strewn path, Scarlet and her team moved like oil, each knowing the other's mind inside out. Turning to Castillo, the Englishwoman said, "How do you say hands up in Spanish?"

On the top floor now, Camacho and Nikolai covered the rear. Reaper kicked the door down and Scarlet was first inside, gun raised and ready to fire. The apartment was filthy. Used heroin needles littered the floor and open bags of refuse piled up at the bottom of the stairs.

"Clear!" Reaper returned from the kitchen.

Camacho swung his gun into the toilet. "Clear!"

Scarlet and Castillo were already halfway up the stairs with Reaper a step behind. The Mexican swung around and covered her by aiming his weapon up at the bannisters running around the top floor, but there was no one there. At the top, Scarlet kicked open the first door and found nothing but more junk. "Clear!"

Reaper had advanced ahead of her now, and had already cleared the next room. Camacho and Nikolai stayed downstairs, covering the entrance and making sure no Serpents entered the property and trapped them inside.

At the final door, Scarlet saw a shadow moving on the threshold strip. "Down!"

She and Reaper dived for the cover of other rooms, and Castillo slammed his body back inside the stairwell just as bullets raked through the shut door. They tucked their heads down as the rounds blasted dozens of holes in the cheap hollow-core door. A few seconds of gunfire reduced the door to shredded splinters.

Scarlet and Reaper spun out of the rooms, returning fire on the shooter, but the man was undeterred by their assault. He took cover behind an upturned sofa just out of their view and fired back. The cracking of his gun was sharp and impossibly loud in the confined space of the living room, and the stench of gun-smoke reeked in the humid, sweaty air. Another man had been out of sight, reloading, and now added to the fusillade.

Scarlet and Reaper took cover again, each reloading and assessing the situation.

"There's two of the bastards, Reap."

"And four of us."

"Can't get four in this corridor – it's a bottleneck."

"Grenade?"

She shook her head. "We need to talk to one of them, at least."

"So, it's two versus two, then," he said with a shrug. "We have been through worse."

"I think this time, it's two versus one," she said. "No way are we both getting down into that room at the same time."

More gunfire and angry screams in Spanish.

"Everyone okay downstairs?" Scarlet called out.

"Hell yeah!" Nikolai shouted from downstairs. "I'm having the time of my life. You?"

"Just asking."

After more Spanish insults, another wave of bullets chewed some chunks out of what was left of the door's upper casing and punched a neat line up the plaster above their heads.

"You want me to go first?" Reaper said.

She laughed. "You? You move like a grizzly bear, Reap."

"I can still get into that room."

"Not this time, old friend." She smacked a fresh magazine into the grip of her weapon and got to her haunches. "This time, it's down to me."

Reaper put his hand on her shoulder. "Then, I pity them. Here, take my gun, too."

She was gone without another word, sprinting down the smoky corridor as if demons were nipping at her heels. She had only one thing on her mind, and that was taking one of them alive. The fourth vial was still out there, and this might be their last chance of getting its location.

Reaching the end, she dived into the room and twisted around just before she hit the ground. Raising both handguns, she fired ferociously on the men, emptying both mags by the time she crashed down into the carpet. In the onslaught, she had wrecked most of the room, torn plaster from the walls, blown out the TV set and window and exploded a large glass reptile enclosure beside a brown Ezy Rest recliner.

With half a dozen bearded dragons scattering all over the room in every direction, Loza's men dived back down behind the sofa and reloaded.

"Manos arriba, arseholes!"

The men ignored her and fired again. She fired back and the impact of her rounds spun one of the men around and knocked him into the wall. He slid slowly down, his face grinding against the roughly hewn rocky walls, then lurched to the side and smacked into the ground.

The other man fired on her, causing her to dive once again for cover. She landed hard and it hurt, but returned fire as she went. *I'm getting too old for this bullshit*, she thought. The assault had badly wounded the other man.

He dropped his gun and fell back into a pile of glass splinters. One of the dragons scooted over his body, darting under the upturned sofa.

She walked over to him and pointed her gun at his head. "We're all clear, guys."

The twin shadows of Reaper and Castillo crossed the messy carpet as the two men stood beside her. The Frenchman peered outside through the smashed window, scanning the street for trouble while Castillo spoke to the man in quiet Spanish. After a brief conversation, the man tipped his head back, closed his eyes and died.

Castillo muttered a prayer and made the sign of the cross. Turning his sad, puffy eyes up to Scarlet, he said, "He says the plan is to set off the fourth device somewhere in the airport."

"How did you get that out of him?"

"Que?"

"I mean, is it reliable information?"

He nodded. "He was dying, Cairo. He asked for forgiveness, and I gave it to him."

She holstered her gun and looked at a lizard on the carpet. It looked back up at her, and then zoomed under the smashed TV. Outside, she heard police sirens. "All right, we got what we needed. Let's get out of this dump."

*

Parked up in the street, Cougar also heard the sirens. She glanced in the Sierra's side mirror, seeing several police cars screeching around the corner into Ordaz's street. The small battle inside the apartment had not gone unnoticed by the neighbors, and now the place was seconds away from being swamped with law enforcement officials.

Dressed in plain black jeans and a leather jacket and a baseball cap tugged down low over her face, she was innocuous enough, but it didn't pay to take risks. Pretending to read a magazine, she watched as the fat Mexican policeman led the ECHO team out of the apartment block and into the white Chrysler. Seconds later they were cruising past her and then they were gone, turning the corner at the opposite end of the street to where the police had entered.

Cougar tossed the magazine down on the seat, turned on the engine and slowly pulled out in pursuit of the Chrysler. Any later and the cops would have been on her tail too, but as it was, they were too busy at the far end of the street, screeching to a halt outside the smoking warzone.

So far, she considered patiently, Mexico City had proved a poor hunting ground. At no point since she landed had the right opportunity to take out Target 4 presented itself. The confines of the busy city were too claustrophobic for a long-range sniper. Her modus operandi was to shoot and flee, making herself disappear before anyone knew even the vague direction of the bullet's trajectory.

This place offered nothing like that.

And yet time was running out and she had to get the job done. Sighing, she floored the throttle, the automatic gearbox dropping down into third. She was maintaining a safe distance behind the EHCO team, always at least three cars back, and now they were heading east. If the road signs were anything to go by, it looked like they were heading to the airport.

Airports meant airfields. Wide open airfields.

Maybe things were looking up after all.

CHAPTER THIRTY-TWO

The Dove kicked over the desk beside his bed and padded around the penthouse suite like a hungry wolf. He was known for keeping his cool, but right now he felt nothing but a deep, burning rage. How had ECHO not only got to Mexico so fast, but also taken out three of the four supervirus bombs? This was three-quarters of the payload Zamkov had ordered him to deploy across the city.

ECHO were too good, and if he didn't act fast they would soon track down the last supervirus device, and that meant tracking him down, too. If Rodrigues and Barbosa successfully deployed their supervirus vials in Paris and Hong Kong, Zamkov would take a very dim view of his failure in Mexico.

He heard the door open and turned to see Ramiro Loza walk into the room, flanked by thugs.

"Your men failed again."

El Jefe was starting to look nervous now. "You still have the fourth bomb?"

"Yes, and I will deploy this personally. Your men are useless."

"My men are fighting a Special Ops team that you never told me about. We already talked about this."

"Don't make me come after you, Loza," he said, almost in a whisper. "Because if you fail me again, I will track you down and kill you, but your death will not be quick and painless. For you, I will make it last days, and I will not do it until you have watched me kill everyone you ever loved."

The man they called El Jefe bristled, but fought down the impulse to threaten the Dove. Something told him he was not the sort of man who responded well to threats. Better simply to act than to let him see how angry he was. A man like the Dove didn't care about words, only action. No one threatened El Jefe in front of his men, and for this alone, the Brazilian would suffer a terrible and painful end.

But not now.

For now, he would suck it up and do as he was told. "I presume Zamkov still intends to pay me for all the trouble I have gone to?"

"You failed your task."

"I still have two of the ECHO team. If you want me to kill them, then I want to be paid."

"Yes, those are the cards you hold."

"I can always let them go and tell them where you are."

The Dove gave the matter some thought. "I still have to deploy the last device. You will get your money, but only on the condition you keep ECHO away from me."

Loza smiled. Ten million dollars would go a long way in expanding his criminal empire. It was good money, especially for less than a few days' work. Extorting and stealing that sort of cash would normally take months of much more risky work.

"Don't worry," he drawled, working hard to look calm and in control. "We'll get them off your back. When the rest of their team see me execute the woman live on their little phone screens, they will back down and pull out of the mission."

"I pray you are right," the Dove said.

"I know what I'm doing. I've done this hundreds of times before. No one can continue a mission after seeing the terrible way I will kill her, and with the added threat of the same thing happening to Bale, they will soon back down and scuttle away."

"The terrible way you will kill her?"

Loza scratched his stubbly chin and grinned. "Tell me, are you aware of the giant peccaries you have in Brazil?"

The Dove's face crumpled back into impatient anger. "What the hell are you talking about?"

"Pigs," Loza said. "They are like pigs."

"I know what they are."

"Then you know they can be very aggressive, especially when running in a herd."

The Dove sighed. "This had better be going somewhere, Loza, because if – wait, you're not suggesting what I think you are?"

Loza smiled coldly. "What am I suggesting?"

"They told me you were fucked up, but not even I would do something like that. When I kill, it's a matter of professional pride. Clean and quick, although as I say, I would make an exception for you."

"I'm touched, but I am *not* you – we have very different stories, you and me. For me, taking a woman like Donovan and feeding her to a herd of wild peccaries is simple meat and potatoes. I like hearing the screams."

The Dove froze. "You mean the squeals of the pigs, right?"

"I mean the screams of the victim. When I feed someone to my peccaries, they are always alive. If you want to watch, then come with me and see what I am made of."

The Dove kept his disgust hidden from the gangster. "No, but thank you. I have work to do deploying the device in the airport, as you well know. You go to the ranch and do whatever you have to do to make sure the rest of the ECHO team understand what will happen to their friends if they don't pull back and leave me alone to deploy the final bomb."

Loza shrugged. "No problemo, I can set up a camera easily enough. We can livestream the event and make sure they get the picture that way."

"Don't screw this up, Loza. This is your final chance."

"You worry too much, stranger. Leave it with me. Lea Donovan will be pig food within the next few hours."

CHAPTER THIRTY-THREE

Lexi pulled the truck up on the side of the road. As she activated the air brakes, the badly scarred and shot-up eighty ton Kenworth breathed a massive sigh of relief, and she switched off the engine. They were parked up on a ridge in a high, desert pass, overlooking the valley where El Jefe's Buena Vista ranch was located, a few miles west of a town called *Paraíso*. The only sound was the hot wind blowing in through the cracks in the shattered windshield.

"That wind is like a hairdryer," Lexi said.

"Then be grateful we're not further south," Franco said. "The Tehuano wind is ten times worse."

Hawke surveyed the compound with his pocket monocular. "The only thing missing from up here is a rolling tumbleweed, but down on the ranch it's all go."

Lexi swung open the driver's door and another blast of air rushed into the cab. She stepped down on the stainless-steel tank wrap and jumped down to the ground. One by one, the rest of the team joined her at the edge of the ridge.

"Hey, hold your horses," Hawke said, swerving the monocular into the eastern sky. "What have we here?"

"What is it?" Zeke asked.

"Looks like a chopper."

"This has to be El Jefe," Franco said.

Lexi shielded the sun from her eyes, watching the helicopter zoom over the ridge behind the ranch and make its descent. "It's landing."

They watched it touch down. Men dressed in jeans and exposed shoulder holsters over their shirts climbed out and checked the coast was clear. Moments later, El Jefe stepped out of the chopper into the shimmering Mexican afternoon.

"We need to be careful, friends," Franco said. "Loza has ordered the murders of hundreds of men and women, and even some children. He has personally killed at least fourteen people, and his methods are not clean or quick. He fed one rival gang leader to his peccaries."

Zeke looked confused. "What is that?"

"It's a type of pig," Hawke said. "Indigenous to central and South America."

"I thought they were herbivores," said Lexi.

"No, omnivores," Franco said. "Believe me, I got to one of his properties the day after one of his sessions. Thanks to what I found there, I had nightmares for a month."

"He sounds like a pig himself," Lexi said.

Zeke leaned against the side of the truck's engine cab and shook his head. "This Loza has evil running through his veins."

"You believe in evil?" Franco said.

"Sure do. This world ain't so hard to understand. There is good and there is evil. Black and white. Loza feeds men to pigs. Evil. He has a black void where his soul should be, and there is no saving a man like this. No chance of redemption. You disagree with me?"

Franco thought about it. "I have seen men rehabilitated."

"Not men like Loza," said the Texan in his thick, slow accent.

"No, not men like Loza."

"Then if he can't be saved, there is evil." Zeke said. "And what do you do with evil?"

"You destroy it," Lexi said, her face twisted momentarily by the memory of her parents' murder.

"He is still a man," Franco protested. "No one is destroying him. He is to be arrested and taken back to the city to face trial. That is our legal system. We are not vigilantes."

Zeke shrugged. "I'm no vigilante. I am a simple soldier but I'm also a religious man. That is why I know evil when I see it. Today, we play by your rules and we take this evil and we lock it up in a cage. After that, it is still your problem, but we will have saved our friends."

"Yes, we play by my rules. No one is to kill Loza unless it is in self-defense. If any of you kill him without a good legal reason, I will arrest you on the spot and you will be charged with murder. Is that understood?"

Hawke slapped him on the back. "Take it easy, Franco. We're not here to kill anyone. We're here to rescue Lea and Ryan. No one on my team will kill anyone today unless it's in self-defense, just as you say. But if anyone dies in the crossfire, then that's another thing. And there will be a lot of crossfire."

"I understand. When do we go in? Do you want to wait until it's dark?"

Hawke shook his head. "Ideally, yes, but nightfall is just too far away, and this mission is time critical. That means we're going in as soon as possible. Full daylight."

Franco sucked his teeth. "This is very risky, Hawke."

Lexi said, "Most of the stuff we do is very risky."

The Mexican shook his head. "There must be at least twenty or thirty men down there in the compound, and yet there are only four of us. I don't see how we can attack them without getting killed. At least if we wait until the cover of night, we stand a chance."

Lexi sighed, struggling once again to control her temper. "I didn't drive that thing all the way out here to sit around with my thumb up my —."

"What my friend and colleague is trying to say," Hawke said, "is that waiting another six or seven hours for darkness is out of the question. In other words, get ready to go into battle."

"In that case, please tell me we have a plan," Zeke said.

"Of course we have a plan." The big grin on Hawke's face filled Franco with terror. "We're going to break into the ranch house with a battering ram and see what happens next."

"Oh no…" Franco looked like he was going to be sick. "More madness."

"Chin up, Manny," Hawke said. "It'll all be over before you know it."

*

Lea closed her eyes and fought her fears down. Keeping the thought of her own execution in check wasn't easy, but letting it get to her meant they had won. It also meant she was weak, and she hadn't come this far to be broken by a man like El Jefe. More than that, she had to stay strong for Ryan.

For all his bluster and fitness regimen and tattoos and cigarettes, she knew better than anyone that he was still, at heart, the same man she had married all those years ago. Just two stupid kids setting out into the world together, they had held each other up in different ways, but she was always the strong one. If she let go of the situation now, she wouldn't just be failing herself, but Ryan too.

Her first thought was assessing their chances of escape. Realistically, their current situation offered few opportunities. The room was sparsely furnished, the door was locked and the windows were barred with decorative metals grilles and then shutters. There was no way out, and that was presuming they could free themselves from the chairs, which they could not.

Escape, at this moment, was out.

That meant waiting for something to happen. This strategy was always her last resort because it put the power in the hands of her enemy, but right now she had little choice. She was confident they would get a chance to escape, but only if someone cut through the multiple layers of duct tape biting into their wrists and ankles. Until that happened, they were going nowhere, and she was starting to feel tired.

More than that, she felt exhausted. Here she was, in the middle of another nightmare, another battle for her soul, covered in cuts and bruises, betrayed by her aching bones and muscles. It had been a long road. Her life flicked before her eyes. Her father's murder melted into the first time Eden had mentioned ECHO to her. This blurred into the fateful day she met Hawke in London and then her mind filled with images of the Oracle and his Athanatoi henchmen.

The elixir.

The gods.

Undiscovered secrets.

A long road, indeed.

*

Ryan was scared. While he would never say so to Lea, he felt no shame in admitting it to himself, at least. Taped down to a chair in an isolated, rural property owned by one of Mexico's most dangerous gangs was not the best place to be, and he knew it. Ever since El Jefe's thugs had dragged him into the panel van outside the airport, he had felt his life expectancy slowly getting shorter. He wondered if his death was inevitable.

He kept his worries from Lea with good reason. In their marriage, she had always been the rock and the last thing he wanted was to make her think she had to keep him calm and talk him down from his fears. She was living through her own personal hell right now; he just knew it. Who wouldn't be? She was in the exact same boat as he was and processing it in her own way. No, he had to hold it together and stay calm.

But it was hard. Thoughts of his immediate death rose in his mind like wraths; grim portents of what was to come and impossible to push away. Would the end be swift and painless, or would El Jefe make it last for hours just for his amusement? Maybe he would livestream it on the internet just for kicks, or to terrorize the rest of the team into submission.

If the Mexican was stupid enough to think that, he had a big surprise coming. If there was one thing Ryan Bale was more certain of than anything else, it was that the rest of the ECHO team would extract a bloody price in revenge if El Jefe ordered their executions. That, at least, was a comforting thought.

He had never given his death any real thought. Why would he? He was still a young man, and looking ahead in his life meant seeing decade after decade stretched out before him. To him, the future meant endless years of pleasures and experiences. It meant ranging the world with his ECHO friends, seeing things and places most people could only dream about.

It meant meeting someone and falling in love again. It meant starting a family. Maybe it even meant leaving

ECHO one day and settling down for good. The idea everything would end today in a decrepit Mexican farmhouse was so ridiculous it seemed impossible to harbor in his young mind.

Was that a shadow under the door? Was someone out in the hallway, on their way to kill them? He'd read more than enough about the brutality of some of Mexico's gangs, and some of their execution methods were notorious among the criminal underworld. Hours of torture were not uncommon, neither was being decapitated and dumped in the desert for those unwitting accomplices, the coyotes.

He stopped thinking about it and silently cursed himself for letting his fears run away with him. This was typical Bale, he thought. Right now, Lea would no doubt be thinking about how to escape from this place, and these men. She would be ranking them on their abilities and weaknesses, on who would be the easiest to pick off first. How to disarm one of them or failing that, what she could use as a weapon.

And what was he doing?

Practically ordering his own funeral flowers.

Get it together, Ryan. Show her you can be strong.

Then things changed.

"Lea! I hear someone."

"Me too," she said.

Someone scraped a key in the lock, and the door opened to reveal several men standing in the shadows.

CHAPTER THIRTY-FOUR

Ramiro Loza liked the smell of fear. He liked the way it looked, too, but today he was disappointed. If either of the two people tied down to chairs in front of him were frightened, they weren't showing it. This displeased him, but he would keep his anger to himself, just as his prisoners were doing. This was, after all, a game only he could win.

After landing at Buena Vista, he had made his way straight over to see the new prisoners, and now he stood in the shadows with Vicente Alonso at the back of the room and watched them. They knew he was here, but he wanted to make them sweat. He wanted to tenderize them, but the Dove's timetable meant things had to move along.

"If you're going to kill us, then get on with it."

The woman.

He stepped out of the shadows and caressed her face. "You're very feisty."

"Get your hands off me, you filthy maggot."

He slapped her hard but she swallowed her scream. Staring up at him with blood trickling over her lower lip, she smiled. "Is that all you've got?"

He started to chuckle. "You do not want to know what I have in store for you."

"Fuck you and the horse you rode in on, Loza."

He stopped laughing and gently scraped the tip of his bowie knife across her forehead, and then down her temple and over her cheek. He swivelled it around and slid it under the jaw until it was pushing into her neck.

239

"I would love to kill you," he said quietly. "I love to kill people."

"I don't fear death, and I don't fear you."

Loza nodded as if he understood. "I am the same, I do not fear death either. It seems you and I have something in common. I have made my peace with the devil, have you?"

"I worship no devil."

Loza saw that his captive was cut from a different cloth to the men and women who usually ended up in front of him. The brave young woman looked back up at him, caught his eye and held his gaze without any fear. He recognized the look in those eyes. He saw the pain and the suffering this woman had experienced; he had known it himself. In that way, he felt a common bond with his prisoner, but he would still kill her, and then the boy. And he would enjoy doing it. It was just the way he was.

"My friends are not the sort of people you want to upset," Lea said.

Loza laughed long and hard. "My gang are not the sort of people you want to upset. I doubt very much that your friends could lay a finger on any of them. These are the toughest, hardest men in the Mexican underworld. They are not frightened of your friends, and neither am I. They might have deactivated the Dove's bombs, but when they come here to rescue you, they will find nothing but death."

"Yeah – yours," Ryan said.

Loza looked down at him. Hours ago, he had slapped him so hard he had knocked him over in his chair to the floor. He was still there.

"I think not, little worm."

"Fuck off."

Alonso slowly pushed the sole of his boot down on Ryan's face, gradually increasing pressure until his cheek was squashed up against his teeth. "A man in your position should be much more polite."

"Fuck off, please."

"Enough of this!" Loza snapped. "It is time to send a strong message to the rest of your team."

As Alonso scowled and removed his boot, Lea said, "The team will never compromise the mission. Not even to save us."

"I think you are very wrong," he said. "What would you do, if you saw your beloved Joe Hawke being fed alive to wild animals, and the only way you could stop it and keep him alive was if you stood down, and gave up on your mission?"

Lea felt sick, but fought the desire to vomit. "Fed to animals? What are you talking about?"

"You will find out soon enough," he said. "The only question is who will be the canary in the coal mine? You..." he turned his pointing finger down to Ryan. "Or you?"

Loza turned to the men standing behind him. "Bring them both to the arena."

When she felt the men's hands all over her, Lea screamed, but with her hands and legs taped down to the chair there was nothing she could do to protect herself. Ryan was in the same situation, and neither of them could do anything to stop the horror that was unfolding around them.

Loza led the men carrying Lea and Ryan, still taped to the chairs, out of the room and along a short corridor. At the end, he turned a ceramic handle and opened a white-painted door. Sunlight flooded into the house, and then they were outside in the dry, dusty air, heading toward a ramshackle barn.

"Is the livestream all set up?" Loza asked Alonso.

Alonso swung open the barn door and the group moved back into the shade. "Si."

Lea's eyes adjusted to the new gloom just in time to see Loza order his men to lift a trapdoor in the center of the barn. After clearing piles of hay and dust out of the way, the men used a leather strap to open a large wooden hatch in the barn floor, and Loza ordered them to take the prisoners down into the hole.

As Alonso and the men carried her down a dirty slope into the darkness, she twisted her head to look up at Loza who was still standing on the barn floor above her. "You can't do this to us, you fucking psycho!"

After a pause, he said, "Yes, very feisty."

When they reached the bottom of the slope, the men set her down on the chair and Alonso tugged on a dirty pullcord. A light came on in response and what Lea saw filled her with a fear she had never felt before.

The room beneath the barn was a specially constructed pit with chairs placed around it in a semi-circle, arranged for people to view the depraved horror shows Loza obviously used this place for. Staring into the pit, things got worse. Behind a metal fence at one end of the pit, she saw wooden gates placed around the outside of the dugout. On the floor in the corner, partially covered in dirt and rags, she saw a pile of what could only be human bones.

"Ryan!" she cried out. "Are you in here?"

The men slammed his chair down beside hers. "Unfortunately, yes, and... wait – are those...?"

"Yes, I think so," she said. "They're human remains."

"Bloody hell, Lea, this isn't good."

"Are you trying to be funny? Of course it's not freaking good! If my hands weren't taped down I'd slap you for that comment."

With his hands in his pockets, Loza walked over to them and grinned. "Welcome to my favorite place in the whole world – the Buena Vista Arena!"

Lea shook her head, lost and afraid. "You're the sickest son of a bitch I have *ever* known."

"Please – stop! You'll make me blush. Vicente! Get these two down into the pit and then open the gates."

"No!" Ryan yelled.

"And Vicente," Loza lowered his voice into a conspiratorial whisper, just loud enough for his prisoners to hear. "Make sure you get out first, I've been starving them for days."

CHAPTER THIRTY-FIVE

"But we don't have a battering ram," Franco said.

Hawke grinned at him. "Yeah, we do."

"I don't think so, Joe," Zeke said. "There is no battering ram in *my* pack, at least."

Lexi grinned.

"Don't look at me," Franco said. "I have only my regulation sidearm."

Zeke turned to face the Chinese assassin. "Why are you smirking?"

"Because she knows me better than you do," Hawke said.

"I still don't get it," said the Texan.

"Me neither," Franco added, lifting his watch for all to see. "And I'm sure I don't need to remind you that time is running out fast. Zamkov is planning on releasing the supervirus on the Day of the Dead, and the day is rapidly running out!"

"No, you don't need to remind us," Lexi said.

Zeke sighed. "So where is the battering ram?"

With her arms still crossed over her chest, Lexi leaned in closer to the monk. "You're leaning on it, Billy Bob."

Now he got it, and so did the Mexican agent standing beside him. Zeke looked like he appreciated the update, but Franco was horrified. "You want to drive this truck *through* El Jefe's compound?"

Hawke nodded, as if he were still mulling it over. He wasn't; the decision was made and he turned to get back into the cab. "Right up to the front door and through the other side, amigo."

"This is insane! You are insane."

"It's the best shot we've got against so many men," Lexi said. The chrome zipper on her leather jacket shone on the hot sun, momentarily dazzling Franco. He looked away, blinked, then returned his gaze to her. "No, it's *crazy*, and so are you for agreeing to it."

"Why crazy?" Zeke asked. "This truck is an irresistible force, but unfortunately for El Jefe, his ranch is not an immovable object. Simple physics says he is completely screwed."

"It's still nuts!" Franco protested. "For one thing, your friends are in there!"

"Our friends are over there in that barn," Lexi said. "We already know that. We just saw both of them as Loza's men dragged them out there. I don't know if you noticed or not, but they were surrounded by about thirty men with guns."

"Yes, I saw that."

"If not the truck," Zeke drawled, "then what do you suggest we do?"

"You know what I'm going to say." Franco was exasperated. "We call for…"

"Don't say it, Franco," Lexi said. "You know why we can't call backup. This problem is all ours, and we need to use every weapon at our disposal."

Hawke climbed up on the next step and hung onto the grab handle. "True story. As my old drill sergeant used to say, use what you can get and get what you can use."

With Franco's protests falling on deaf ears, Hawke turned to Lexi. "You know what to do, right?"

She nodded and pulled her gun. We'll go over to the ridge in the west and wait until you knock on the door. Then we wait until the panic starts and hit the barn. What about you?"

ROB JONES

"If she's up to it, I'll bring the truck around to the barn after demolishing the ranch house."

"Be sure to do as much damage as you can on the way."

Hawke winked. "You know I will, Lex. Tell me again, where the hell is second gear?"

"You're kidding, right?"

"Sure. I watched you drive it back on the highway and getting up to sixth seems easy enough."

She looked from the truck down to the compound, then back up to the war-torn ex-commando. "You're not going to need all six to smash that ranch up."

"That's what I figured. Wish me luck."

She leaned up and kissed him on the cheek for the second time that day. "Like you need it."

Hawke let the kiss slide without comment. The truth was he appreciated it. She was an old friend and a good-looking woman, and there was no way she would get in the middle of him and Lea. She was just being all Lexi about things, and he got that.

Zeke looked up at him now, a look of regret on his face. "I'm sorry, but there is no kiss from me. I'm way too shy."

Hawke couldn't resist smiling. "I'll get over it, Zeke." Hawke climbed up into the cab and slammed the door. "It won't be easy, but in time, I'll get there."

The Texan grinned back and gave him the thumbs up. "Go wreck that place, man."

The Englishman fired up the truck, revving the colossal engine to produce a low, earth-rumbling roar. Leaning out of the window, he called down to Lexi. "I'm not going to get far before they see me and start firing. I'll handle that, but don't wait for me if anything goes wrong and I get hit. Use whatever chaos the truck causes to your

246

advantage and get Lea and Ryan out of that barn and to safety."

Lexi rolled her eyes. "You're my hero, did you know that?"

"Fuck off, Lex."

He selected first gear and pulled the truck away from the siding. Checking his mirror, he saw Lexi was already leading Zeke and Franco off the road, using the cover of some cypress trees to reach their position. For a few moments, he was able to look out of the cab window to watch them as he drove along the road, but then they moved out of sight and went deeper into the forest to traverse the valley west of the compound.

He shifted into second, then third, steering the truck around a bend, slowly getting closer to the ridge where he intended on leaving the road and ploughing down into the compound. Franco had been right when he said it was insane, and he knew it, too. But he had counted at least fifty men in the compound, and some of them had automatic weapons over their shoulders.

Both he and Lexi knew there was no way a unit of four people with sidearms were taking out a small army like that without some extra help. He'd seen enough action movies to know what directors and screenwriters thought special ops soldiers could do, but most of it was ridiculous. Even a highly trained commando had only so much power against fifty armed men. He would stand a better chance if he could have attacked at night and used the darkness as cover to create confusion, but waiting for nightfall just wasn't an option.

Only the insane truck thing was an option.

CHAPTER THIRTY-SIX

He gripped the steering wheel, swinging the massive Kenworth off the road and down onto the slope above the Buena Vista Ranch. The colossal engine roared and growled as the mighty tires of the tractor unit rumbled over the loose rock and desert scree. Hawke fought to keep the truck in a straight line.

"Not long now, boys." The truck hit the bottom of the slope with a metal-screeching smash. Stamping on the throttle and shifting up, the engine howled like an animal in pain. "That is *definitely* not the right gear."

Ahead, Loza's men had seen the rig and were springing into action, drawing their weapons and taking up defensive positions behind the perimeter wall.

"Really?" Hawke shook his head. "You think a foot-thick drystone wall is going to stop an eighty-ton truck?"

They fired on him, and he ducked down behind the dash as he ploughed the truck through the walls. It broke the defensive line as if it wasn't even there, spraying broken bricks and dead men into the air either side of the cab.

Hawke looked to his right and saw Lexi, Zeke and Franco heading toward an old barn on the ranch's western border. Good, he thought; it's working. The Serpents were reacting to the truck smashing into their lives and already overlooking other chinks in their armor. The longer he kept the show going over here, the longer Lexi had to see whatever the hell was going on in that barn.

In a wild hail of bullets, he swung the truck to the right and aimed it right at the main ranch house. The chopper was his prime target, but he couldn't even see it. Judging by where it had landed, he guessed the quickest way to it was right through Loza's Home Sweet Home.

Closing in on the center of El Jefe's criminal empire, the shooting grew wilder and more desperate. Dozens of gangsters swarmed like ants, fanning out around the truck as he drove it through a line of parked pickup trucks. The Kenworth batted them aside as if they were toys, but it was taking damage. Bullets streaked up its side, punching holes in the windows and up the exhaust stacks.

Hawke carried on regardless, steering the monster further around to the right until he was lined up with the ranch house. Most of the men were armed with sidearms or rifles, but now he saw the men who had climbed out of the chopper with Loza. He was disappointed to see they had upgraded their pistols to a mini RPG launcher.

"Shit," he muttered, revving the engine. "This could be a problem."

The question was, could he gun the truck over the top of their position before they could load and launch the RPG? The answer came in bone-crunching carnage as he piled the Kenworth over the top of their truck and killed both of them instantly. He steered left and headed back toward the ranch house, but his celebrations were cut short when he saw two more men on top of a grain silo to the south.

They were aiming another RPG at him, and this time the silo was too far away to take out before they fired. He had no choice but to point the truck at the ranch house, wedge the throttle pedal down and dive to safety. Using a twelve-inch spanner from the toolbox in the footwell, he managed to jam the pedal to the metal just as the men loosed the RPG.

A trail of white smoke drifted out behind the lethal projectile as it screeched across the hot sky like a wild banshee, aimed right for his windshield.

"Shite alight!" he yelled, swinging open the door and diving out of the cab as another fusillade of bullets fired from his left. He crashed into the ground just as the RPG made contact with the truck, but what he saw next left him speechless.

The RPG ripped through the driver's window, through the inside of the cab and out of the other window, leaving no more damage than a twisting white column of exhaust smoke inside the cab. It continued on its way across the front yard and smashed into another grain silo, blowing it sky-high in a fierce, raging fireball.

The truck growled the last few yards before piling into the front of Loza's ranch house, breaking down the walls and collapsing a good chunk of the red-tiled roof. Tiles, skylights and vent pipes blew up into the air as the gables snapped and the main trusses buckled and collapsed.

In the collision, the trailer with the one surviving supercar on board had become disconnected from the tractor unit, and was jack-knifed out at a fifty degree angle. Hawke now took cover behind the bright yellow McLaren 702s at the front of the trailer and fired on the ranch house as Serpents streamed out of it covered in plaster dust, cuts and bruises. They fought back hard, but he was ready and unloaded an entire mag on them. Screaming in the chaos, four of them were killed instantly and the others dispersed in search of cover.

A second wave of men emerged from the dust and smoke, took up defensive positions in the rubble of the exploded grain silo and fired on him. The Englishman reloaded and returned fire, knowing every second he kept them busy gave Lexi a better chance of finding Lea and Ryan, but then all the men he was fighting turned and fled.

"I wasn't doing that well!" he said. "Unless…"

When he turned and looked over his shoulder, he saw what had made the men run for their lives. Another RPG was spiralling down at him out of the clear blue sky and was no more than three seconds away from him.

*

Lea watched in terror as Alonso yanked out a rusty bolt, slid up the wooden gate and sprinted like crazy for the chipped, gnawed ladder. By the time the first peccary had appeared in the hole, he was pulling the ladder with shaking hands, and making the sign of the cross over his head and chest.

"That thing is much bigger than I was expecting," Lea said, straining against the duct tape binding her to the chair.

"What did you think they were going to unleash on us?" Ryan said. "Some guinea pigs?"

"Don't start, Ry!"

The heavy-set animal emerged from the hole with an angry squeal, while another moved around in the darkness behind it. As the first one moved closer, the second came out into the pit and the entire pack bundled out behind it.

"Fuck me," Lea said. "There must be at least a dozen of them."

"There's fourteen," Ryan said.

"I'd forgotten how you can count so fast."

The animals grew in excitement, growling, snorting and roaring and running around the outside of the pit. In between them and the two ECHO members was the one single metal fence which divided the area with the wooden gates from the rest of El Jefe's insane arena.

Ryan wrenched at the tape but without even a millimetre to work with, there was no hope of breaking free. "They're circling us, and they look really hungry."

Lea heard the men behind her laugh.

"That's because they *are* hungry, you fools!" Loza shouted. "I have starved them for this very occasion. They want their dinner, and *you* are their dinner."

As they moved cautiously closer again, Lea saw one of them open its mouth to reveal four enormous, yellow fangs as sharp as razors. The only thing between her and that disgusting, gaping mouth full of sharp teeth was the metal fence.

"Make sure the livestream is working," Loza called out in Spanish.

Ryan translated what he said, and Lea paled.

"It's all good to go, boss," Alonso called back.

Loza laughed and stuck a cigar in his mouth. "Good, then the show is about to begin."

CHAPTER THIRTY-SEVEN

Hawke dived away from the truck's trailer, slamming into the dry baked earth just as the RPG ripped into the side of the McLaren and blew it to pieces. He swore loud and hard as the explosives blasted the supercar into a million pieces of twisted, blackened metal, burning rubber and smoldering plastic.

Nuts and bolts spiralled out like shrapnel from a nail bomb. He heard a colossal thud a few yards to his right and turned to see the entire engine block half-buried in the dirt beside him. The force of the detonation must have blown it at least three hundred feet into the air.

In the bedlam, one of the Serpents made a move for him, breaking cover and pulling his weapon. As wheel arches and sill panels rained back down to earth all around him, a smoking forged alloy wheel fell from the sky and crashed into the man's head, smashing his skull open, felling him like a tree trunk.

"The sun shines on the righteous." Hawke rolled into the cover of the tractor unit a few yards away. Emptying another mag into more men fleeing what was left of the ranch house, he prayed Lexi had pulled off her part of the mission. A gangster loped to the end of the ruins and slipped around the corner but he fired again, just catching him in the back.

Others ran for their lives now, but he fired again in a relentless barrage. Four more went down, dead before they hit the ground, but the rest scattered. Some got back into the smouldering ruins, others dived for the cover of the parked cars.

Using the rear wheel axle to climb up the side of the upturned trailer, Hawke sprinted along its length until he reached the end. El Jefe's men saw him and opened fire, but he leaped from the end of the trailer onto the remaining part of the roof. It was a good distance and while he knew his twenty-year old self could easily make it, the older version made the jump on a wing and prayer.

And missed.

The gutter scraped down his stomach as he slid down to the ground but he just managed to grab a vent pipe and stop his fall. Smelling blood, the Serpents broke cover and ran out into the yard, raising their guns and aiming at his back. He made a snap judgement that dropping into the ruined portico would get him out of the line of fire faster than trying to clamber up on the roof, especially since so many of them had been loosened by the crash.

He released his grip on the vent pipe and fell, just as they opened fire. Bullets ripped into the soffits and drainpipes, splitting the terracotta tiles into shards and ricocheting in all directions.

He hit the ground hard, narrowly missing a brick which would have twisted his ankle and left him vulnerable. Scrambling to his feet, he smacked another mag into his Glock and sprinted for the cover of what had once been the main hall. He scanned the area. The bottom part of an elaborate mahogany staircase ended abruptly halfway up. The upper part had been torn away by the truck's cab, which he now saw at the back of the house in what looked like the kitchen.

What had once been the top of the stairs was now an isolated mezzanine balcony, and stranded on it were several men, but none of them was Loza. It didn't matter. He'd done his job and delivered the mother of all distractions. Men from all over the ranch were streaming into the main house, all baying for his blood and trying to impress El Jefe.

He fired on the mezzanine, driving the men back into the room they had come from. They would be back in seconds, just as soon as they had loaded their weapons and organized a plan of attack. He used those seconds to sprint under the mezzanine and over to the rubble-covered truck. Climbing up into the cab, he raised his palm mic to his mouth.

"Anyone around?"

"I hear you, Hawke."

Lexi's voice, and whenever she called him, that meant she was usually under fire.

"All good?"

"We're under pressure."

"They're putting up a fight?"

"Well, I'm not singing the fucking Queen song, am I?"

"I suppose not. How many?"

"More than we thought. Turns out it wasn't just a barn, but there was a suite of offices in here, too. It also turns out Loza's men are not as stupid as we thought."

"They knew the truck was just a distraction?"

"I wouldn't say…*fuck!*"

"Lex?"

"I'm fine – it was just a bullet."

Only Agent Dragonfly, he thought.

"And take that you ass nuggets!"

He heard a rapid burst of sidearm fire as he crunched the gears into reverse and began driving the truck back out into the rubble. "Arse nuggets?"

"I'm just riffing, Hawke, and in my *fifth* language. Got a problem with that?"

The truck crunched over the bodies of some of El Jefe's fallen goons. "I absolutely do not have the balls to have a problem with that, Lexi."

"Good. Now, is there a reason for this call?"

"I just called to say I love you, Lex, and that I'm on my way over to you now. Expect a twenty-thousand-pound cab to drive through the east side of the office suite in about two minutes."

"Tractor unit."

"Eh?"

"You're sitting in a cab, but that's sitting on a tractor unit. Do they teach you nothing in the British Army?"

"They actually do teach very little in the British Army, but luckily I was never in the British Army. I was in the Marines and then the SBS. We're altogether better informed."

"Nothing like a bit of inter-service rivalry, Hawke, but as much as I'd like to join in, I'm up to my ass in Mexican bandits."

"I hear you, Lex. I'm on my way."

Both rear-view mirrors had been ripped off in the crash, but he didn't need either to know Loza's men were behind the truck and firing on him. The location of two gas tanks on the outside of the cab – tractor unit, he corrected himself – were dangerous, but he knew what the shooters did not know. All the tanks were nearly empty and he was running the Kenworth on fumes.

*

At the western edge of the property, Lexi Zhang slammed into the dirt and reloaded her gun. She flicked her head over her shoulder to check Zeke and Franco were safe. She knew Zeke had experience of fire fights, but she

guessed the inexperienced CNO agent had only ever
squeezed off a few rounds on his annual trip to the range.

"You guys all right?"

Two nods. Zeke said, "But that truck made a hell of a
mess of the ranch. I hope Hawke's all right."

"He's fine," she said. "I just talked to him. We have to
worry about ourselves right now, not him – got it?"

They both got it.

Up ahead, they watched half a dozen more men
running out of the barn's main entrance. They weaved
around some parked pickup trucks, drew their weapons
and ran over to the smouldering ruins of El Jefe's country
retreat.

Lexi slid a round into the chamber. "All right, go go
go!"

She scrambled to her feet and ran across the gravel to
the barn's side door. The two men followed but she had
already reached the door and shot the lock to pieces by
the time they caught up with her.

She ran inside, gun raised into the aim and swept it
from side to side, but she saw nothing except an empty
barn. "What the hell?"

"They definitely came in here," Zeke said.

Franco searched the dusty barn but saw nothing except
old rusting farm equipment. "So, where the hell are
they?"

"There!" Lexi said. "Look on the floor in the corner –
it's a trap door."

They sprinted over and saw what she had found. A
black metal hoop was attached to a series of wooden
planks nailed together. It looked old and poorly made, but
it was still a trap door.

Zeke shook his head. "I'm not liking the look of this,
Lexi."

"Me neither," she said.

"And what the hell is that noise?" Zeke asked. "Sounds like pigs or something."

"This is freaking me out," Lexi said. "Why would anyone need a secret room underneath a barn in the middle of a ranch this isolated?"

"I'll tell you why," Franco said. "But first, drop your guns, kick them over there and raise your hands, or I will blow both of your heads off."

258

CHAPTER THIRTY-EIGHT

"You son of a bitch," Lexi said. "You're working for Loza."

Franco nodded, and kicked their guns across the barn floor. "If you do as you're told, he will kill you quickly. Believe me, you want him to kill you quickly."

Lexi's eyes darted over to their guns. They were too far to run to, for sure. Franco would rake her full of lead before she had even got halfway over to them. She had to stall for more time. "When did he get to you?"

"Two years ago, on a drugs raid in Tepito. He threatened my family. He kidnapped my daughter to show how serious he was. When I swore loyalty to him, he released her with a nice long scar down her cheek. If I step out of line, he will kill my whole family and make me watch. He has done it before, to others. He feeds people to his pigs. That's what you can hear."

Zeke's lip curled in disgust. "Then why not join us and kill him, man?"

"He is too powerful. Only this way can I ensure the safety of my family."

"You are a pathetic coward," the Texan said.

"But I am alive. Now, get down into the basement."

Lexi raised her hands and moved down the slope into the darkness. Beside her, the Texan tank commander was silent, but she saw an unusual rage burning in his blue eyes.

"Señor Loza!" Franco called out.

Startled, the leader of the Serpents turned to see the CNI agent marching Lexi and Zeke down the slope into the viewing area round the pit.

"Agent Franco," Loza said. "How good to see you! And you have brought me some more food, I see."

"Lex!" Lea called out. "Get out of here! For god's sake." Then she saw Franco's gun at their backs. "Damn it."

Lexi was crestfallen. "Sorry, Lea. I blew it."

"No," Zeke said. "We were betrayed by this bastard. This is not the same thing."

"It doesn't change where we are," Lexi said, hate smoldering in her dark eyes.

Franco walked them over to Loza. "There is one more up top," he said. "Hawke."

"I know, he's trashing the ranch with a truck," Loza said. "But not for long. I'm going to call him now and send him the livestream of his friends being fed alive to my pets, one by one. The slower he complies with my orders and retreats, the less Christmas cards he will need this year. Release the peccaries!"

The metal grate scraped up through the rusty runner and the peccaries burst out into the pit, growling and snorting as they headed straight for Lea and Ryan. They squealed and belched and growled as they drew closer to their meals.

No one down in the pit had ever heard the noise an eighty ton truck makes as it drives through a barn, but at the same time Loza unleashed his beasts, Hawke drove the Kenworth into the eastern wall of the barn and the entire building collapsed down around it.

"My god!" Loza screamed at his men. "Get up there and kill him!"

They had no chance. The colossal weight of the tractor unit was too much for the poorly built dug-out beneath the barn, and now the front end of the cab crashed through the roof in a shower of dirt, snapping timber support posts like toothpicks. Franco was directly underneath, and the last thing anyone saw of him was the Kenworth's heavy duty louvred grille crushing him flat as it hit the ground with a juddering, earth-shaking halt.

"Talk about working flat-out for someone!" Ryan said.

Lea didn't hear the quip; she was too busy snarling and screaming at the peccaries snapping at her ankles. Lexi and Zeke had snatched the few seconds of mayhem to disarm two of Loza's men and roll into cover behind the truck. In the middle of it all, Joe Hawke was kicking his way through the broken windshield and crawling out of the cab, gun in hand. He saw Lea and Ryan and charged over to them, firing on the peccaries, scattering them to the outside of the pit.

To his right, Vicente Alonso was running up the slope on his way back up into the ruins of the barn. Hawke spun around and fired on him, planting three rounds in his torso and a fourth in the side of his head. As the Mexican's bullet-riddled corpse rolled down the slope, Hawke ran over to Lea and Ryan.

"Sorry I'm late," he said.

"Better late than never!" Lea rubbed her freed wrists. "That was close."

"You can say that again," Hawke said. "When I said you two should go out for dinner together, I meant in a restaurant, Ryan."

"I'm the funny one, Joe," Ryan said, deadpan. "Leave it to the experts."

"Where's *El Jefe*?" Lea asked, her voice full of contempt.

Hawke finished untying them. "Unfortunately for him, he just got introduced to Lexi Zhang. Let's get out of here! Zeke! The ladder."

The Texan lowered the wooden ladder and the three of them climbed away from the enraged, squealing animals. Across the other side of the pit, things were looking bleak for Ramiro Loza. With his guard of Serpents wiped out and Franco crushed to death, he was alone and running scared. He snatched at a gun on the floor, but Lexi kicked it away, then fired another kick into his face. The blow knocked him off his balance and he tumbled into the mess of squirming, snorting peccaries below him in the pit.

As they fought with each other to rip chunks from his face, Lea winced and looked away. Only seconds ago, this wild, heaving nightmare of snapping jaws and jets of arterial blood and human screams had been her fate.

Ryan peered down and felt sick, but still managed to find himself. Wrapping an arm around Lexi, he thanked them all for saving their lives. As they emerged into the daylight and smoking ruins of the barn, he looked up at the sky with a smile and breathed a deep sigh of heartfelt relief. After a short silence, he said, "What do you call a Mexican pig?"

Lea rolled her eyes, only just feeling safe enough to believe it was really over. "I don't know, Ry – what do you call a Mexican pig?"

"Porque."

Lexi slapped his shoulder. "Your face is funny, but what comes out of it, not so much."

Hawke's phone rang. "It's Cairo. She just found out the Dove is heading to the airport and he still has a vial of the supervirus with him, just in case Loza screwed up."

"My god," Lea said. "It'll be all over the entire world within a few hours. We have to get over there right now."

"Yeah, you know the arse end of nowhere, right?" Ryan said. "Well, that's where people from where we are *right now* go on holiday to liven up their lives."

"He's right," Lea said. "This one's down to Cairo – we're too far out to help and we can't exactly take the truck. We're stuck here."

"And that's where you're wrong," Hawke said. "Loza arrived on a neat little executive chopper parked up around the back of the ranch house. I was going to drive over the top of it to stop him getting away, but luckily I was somewhat curtailed by events."

Lexi holstered her gun and started walking off into the late afternoon sun. "Looks like Cairo isn't going to have all the fun after all."

With their shadows stretched out ahead of them on the dusty dirt of the Buena Vista ranch's front yard, the ECHO team made their way over to Loza's helicopter, each in their own hearts knowing the battle was nowhere near being over yet.

*

Always in the dark, Alex Reeve considered. Since being brought to this place, this hell, this Tartarus, she had been kept in the dark nearly the entire time. And alone. She buried a sob in her hands and wiped the tears from her eye. The loneliness was worse than the dark, she considered. If only she had someone to talk to, even the darkness might be bearable.

From somewhere deep within, she found some more strength and got herself together for the thousandth time since Faulkner had stormed into the Oval Office and seized power from her father. Running her tongue over the hole in her gum, a shiver went down her spine. She knew Blanchard had threatened to let Mahoe finish the job if her father didn't back down, and now all she could do was sit in the dark and wait for the knock at the cell door.

Was there any chance Joe Hawke and the rest of the team could find them and save them from this nightmare? She doubted it. They had been here for days now. If ECHO knew their location they would have mounted a rescue operation by now. Maybe Faulkner had killed them all?

She felt her heart sink. What had started as a simple crush on Hawke had grown into something much more serious, and while she knew he was with Lea, she still wanted to tell him how she felt. Now, she would never get the chance. The moment was gone, and he would never know. The thousand different life paths she had thought about, wondering which one she would end up following, had all converged into this terrible, inescapable hell.

Maybe, she thought grimly, she was the only one out of all her friends left alive? Maybe Faulkner had ordered Blanchard to keep her in the darkness of this isolation cell for the rest of her life.

The sobs turned into a wail, and drowning in helplessness and desolation, she felt the mother of all panic attacks rising like a tsunami. This, then, would be her life from now on. Sitting in the dark, waiting to be told her father was dead, or that she was going to be tortured.

Without knowing it, her life had become a hell on earth.

CHAPTER THIRTY-NINE

A round of applause from Scarlet's team burst out spontaneously when Hawke booted open the door and Lea and Ryan walked into the room. Both teams were gathered together once again in a cheap motel room in Mexico City's Tacubaya district, and shared quick stories of their own personal nightmares before collapsing on various chairs and beds.

"Here," Scarlet said, throwing Lea a cold beer. "You look like you need it."

"What about me?" Ryan said.

"I ordered a root beer for you."

"My sides are aching," he said, "and not from the beating back at the ranch. Oh no, they're aching because of how funny you are."

"Catch," she said, throwing him another bottle from the fridge. "I'm only kidding, pissflaps."

He caught it one hand and levered the top off with his teeth. "I knew it in my heart."

"I still cannot believe Franco was working for El Jefe," Castillo said. "I have known him for many years. I know his wife and children. They will be devastated by his death."

"I know how they feel," Lexi said, grabbing her own beer. "I was sort of devastated when the bastard pulled a gun on me."

"I understand how you feel, but his family must never learn the truth about him. His life might been destroyed by Loza, but at least give him the chance to have some dignity in death. Let me tell them he died fighting Loza and his men, not *for* them."

Lexi raised her hands. One was still gripping a cold beer bottle. "Hey, whatever floats your boat. I can't see any reason to let his kids know the truth about him."

"Thank you."

"Thank god you got out of there in time," Camacho said. "Those pigs sound grim."

"They were, believe me," Lea said.

Zeke chinked beer bottled with Ryan. "Good to have you back, man. Sounds like a helluva time."

"It was," Ryan said. "I was okay, but Lea needed a lot of support."

Lea rolled her eyes, but felt too relieved to comment.

"What about the other teams?" Lea said. "I've been pretty tied up the last few hours so I'm kinda out of the loop."

Scarlet said, "We haven't heard anything from Orlando, Bravo Troop or the Raiders for hours, but we can't worry about them. We have our own mission to think of."

Lea nodded. "What have we got on the Dove? Is he at the airport yet?"

Castillo's briefing was short and to the point. "My contacts at the CNI tell me he has not arrived at the airport yet, so we still have time to get over there and stop him before he releases the supervirus. Cortez tells me he is still in Loza's penthouse suite."

"In that case," Camacho said, smacking his hands together. "We have time to eat."

"It's a good idea," Hawke said. "I haven't eaten for twenty-four hours."

When room service brought their meals up, Camacho thanked the woman and wheeled the cart into the center of the room. Pulling the white cloth away with a theatrical *ta-dah*, their eyes feasted on a vast array of fine foods – grilled rib eye, Chilean salmon with sautéed vegetables, truffled French fries and Russet mashed potatoes.

"You even remembered dessert," Scarlet said, eyeing up a vanilla petit gateau and a lemon sorbet. "Alby, please tell me the Dove is still in the penthouse and we have time to sample this."

Castillo snapped his phone shut and gave an apologetic smile. "I'm sorry, but he's already on the way. He took a cab to the airport less than two minutes ago."

"Oh bugger," she said with a long sigh.

"I have a friend at the airport who might be able to help us," Castillo said. "I'm guessing with Loza out of the way, your friends safe and only one supervirus device on the loose, you have no objections if I bring in someone from the outside now?"

"Good idea," Lea said.

"I'll get on it."

As she walked to the door, Scarlet picked up a single chocolate-dipped strawberry and popped it into her mouth. "Heaven."

"But now it's time for hell," Lea said.

"Lea's right," Hawke said. "So let's get on with it. Tool up everyone."

*

Cotillard used another ID card to get Bravo Troop through the Eiffel Tower's security and seconds later they were in the elevator heading up to the top floor. Hudson was ice cool, inside and out, but Mack and Danny were revved up and ready to take Rodrigues out once and for all. In the corner of the elevator, Kyra and Cotillard spoke in quiet French, and were both startled when they reached their destination.

Stepping out onto the top floor, Kyra gasped when she saw the city. She had never been to the top of the Eiffel Tower before, but it delivered everything she had ever thought it would, and a lot more. The lights of the famous city sparkled all the way to the horizon, and far below, across the River Seine, boulevards lined with floodlit plane trees and French flags stretched away from the Trocadero Gardens into the mysteries of upmarket Chaillot.

"Woah," she said. "The guidebooks never said anything about this."

Danny laughed. "They didn't say nothing about the psychopath lurking at the top of this tower, neither, darlin'."

He pulled his gun and scanned the cramped space around them. The thousand foot drop below them was fenced off behind a steel mesh, with gaps just big enough for tourists to snap pictures of the city, and the narrow walkway between the fence and the tower was dotted with bolted-down telescopes. Drop a few coins in one and get a great view of Paris, Danny thought. *Yeah, but not tonight.*

"Any sign of Rodrigues?" Hudson asked.

"Not around here," Mack called out. He was alone on the southwest side of the tower.

Just visible through the iron girders, Cotillard and Kyra also replied from the northwest section. "Not here."

Hudson walked up the small staircase to the upper viewing level. Set further back away from the edge, it was higher than the metal safety fence and allowed a better view without being dangerous. "Damn it all…" He turned and stared out across the most famous view of all – the

Champ de Mars, and felt a wave of defeat fast approaching. "Maybe it was a ruse. Maybe they planned to… wait – I see something moving in the shadows!"

It was too late. Rodrigues had been hiding the suitcase IED in the iron girders above his head, and now he jumped him from above, forcing Hudson to the floor.

Hudson tried to turn and fire but there wasn't enough time. He crumpled beneath the weight of the Mexican as he piled into him and crushed him against the metal plate flooring.

He tried to call out, but Rodrigues punched him in the mouth and batted the gun out of his hand. It smacked down on the riveted floor plates, tipped over the edge beneath the balcony and clattered down to the lower viewing level.

As the man pulled back an arm to lay another punch on him, Hudson seized the moment, twisted his body up and headbutted him in the face.

Rodrigues cried out and tumbled away from him, bringing his hands up instinctively to check his smashed nose, now flattened all over his face.

Hudson was on his feet, but unarmed. He rushed the Mexican, swung his leg back and kicked him in the head. Rodrigues grunted in pain and crashed down to the metal plates with a wet smack.

The former SAS major lunged forward in a bid to get hold of Rodrigues's gun, but there was still some fight in the Mexican and he ripped the pistol from his holster. He wasn't near enough to make the shot a dead cert, but he was close enough to make it dangerous.

It happened in a heartbeat.

Danny turned around the corner, saw what was happening and lifted his gun, but Rodrigues's weapon was already cocked and raised into the aim. He spun around and fired once, and the round made it home, burying itself in Danny's stomach. He fired a second time before Danny had reacted, and this time the bullet tore through his bicep and ripped out the other side, blasting a cloud of blood and muscle matter into the air.

Danny cried out in pain and fell to the ground. Rodrigues took a step back, distracted by Kyra Harpenden, who had screamed out loud and without shame when the bullets tore into her friend.

Mack had turned the other corner behind the Mexican, and now fired three times into the man's back. Hudson, Kyra and Cotillard watched solemnly as the bullets blasted out of his chest, blowing out a spray of blood-mist across the viewing platform.

"Shoot my fuckin' pal!" Mack growled. "And you're fuckin' done, mate."

But Rodrigues wasn't done. On his knees now, and with blood pouring out of his mouth and running down over his chin, the Mexican gangster had one trick up his sleeve. Reaching down to his ankle, he pulled a throwing knife from a concealed holster and flicked it across the platform at anyone he could hit.

It landed in Hudson's leg, slashing a half-inch cut before clattering to the floor.

Hudson grunted and clutched at the blood pouring from his leg. Mack fired on Rodrigues a fourth time, blowing the back of his skull out, killing him instantly. Holstering his smoking gun, he ran across to Danny.

"We need a medivac right now," Mack said. "He's gone in minutes without it, boss."

Kyra was already on the phone. "I'm on it, Mack."

Hudson said, "Good work, Kyra. Tell them he'll be on the ground on the southeast side of the tower near the Avenue Gustave Eiffel. They'll know where to get him."

270

"What about you?"

"I'm fine – it's just a flesh wound. Listen, I want you and Mack to stay with Danny until the ambulance arrives, then you both get the hell away."

"What about Danny?" Kyra asked.

"He came out of nappies a long time ago, Kyra," Mack said.

"Huh?"

"Diapers," Hudson said. "There isn't a hospital in France that can hold Danny Plane against his will, or a prison. Let them sort him out and then he'll get back to us. In the meantime, we can't risk any of us being taken into custody."

She gave a reluctant nod as Mack lifted the mumbling Danny into his arms and headed toward the elevator. "C'mon, you big baby," Mack said.

Cotillard was pacing up and down like a condemned man. "What about the bomb!"

"We have to destroy it," Hudson said.

"But how?"

Behind Cotillard, Hudson saw Mack, Kyra and Danny disappear into the elevator and head down to the ground. "Cairo's intel is clear. We need to disconnect this mechanism to stop it from firing the cartridges into the air. That way when we blow up the C4 in this case, it can burn the virus to death."

"This sounds very risky."

"So is handing it over to the authorities when any one of them could be working for Nikita Zamkov."

"Then it's down to us."

Hudson was already on it, carefully breaking the connection between the cartridges holding the supervirus vials and the motor that was designed to propel them away from the explosion and spray them as wide as possible for maximum dispersal.

"We're done," Hud said, taking note of the numbers Cairo had warned him about.

The French detective peered down at him. "What are you doing?"

"We think these numbers are significant – a message to the men who delivered the bombs around the world."

"Like what? Bank accounts?"

"No," Hudson shook his head and slammed the case shut. "Our theory is that they're coordinates to their boss's secret base."

"I see – but now what do we do with this thing?" Cotillard said. "We can't blow it up here – it will blow up the entire top floor of the tower!"

Hudson picked up the case, pulled his weapon from his holster, cocked the hammer and swung the case back as far as he could. "I hope you like fireworks, Jean."

"Oh, non! Non, non, non!"

It was too late. Hudson heaved the case out over the top of the lower viewing platform's safety fence and the two men watched it spin out away from the tower, one thousand feet above the city. Then he took aim and fired on it.

One, two, three rounds fired in as many seconds.

The rounds hit the detonator inside the case, triggering the C4.

A dazzling, violent fireball erupted over the city, exploding with a deep roar and firing a heavy shockwave back to the platform. Hudson and Cotillard both felt the heat and shockwave of the blast as they watched the fragments of the case and the burning fireball enveloping it as they fell out of the sky.

"And we're out of here." Hudson holstered his weapon and limped over to the elevators.

"My god..." Cotillard said. "That was unbelievable."

"Now, Jean! We can't be anywhere near here when things get busy."

And with that, the two men stepped into the elevator and prepared to disappear into the Parisian night.

CHAPTER FORTY

Jed Mason had never been the same since he'd discovered Cleopatra's tomb and the Book of Thoth. Learning that the ancient Egyptian God of Magic had been real and actually walked the earth had been a steep curve for him. He'd heard rumors about ECHO and what they had done, but not until the moment when he'd held that crumbling book in his hands did he truly believe it.

That belief had been a guiding force when choosing to accept ECHO's request for assistance and help them track down Zamkov's devices. Now, as he drove through the Hong Kong dawn and descended into the tunnel beneath Victoria Harbour, he found himself once again questioning what he had learnt about Thoth, and everything he had heard about the exploits of the world-famous ECHO team.

"All good?"

It was Ella Makepeace. The team's organizer-in-chief and famous TV hypnotist was sitting beside him in the back of Maggie Lai's Nissan SUV. The soft glow of the Cross-Harbour Tunnel lights were shining in her long hair. It looked like she had a halo.

"Yeah, all good," he said with an uncertain smile. "But life was simpler when I was in the army."

"Jed Mason, British Army Boxing Champion of 1972."

"Less of it, Ells. It was 1992."

"Not sure that sounds much better."

"No," his smile faded. "Not sure it does."

Maggie blew the horn at someone and swerved around them, waving her fist and shouting in Cantonese. Turning, the former MI6 agent gave them all a serious look. "We're ten minutes out."

"Lucky old us," Caleb said, yawning and stretching his arms. "I can't wait till this is over and I'm on a plane back to my ranch in Arizona. No offense, Maggie."

"None taken."

He nodded. "Got me a ton of work to do out there."

"What about you, Milo?" Maggie asked. "What will you do when this is over?"

He shrugged. "Thinking about getting into blockchain in a big way and retiring in New Zealand."

"Why New Zealand?" she asked.

"Just like Hobbits."

"Cool." She changed lanes. "And you, Ella?"

"Go back to London. Some producers contacted me about another TV show."

"Even cooler."

Mason turned to Zara. "You're going back to LA?"

The former LAPD cop sounded distant when she spoke. "Maybe, but I'm thinking of retracing my Dad's last tour."

Maggie looked at her in the mirror. "Your Dad's tour?"

"Dad was a blues guitarist."

"A blues guitarist?" Milo said. "Stop being modest. Jimmy Dietrich was one of the greatest blues guitarists of all time. Even Stevie Ray Vaughan supported him once."

"Yeah…" her voice trailed.

Caleb stepped in. "And *that* boys and girls, is the coolest thing of all. Jed – what about you?"

"Not a clue, mate. Just take life one day at a time."

Maggie signalled to pull south into Magazine Gap. "I thought you were all working for Ezra Haven at Titanfort?"

A long silence.

"Was it something I said?"

"We work for Ezra Haven all right," Mason said. "But we're not kept in cages in his basement. I'm sorry, Maggie, beyond that, none of us can say anything more. To say Titanfort is secretive is the greatest understatement of the new millennium."

"Ah, no problem. Anyway, here we are."

Mason looked out of the window as Maggie drove the SUV up towards The Peak, an eighteen hundred-foot-high hill on Hong Kong island. Her intel had placed Tony Barbosa at the sight on no fewer than three occasions in the last sixteen hours, and they all knew what that meant – he was casing the popular tourist destination for somewhere to set the device.

Turning west and driving toward Mount Austin, a magnificent view of Central Hong Kong stretched out to their right. "That's really something," Zara said. "All those skyscrapers, all those people."

"Sure is," Mason said.

"There's the viewing platform where Jonny last saw Barbosa," Maggie said, pulling up and switching off the engine. "He was seen coming up here with the case and leaving without it, so this is where I love you and leave you."

"Thanks Maggie," Mason said. "You've been a massive help."

They watched her drive away and headed over to the platform. "We know the case is up here somewhere," Mason said. "So get searching."

They split up into groups and began to search the center, quietly working around the tourists so as not to startle or frighten them. Ella wandered over to some of the telescopes and peered over the balcony. "Nothing down there, either."

Their plan ended abruptly when a bullet struck her elbow, shattering the bone and making her cry out and fall to the floor. Caleb spun on his heel and sprinted over to her. "Hold still, Ells. I'm on my way!"

"No!" Mason said. "He's still up here!"

Zara's eyes filled with despair as she watched Barbosa emptying his weapon into Caleb's back. Nine mil rounds peppered the Arizonan's black leather jacket, punching holes into her friend's broad, muscly back. She thought the onslaught would bring him down, but he kept going against all odds, more determined than ever to drag Ella out of the line of fire.

"Cal!"

He ignored her and staggered closer to Ella.

Zara and Jed exchanged a glance of disbelief as they took in the almost impossible sight of Caleb Jackson pounding across the smooth flagstones with half a dozen holes drilled into his back.

"Cal!" Her voice was quieter now, almost a whisper. She said it for herself more than her friend, who she knew could no longer hear her.

"Let him go, Zara," Jed said. "He's made the choice."

Zara knew what he had said was right, but squeezed her fingers around the grip of her handgun until her knuckles went white. Rage rose inside her like acid and she made a scan of the center's roof to find Barbosa. "Bastard son of a bitch has to be up there somewhere, Jed!"

Caleb was with Ella now, and heaving her up over his shoulders. As he moved, the hem of his leather jacket lifted up and they all saw the blood pouring out of his back, staining his white shirt a dark crimson red.

More shots rained down. This time they were aimed at him as he started to jog back over to them with Ella on his shoulders. They missed, pinging into the stone tiles and ricocheting off into the humid morning air hanging over The Peak. The few remaining tourists still on the tower screamed once again, ducking their heads as they sprinted inside the building to find a refuge from the bloody terror unfolding on the viewing platform.

"There!" Mason said. "I see the bastard. He's on the eastern end of the center's roof!"

Cal struggled on, bringing Ella to safety. Six shots in six seconds, all direct hits. There would be no way to staunch such a massive blood-flow, and they all knew it. Caleb knew it, too, and now Ella was safely out of the line of fire, he dropped to his knees and fell to the side of her, crashing into the glass safety panel that ran around the viewing platform.

He smiled and tried to laugh, but blood bubbled out of his lips and he started coughing. As he slumped further down to the ground, his hand slipped and he went all the way to the flagstones until he was lying on his side, just as if he was about to go to sleep. Behind him, Zara saw the Hong Kong skyline through the glass screen, now smeared with the blood of her dying friend. She felt like crying, but held it in.

"You're going to be okay, Cal."

He coughed. "You can't kid a kidder, kid."

"I'm sorry…" she said.

Coughing, he said, "Hey, you're doing real well…"

She raised an eyebrow. "This ain't my first rodeo, chief, and…"

She felt his body go limp and knew he was gone. It had happened so fast, she barely knew how to react, except to indulge the rage rising in her heart. "Barbosa is a dead man, Jed. He's mine!"

"We have to get him first! Milo, you wait here, call an ambulance and make sure Ella gets to hospital. We can't do anything for Cal right now."

"And you?" Milo asked.

"Zara and I are going to hunt down Barbosa, destroy the device and make sure the bastard pays for what he did to Cal."

Mason and Zara left Ella and Milo with Caleb's body as they sprinted through the sniper fire toward the viewing platform roof. Chaos had erupted with the shot that nearly killed Ella and now they fought through the screaming tourists to reach the man who had murdered their friend.

"I see him!" Mason yelled.

"He's mine, Jed! Damn it!"

Mason knew why she was reacting like this. After her father's death, Caleb had always been there for her. This was like watching her dad die all over again. "Just take it easy, Zara – we don't know where the device is yet."

"You think he's got it on him?"

Mason shrugged. "Maybe, maybe not. He might have hidden it somewhere."

Zara was climbing onto the roof now, turning and looking back at Caleb's dead body. The blood had started to pool around the giant man and was already congealing into a thick black puddle. "And what then?"

Mason's response was sanguine. "Then, I'll ask him to tell me where they are, and he'll oblige me." He smacked a fresh mag into the grip of his gun and stuffed the weapon into his shoulder holster. "I guarantee it."

"And then he pays for Cal," Zara said. "There he is!"

Barbosa was trapped on the edge of the roof, partially obscured by a line of AC units and holding the IED case. "Get back, you bastards! Get back or I will detonate this right here, right now!"

Zara had years of shooting fleeing perps tucked away under belt, and knew what had to happen next. Mason had hesitated, but she felt no conflict inside her. She lifted her gun and shot Barbosa in the head before he could even think of making another threat. The report of her gun firing in the hot, humid Hong Kong air made even Mason jump, but then it was over, and Barbosa's limp body tumbled down onto the roof.

"Jesus, Z!"

"He killed Cal."

They approached his dead body and retrieved the case. "ECHO says we have to cut the cables joining the... wait a minute, Zara! He'd already activated it before we caught up with him – it's going to blow in less than a minute."

"Then work faster!"

Mason opened the case and tried to remember ECHO's instructions. It wasn't easy work – the humidity was crushing into him and sweat ran from his forehead into the device. He felt the intense tropical sun burning on his neck, and images of Cal's dead face swirled in his fevered mind.

Snapping a picture of the numbers on the timer display, he staggered to his feet. "I think I've done it."

"You think?"

"No time to know and the C4 timer is still running down! Ten seconds!"

"We have to get it away from the building!"

"No time to throw it anywhere! Run!"

They scrambled away from the case and dived over the edge of the roof. Behind them, a massive explosion ripped across the zinc flashing of the roof, blasting the air-conditioner units into the air as if they were made of balsa wood.

Mason and Zara slammed into the flagstone tiles around the base of the tourist center and rolled to a stop. "Would have been easier if we could have taken our time and shot it," he said.

"But we still did it."

Staggering over to the others, they took in the carnage. Smoke billowed from the tourist center's shattered windows, swirling in the hot air above the viewing platform and dissipating up into the sky. A loosened chunk of masonry tumbled off the top of the building and plummeted through the air, landing on a parked car and punching a fridge-sized dent in its steel roof. The alarm was instantly triggered, and its ear-piercing shriek added to the cocktail of fear and confusion all over The Peak.

Mason looked down at Barbosa's obliterated, charred remains, then back up at the terrified people around the tourist center. When he looked over at Caleb's body, his lip curled. "Get these numbers over to ECHO. If they're the coordinates for Zamkov's base, then we have one more account to settle."

CHAPTER FORTY-ONE

In the gentle hum of the SUV, Hawke and Lea shared a glance, but neither said a word. They both knew how close they had come to losing each other on this mission, and it was still far from over. Neither of them, nor anyone else on the team could believe this nightmare had unfolded in less than twenty-four hours. It had been a punishing test of their endurance but the final battle still awaited them.

Swerving into the parking lot, Reaper put the handbrake on and killed the engine. "Nous sommes ici, mes enfants."

"Thanks *dad*," Ryan said.

"To the HVAC room, everyone," Castillo said. "My contact says he followed the Dove there on the internal CCTV."

Baseball caps pulled down over their faces, they made their way inside the airport and headed straight over to the HVAC room at the top of the main departure lounge. The Heating, Ventilating, and Air-Conditioning system for an airport was a beast of a thing, massive in size and requiring its own special area to house the various boilers, chillers and cooling towers.

"Stay on the ball, everyone," Hawke said. "Zamkov's little Day of the Dead surprise is nearly over so they're going to be more desperate than ever to set it off."

As they climbed the steps to the top floor, Lea took a call. After speaking for a few seconds she slipped her phone away and gave a cautious smile. "That was Orlando – Bravo Troop took out Rodrigues in Paris and burned the virus, and the Raiders took out Barbosa in Hong Kong. They both sent us the coordinates from their devices, so it's just down to us now."

"Bastards beat us," Ryan said.

"They never had a kidnapping to deal with," Scarlet said.

"Forget about it. We've got our own fish to fry," Lea said. "And it's time to get the frying pan out."

*

The inside of the HVAC suite was a labyrinth of pipes, vents, ducts and big, fat insulated cables running all over the walls and ceiling. This part of the building was landside, which meant the team still had their weapons. They drew their guns and fanned out, beginning their search for the final supervirus device and the Dove.

"Over there is the most obvious place," Ryan said. "Connected to one of the cold coil rigs – from there the air comes right out through to the blowers and is dispersed throughout the entire airport. Look for the big square units – they're the compressors. From there follow the tubes and you'll get to the coils."

"How many compressors are there in this monster?" Camacho asked. "I count at least three."

"I think there are five," Ryan said. "If we split up and…"

The shot was deafening inside the HVAC suite's cold metal walls. The bullet ricocheted off an expansion valve above Ryan's head and blasted him with refrigerant gas. He screamed in shock and rolled away onto the floor.

Chaos erupted as Hawke ordered everyone into cover and returned fire, but the Dove was no more than a shadow. He slipped away into the cloud of high-pressure freon escaping from the cracked valve.

"He's over there!" Zeke called out. "Climbing up onto the mezzanine above the compressors."

Hawke gave chase, powered forward not by the thought of the deaths of billions of anonymous people, but by the simple image of Lea tied up in Loza's barn. The Dove had been a part of that plan, and now he was going to pay the toll.

He reached the mezzanine and heard several more shots. More Freon burst into the air from more valves. The Brazilian was trapped and the only way he could get away was if he became invisible.

Castillo strained to see in the gas. "This is chaos!"

"I can't see a thing!" Lea shouted.

"Me neither," said Ryan.

"Just as well, with your face, boy." Scarlet's voice, coming from somewhere below him.

Hawke almost grinned – could anything stop Cairo Sloane's juggernaut of bitchy humor? He doubted it, but his mind was focused on the hunt. The Dove was a hitman, but up here, now, surrounded by the ECHO team attack dogs, Hawke was the hunter and the Brazilian was the fox.

"No point in surrendering, dickhead," Hawke called out. "I'm going to kill you whatever you do, so you may as well fight to the end."

"I've got the device!" Ryan was on his knees on the lower level, peering down beneath the base of the industrial compressor as he studied the matte black case. "It's just as you described the others."

"I'm on my way," said Camacho. "I can disconnect it in seconds. Hang on."

"You hear that, arsehole?" Lea said. "It's over, and your little plan failed."

"I don't think so," the Dove called out. "The Butcher has another vial of the supervirus down in his base. He's going to release it into the jet stream. You all failed. Everything you did was for nothing!"

A gunshot, muffled by the escaping gas, and the sound of a round tracing past his head. Hawke dived behind a compressor and fired back, watching his own bullet split the freon like a knife through butter. He fired again, and the Dove lost his nerve.

Making a break for the stairs at the other end of the mezzanine, Hawke fired, planting three bullets in his back. The Brazilian froze in sheer terror and seemed to hover at the top of the steps.

"Joe!" Lea's voice. "Are you okay?"

"I'm all good, and the Dove's wings are clipped. Permanently."

"Thank god!"

He heard whoops of joy and watched the Brazilian tumble down the stairs. He was dead before he hit the bottom step.

"You get that damned device sorted out, Jack?"

"Yeah, it's done, but we have to burn the virus."

Hawke made his way back down the stairs, stepped over the Dove's dead, crumpled body and took the IED case from Camacho. "We need the last coordinates," he said. "This was the only way our dead friend over there would have been able to crawl back to Zamkov."

Lea took a picture of the numbers on the LED display on the device. "All done."

"They're definitely geographical coordinates," Ryan said. "And if I'm right, they're giving the location of somewhere *very* far south."

ROB JONES

"He's right," Hawke said. "Whatever it is, it's nearly eighty degrees south, and that means well into Antarctica."

"Antarctica?" Nikolai said.

Castillo holstered his gun. "My god…"

Now, a devilish smile danced on Lea's lips as she looked up at Hawke. "Are you thinking what I'm thinking?"

"Zamkov," she and Hawke said together.

"Just as we thought," said Scarlet.

Ryan scratched his stubbly chin and nodded at the conclusion. "He planned to give the Dove and the other two warriors the location of his base, but only if they succeeded in activating the timer."

"How very thoughtful of him," Lexi said. "But we already guessed this might be what these numbers were."

Hawke shrugged. "He might be a sociopathic loon, but he kept his word to his warriors. Most of the guys we go up against wouldn't have done that."

"Too bad for him we're the ones showing up in Antarctica, and not his goons," Scarlet said. "Let's put the coordinates into Google Earth and see where this place is."

They all watched with bated breath as the world spun around and zoomed in on a specific location. "Nothing but sodding whiteout," Ryan said.

"But it's *our* sodding whiteout," Hawke said with a grin. "Lea, get Orlando to liaise with Mason and Hud – we're going to Antarctica and we're going mob-handed."

"Cool," Ryan said.

"Yes, it will be," Hawke said. "Very, even at this time of year during the southern hemisphere summer. We need to buy some snow gear on the way, but first, we have to burn this bastard."

286

Placing the case on the floor, he kicked it across to the far end of the suite and aimed his gun at it. "This is going to make a big bang and cause thousands of dollars of damage, but at least there's a sprinkler system, right?"

"Always thinking of others," Lea said. "I love you."

He fired and they sprinted out of the HVAC suite just as the fireball ripped up into the air and mushroomed up in the ceiling.

"Holy crap!" Ryan said, "That really was a big bang."

As the sprinklers came on, Hawke peered over the edge of a balcony outside the HVAC room, seeing security guards running up toward them. "Time we were on our way. They'll be up here in five minutes, minimum."

"So where are we going to get our snow gear?" Lexi asked casually.

"Not here, that's for damn sure. Chile is the best place – it's on the way and there's tons of great ski shops because of the Andes."

"It's on the way?" Ryan said with a sly grin at the coordinates.

"Well, more or less."

"Yeah, give or take," Lea said with a grin. "I hope Orlando's got his wallet ready."

"C'mon everyone." Hawke made his way down the metal steps and climbed down inside a manhole cage at the top of a fire escape ladder. "Let's get out to the jet and get going."

Ryan froze on the spot. "But what about *Tartarus*? And Alex?"

Hawke stopped in the cage and looked up. "We said we'd head up there the second this mission is over, mate. We just found out Zamkov still has a vial of the supervirus and is planning to release it into the southern subtropical jet stream. I don't need to tell you which countries that blows over."

"Peru, Ecuador, Brazil, at least half a dozen African countries, southern India, Sri Lanka, Thailand…"

"Right, so billions of people."

"Why didn't he just do that in the first place, the silly bastard?" Scarlet said.

"Nowhere near as reliable as ground dispersal," Ryan said, tapping his head. "Think about it, Velma."

"If I'm Velma, you're Scrappy."

The banter flowed all the way out of the HVAC system and into the departure lounge, where they passed more security guards running the other way. Hawke turned to Lea, "Please tell me Orlando got us a slot? The airport authorities are already shutting down all flights in and out because of the explosion in the HVAC."

She nodded. "Less than five minutes from now. He's using some influence with the government to let our plane go out, but we have to hurry."

They dumped their guns in a fast food restaurant bin, passed through the small, private customs barrier in the business class lounge and stepped out onto the asphalt apron at the south end of the airport. As the bright Mexican sunshine flooded down onto them, they allowed themselves a moment of celebration, despite the battle to come.

"Bravo Troop did their usual bang-up job," Lea said. "You must be proud, Cairo."

"What can I say? They have a bloody amazing leader."

"I admire Clive Hudson, too," Hawke said with a wink.

"I'm the leader!"

"Really? I thought Hud was the big boss?"

Reaper stepped in. "Don't forget about the Raiders, mes amis… those guys worked hard in Hong Kong to take out Barbosa."

"We'd better watch our backs," Lexi said. "Or these guys are going to make us look like a bunch of…"

Ryan laughed. "Get real, no one's coming close to ECHO."

"Yeah," she said. "For once, our Nerd-in-Chief is right."

"But we couldn't have done it without them," Hawke said. Approaching the private jet, its shiny chrome airstair flashed in the setting sun. "Especially not without Titanfort. Those guys are the intel kings, for sure."

"Not when we get Elysium back up and running," Lea said. Squeezing his hand. "Then we'll give them a run for their money."

Then their world changed forever. In half a second, the joy of their success was shattered, the thrill of the battle to come was split and the heart of the team was torn out.

Scarlet was at the top of the airstair when it happened. She turned and screamed. Time slowed down to a crawl as she reached out, helpless to stop the horror that had already happened. "No!"

*

The bullet hit Jack Camacho in the upper chest. It ripped through his heart, passed through his entire body before continuing on its lethal trajectory, leaving a gaping, bloody hole the size of a melon in his back. His white shirt bloomed red with dark arterial blood as he fell backwards, and they all knew he was dead before he hit the ground.

Scarlet was still screaming in horror as she ran to him, ignoring Hawke's orders for everyone to hit the deck.

Maybe the sniper had two targets tonight, but maybe he didn't. Either way, the former SAS officer couldn't have given a damn as she skidded to a halt beside the man she loved. She knelt on the asphalt, bringing her face close to his.

She gently raised his head from the hard surface and cradled it in her arms, but he was already gone. In her heart, she had known this when she saw the wound from up on the airstair, but she had to hope. She had to have something to cling onto for just a few more seconds. She needed to believe he was alive for as long as possible, to avoid the brutal revelation that her lover had been murdered right in front of her eyes and there was nothing she, nor anyone else, could do about it.

Keeping her head low, her soft whisper was drowned out by the sound of the jets behind her, spooling up ready for the flight. "I know you're gone, Jackie... but now I have to go too."

CHAPTER FORTY-TWO

Agent Cougar watched the chaos unfold as the ECHO team scrambled in response to the latest job in her contract. She knew all their names. Pegasus had briefed her well. The Sloane woman was hugging Camacho now. Brave or foolish? She had sprinted across the apron to her lover, surely knowing he was already dead. Now she was exposed and would make an easy target – all she had to do was line the back of her head up in the sights and fire off another round.

Two down in one job.

But that wasn't her style, and for a very good reason. A second shot would instantly identify her location, at least it would to people as experienced as the ECHO team. No, one shot was enough. One shot meant she was a mystery and would stay that way.

Sweeping the powerful gun's sights across the lot, she watched the leader, a well-built, tall commando with some hefty experience in naval special ops. He had hit the ground within a second of the bullet striking the American CIA agent. He was ordering the others to do the same – not that they needed to be told. All of them had instantly assessed the rough direction of the bullet and had taken appropriate cover to avoid another fatality.

Hawke, that was his name. She watched him now through the sights of her rifle, but he couldn't see her. He was scanning the area for any sign of her; he was in the rough ballpark, but there was no chance. She was crouched down below a concrete wall running around the top of an apartment block in the Moctezuma District, two kilometers north of the airport, tucked away in between two industrial AC units.

Not a chance, baby.

It was a solid location with a clear line of sight across the top of a jumble of other residential buildings and a car rental place, straight over to the private apron at the south of the airport. Adjusting for the wind, she had fired the shot right across the airfield, and the two main runways, in order to take out her fourth target. It was, she silently told herself, one of her more audacious jobs.

Something to tell the grandkids.

Yeah, right.

With a weary heart, she began to disassemble the CheyTac M200 Intervention rifle and pack it away into her bag. And intervened it certainly had today, in the life of John "Jack" Camacho, a former CIA agent turned rogue terrorist, working for the outlawed and highly dangerous ECHO team. Somewhere, a family had a funeral to arrange, and they didn't even know it yet. She sighed as she disconnected the scope and used it as a monocular to check on the team once again.

Led by Hawke, they were making their way inside the private jet Sooke had hired for them. Touchingly, Hawke and the French legionnaire had picked up Camacho's body and were taking him on board.

Danny Devlin, Magnus Lund, Kim Taylor, and now Jack Camacho. That meant four of the central team were down, leaving ten more to go before she moved on to their immediate families. She idly speculated if she would get an order to leave the extended family once the main team was dead. She hoped so. These people were terrorists, and a direct threat to the vital national interest of Uncle Sam, but could she say the same about innocent civilians living quiet lives all over the world?

But that was the contract, and if it was the only way to get the million dollars, then so be it. A million dollars US was nearly twenty million Mexican pesos, and that would go a long way to setting up a bright new life south of the Rio Grande. If that meant taking out Camacho's sister or Vincent Reno's wife and...

Was she about to say his twin boys then?

Really, Jessica? You would kill two young boys just to give your own son a better life?

Hawke and Donovan were one thing, but innocent children?

Her mind became a maelstrom of confusion as she tried to rationalise what she was doing, but there was no way to clear away the thoughts that tortured her, that kept her up night after night. She slipped the scope in her bag, zipped it up and heaved it over her right shoulder. Crossing the roof of the apartment block, she stepped inside the utility door and made her way down the dark concrete stairs until she was on the ground level.

Emerging into the Mexican evening, she walked a block to where her vehicle was parked, opened the doors, placed her bag inside and climbed up after it into the driver's seat. Another job done. Another box ticked. She closed the door, turned the engine on, and felt her shoulders began to relax for the first time since she landed.

Driving away into the Mexican City streets, she made her way back around to the airport where Pegasus had arranged a government jet for her. She was to board it and wait for intel from his office about the destination of the ECHO team's next flight. There, she would track them until the time was right to terminate the fifth target.

It was a living, right?

CHAPTER FORTY-THREE

The flight to Antarctica was bleak. No one spoke a single word from Mexico City to Santiago, where they stopped to refuel and buy their snow gear. From the Chilean capital down to Novolazarevskaya Station on the Antarctica continent, things had progressed to the occasional comment about food or the weather.

At Novo Base, Ryan did the talking. Orlando Sooke, and a former KGB friend in Moscow, had set up a cover story in which the reunited ECHO team played the part of a team of international glaciologists. The story involved them refuelling at the base before heading deeper into the continent to their new base, a joint American-Norwegian enterprise. They were also meeting colleagues from two other scientific teams there.

Bravo Troop and the Raiders.

It was enough to get them what they wanted; the young hacker from London had grifted like a pro, deploying the hours of research he had done on the flight to impress the head of the base.

"I thought there were nine of you in this contingent?" the base commander said, peering at the group.

"Sorry?" Lea said.

"The manifest from Moscow says to expect nine scientists. You are only eight."

Camacho.

"One of us was taken ill," Lea said. "He stayed in Chile."

The man nodded. "I see. But I didn't know there was a new base."

"It's classified," Lea said, causing the Russian to raise an eyebrow. "Highly."

A sullen half hour passed as the plane was fuelled and de-iced, and then the Russians announced the arrival of another aircraft. It touched down and turned off the runway, slowly making its way over to the base. Snow began to fall as the door opened and Clive Hudson emerged at the top of the airstairs.

Reaper looked through the steamed-up window of the base canteen. "Bravo Troop."

"And the Raiders," Lea said. "That's Jed Mason just behind him. They must have coordinated to fly down together."

The teams made their way down the steps, breath pluming in the freezing air. After a brief conversation with the Russian base commander, they stepped inside the canteen. Shutting the door on the snowy wind, a quick round of introductions followed.

"So, you're Joe Hawke," Mason said. "I've heard a lot about you."

"Not all good, I hope."

The two men shook hands and Hawke said, "Sorry to hear about Jackson."

Mason's smile faded. "He was a good man, but he knew what he signed up for."

"Besides," Zara said quietly, "We iced the bastard that killed him."

Behind them, near the door, Scarlet and Hudson shared a hug and a short private conversation. Breaking up, Hudson said, "We're all with you, Cairo."

"I'm sorry to hear about Danny," she said. "Is he okay?"

Hudson nodded. "He's in a critical condition in Paris."

She looked at the bandage around his leg. "And what about you?"

"I'm fine, but are *you* okay?"

Lexi changed the subject, turning to Ryan and Milo. "Wait, if you two actually meet in person, don't you cancel each other out?"

"And this is Lexi Zhang," Ryan said, putting an arm around her shoulder, giving her a brotherly squeeze. "Don't worry, she's only an arsehole about half the time."

"From my experience, having known you less than one minute," Milo said to Lexi, "You're an arsehole one hundred percent of the time."

Lexi said, "Damn, now I've got it in stereo."

Lea turned to Mason. "Where did you join up with Bravo?"

"We met in Cape Town," he said. "Ezra Haven has a contact there who runs a safe house for the CIA. I'm pleased to say, he was very generous in terms of supplying weapons. We have machine pistols, sidearms, grenades, ropes, RPGs, not to mention a dozen high explosive charges. We're ready to go on holiday."

"Sounds like my kind of vacation," Zara said.

"Mine too," said Lea.

Hawke quietened down the hubbub in the small canteen. "Listen up, everyone. We all know why we're here. Zamkov has a base in the interior and not only is he going to attempt to spray the last vial of supervirus into the jet stream, we can presume he's also continuing with his AI program. That's enough motivation for me, but those who want more, know this: two of our good friends have died on this mission."

The atmosphere darkened again.

"Jack Camacho and Caleb Jackson are both gone, murdered by men working for the Butcher, and a third,

Danny Plane, is fighting for his life in Paris. We owe them all a heavy price, and that price will be paid today when we fight in the battle of our lives."

*

They took off once again, headed toward the final coordinates. As they climbed high above Novo Base and turned south, heading deeper into Antarctica, they were struck by the continent's rugged beauty. Leaving its cold, rocky shores and ice shelves behind, they raced south into the unknown.

An hour later, Hawke was first to break the tense silence. "All right, we're here. Everyone get ready."

For twenty minutes the team busied themselves, strapping on parachutes and oxygen-breathing equipment. There was no way Zamkov would approve their jet for landing on his private runway and they also knew he had surface-to-air missiles, so the only way in was a HALO drop.

"High Altitude, Low Opening," Zara said. "That's my kind of entrance."

"Remember to stay focussed," Hawke said. "We're here to destroy the supervirus, take out Zamkov and rescue Kamala. Then ECHO go to Tartarus."

"Please can we retire after that?" Scarlet asked.

Everyone laughed. It was pretty much the first thing she had said since Camacho's death, and everyone wanted to bring her back into the group.

"If that's what you want, then why not?" Lea said, touching her arm. "Kolya, you're ready to do this?"

The Russian nodded. "Reaper has talked me through it very closely. I understand."

"Good, and don't worry about it." Hawke said. "As Rich always says, don't panic if your emergency pullcord doesn't work because you've got the rest of your life to fix it."

Lea groaned. "God, take me back to Buena Vista... the times I've heard that one."

Hawke chortled and fixed his mask into place. "Everyone's oxygen on?"

A row of thumbs-up.

He returned the gesture and signalled to the pilot who closed the cockpit door and depressurized the main cabin. He walked over to the main door and pulled it open. The plane was fully depressurized, so they were spared the theatre of everything being sucked out, but the wind was fierce and roared like a demon.

"Go!"

Reaper was first out, casually stepping out of the racing aircraft and instantly tumbling down toward the raging storm clouds below. Lexi was next, followed by Zeke and Nikolai in the middle. Mason led the Raiders next, and then Hudson, Mack and Kyra followed soon after. Ryan and Lea were the next two out of the door. As they leapt into the freezing sky and dropped away toward the swirling maelstrom below, Reaper was just disappearing into the top of a thunderhead.

"Looks like it's just you and me, darling."

Hawke put his hands on Scarlet's shoulders. "You're like a sister to me, Cairo."

"Jesus, Joe, we slept together."

Through the goggles, she saw his eyes roll. "You know what I mean. I care about you."

"If I didn't have this mask on, I'd push my fingers down my throat and vomit."

"No, you wouldn't. You know we're all here for you?"

298

She nodded.

"Good, now fuck off out of this plane and get some revenge."

A coldness seemed to freeze her eyes, then she gave a thumbs up and jumped from the aircraft. Hawke followed less than two seconds behind her.

CHAPTER FORTY-FOUR

Valentina was surprised when Zamkov walked into her room with Kamala Banks, her shock focussed on the American woman. There was something different about her, something wrong. There was something missing from her eyes.

"Sweetheart, may we come in?" he asked.

The raging wind tore and scratched at the thick safety glass window-wall, howling like a dying animal.

"Of course, my sweetheart, but..."

"Ah, allow me to introduce you to our latest guest. This is K14FZ, or as she will now be known, Kamala."

Valentina took a step back and stared at the AI unit beside Zamkov. She was beautiful. Inwardly, she feared, perhaps more beautiful than she was, but she was only an AI. Thank heaven for small mercies, she thought. I have no reason to be jealous. Niki could never love a robot.

"I don't know what to say. She's spectacular, but where is the..."

"The *real* Kamala Banks?" he said, finishing her sentence for her. "She is in her cell, awaiting execution. She is a traitor, my sweetheart, not one of us. But she will not be lost to the world after death, because I uploaded her entire consciousness into the neural network and downloaded a copy of it into this AI unit. I think you will agree, in terms of capturing the essence of the physical characteristics, this time I have surpassed myself."

"Yes, you have." She felt the dizziness again. All the fears she harbored about not being human began to surface again.

"Kamala, sit down, and tell us about your past."

The AI unit obeyed. "I was born in Washington DC. I used to work for the US Secret Service, but now I work for Zamkov Industries."

Zamkov laughed out loud. "Isn't she amazing?"

Valentina said nothing, but noted the smile fade from his face. "Is there something on your mind?" she asked at last.

"Kamala, please leave us."

K14FZ rose from the seat and walked out of the room. When the door was closed, he turned to Valentina and lowered his voice. "Yes, sweetheart. There is something on my mind. Something heavy, something that has been weighing me down for a long time."

She felt her heart quicken.

Heart? Is that what it really was? Or was it nothing more than electronic signals powered by a lithium-ion powerpack?

"You must tell me, Niki."

"It is difficult for me to find the words, but…"

"Am I one of them?" she asked, nodding at the door K14FZ had just used.

Zamkov dipped his head and wrung his hands. Looking back up at her with tears in his eyes, he spoke in a whisper. "Yes, my sweetheart. Yes, you are an AI."

Valentina refocused her LED eyes on the man she loved, struggling to process what he had just told her. The words he had uttered seemed wrong, somehow. What did he mean, when he had called her a form of artificial intelligence? He had called her a robot, but she knew she was not a robot. She was a person, just like him, with a beating heart and lungs that breathed the same cold, fresh Antarctica air that he did. She was human.

Wasn't she?

If you prick us, do we not bleed?

She felt dizzy, lost. "What are you talking about, sweetheart?" She laughed. She didn't know why, but it just happened. He was teasing her.

"You are not a person, my sweetheart." He held his hands up to her face. "I created you with these hands."

"I am one of your creations?"

"Yes… no! You are more than that. You are my most advanced and precious creation. You are not simply a robot."

None of this was going in. The words were becoming muddied and blurred together. She felt blood pumping in her ears. The dizziness grew worse and she felt nauseous. "It's not true! Why are you doing this to me? Have I done something to offend you? Have I done wrong? Have I hurt your feelings? Is that it?"

"Please… I was hoping your programming could accept this information, but perhaps I will need to make some alterations. Maybe all this was a tremendous mistake. Perhaps I will simply deactivate you and delete the last hour from your memory banks."

She felt herself choke up as tears seeped out of her eyes. Not real tears, she knew now, but some sort of synthetic saline solution. A hideous facsimile of reality. Just like her. A disgusting, loathsome mess of circuit boards, capacitors, soldering, wires, pumps, chips and microprocessors.

She got to her feet, the rage building inside her. "Wait. You're telling me that the real Valentina Kiriyenko is dead?"

He nodded sullenly. "Yes, I'm so sorry."

"So all my memories are nothing but code?"

"No, it's not like that. You are every bit as real as the original."

"The original? You're insane. I was a person!"

He took a step back from the robot. "I know this is hard to understand, but there is no difference. Consciousness is consciousness. It does not matter which vessel it is contained in."

"Only in your insane mind."

"Don't talk like that…"

"How did I die?"

"I…"

"You seem to have forgotten to give me that particular memory."

"That is what I wanted to ask you today."

"What?"

"I don't know how it happened, my dear Valya, but when we were together all those years ago, I entered into a fugue state and when I awoke, you were dead."

She gasped. "You? You murdered me?"

"I don't know what happened."

She began to sob. "And I thought you were going to ask me to marry you."

"We still can! I love you!"

"You're insane."

"I said don't talk like that." He lowered his voice to a mutter. "I need to shut you down. Everything will be all right then. When you wake, you will have no recollection of this conversation. I can start again."

Valentina moved toward him and raised her hand. Was it anger if it was nothing but computer code? Could she hate in the way a person hated? Perhaps, there was a stronger rage than even humans felt. Closer she walked, closer towards the Maker.

"What are you doing?" he asked.

The next thing either of them knew, her robotic hand was around his throat. His face was turning purple as the tiny motors in her hand constricted her fingers tighter and tighter. He choked some words out, but it was too late.

"Stop struggling, Niki. It will all be over in a few seconds."

"You can't kill me..."

"Who said anything about killing you? You will live forever, but now you will be just like me – a robot. I am sure you can have no objection to this."

His swollen purple tongue flicked in and out of flapping, blue lips. "Please..."

"Except I will make some much-needed alterations to your personality."

"No..."

Valentina felt a thrilling rush of pure, electric pleasure as she crushed the human's windpipe and squeezed the last bit of life from him. When she was certain he was dead, she released him, and he dropped to the floor in a heap. Then she walked over to the door and opened it.

"Kamala, I need you to help me."

Kamala entered the room and gasped when she saw Zamkov's corpse. "Oh my God."

"We're taking him to the central neural hub. I need to transfer his consciousness to the network before he becomes fully brain dead."

Kamala obeyed, picking up the corpse and putting him in a fireman's lift.

Following her through the door, Valentina turned and took one look at the impressive penthouse apartment. All mine now, she thought. Just like all of Eschaton Base and its weapons and technology. All mine, and now it will be used to inflict as much suffering on humans as possible, starting with Zamkov's plan to spray the supervirus into the jet stream.

CHAPTER FORTY-FIVE

Scarlet Sloane flew through the freezing cold Antarctic air at terminal velocity. It felt good that her body was now moving at the same speed as her mind, she thought, because her emotions had been at terminal velocity since watching Camacho's death back in Mexico City.

Ahead of her, she saw the swirling black thunderheads high above Eschaton Base swallow up the team members who had jumped before her, starting with Vincent Reno. Those clouds moved like a giant jaw, she considered. A giant jaw powered by the hungry electric storm scouring the concrete and glass HQ below.

She checked her wrist monitor. Minus fifty-three degrees Celsius and travelling at over fifty meters per second. Below her, Queen Maud Land was visible only in snatches as the clouds whipped and bubbled around her. If she closed her eyes and forgot about the pullcord, she would be dead before she knew it and the pain would be gone.

Except that she wasn't the sort of person to think like that. She had loved Jack Camacho for a long time and now he was gone. And this wasn't the first time she has lost a lover, either. Right now, it hurt like hell, but she would fight through it. It's what she did. She was a Sloane. She was ex-SAS. She was ECHO, and people needed her.

Buffeted by the screaming wind and with rain lashing at her face, she made a vow: By the time I hit the ground, I will have moved on. No more words, no more bullshit. Just pack it away in the same place she put her parents' murder and get on with her life. Live hard and laugh long. Crack a cold one and move on.

"You there, Cairo?"

Hawke's voice. He was a few hundred feet above her and off to her right.

"Well, I'm not drinking Sangria in fucking Spain, am I?"

Laughter over the comms.

"Glad to hear it." His voice was weak and breaking up, but they all heard what he said in response. "I can't offer Spain, but I have got a great deal on a little place I know in Antarctica."

More laughter.

"Minus fifty Celsius in summer and it's full of psychopathic killer robots."

"Sounds amazing," Ryan said. "Book me in."

*

Valentina Kiriyenko felt at home behind Zamkov's central control consul. Behind her, Kamala was still holding the Maker's corpse in the fireman's lift, waiting for her next instructions from the new boss. In front of them, down on the main floor, a combination of AI units and humans in boiler suits were busy preparing Zamkov's private Sukhoi jet.

She leaned into a black gooseneck microphone and started to speak, surprised by how loudly her voice was amplified by the public address system. "Unit 423D – report."

The AI unit she had spoken to turned and approached the control consul. "The jet is loaded with the supervirus and ready to take off, but we are still waiting for the storm to pass."

306

"How long?"

"At least another three hours."

She nodded. "Leave the jet in the hangar, but make sure it's fuelled, de-iced and ready to go the instant the storm blows out."

"Yes, Miss Kiriyenko."

She watched the unit scuttle back to its workstation and marvelled over how easy it was to take power from the Butcher. Not one person here, AI or human, had dared to ask her why she was in command. With wild dreams of expanding Zamkov's empire racing through her mind, she was startled when another human beetle in a boiler suit ran over to her.

"We've identified an unknown aircraft flying close to the base."

"Altitude?"

"Forty-two thousand feet."

"Direction?"

"Heading away to the west."

"How close did it get to us?"

"Within two kilometers."

Her razor-sharp AI processor considered thousands of thoughts in a split second. "It could be an airborne team. Prepare a force of fifty men and killer AI units. I want a ring of steel around this base."

"I'm on it."

Valentina had a bad feeling about the mysterious plane. Zamkov had clearly left a trail of breadcrumbs leading back to Eschaton, and now she would have to clear that up. But first, she had other business to attend to. Pulling Zamkov's black scanning helmet off the desk, she scanned his brain into the neural network. Less than three minutes later, she had the entire brain substrates required for a full consciousness transfer. "Kamala, bring me an AI unit. I need to download Mr Zamkov into it."

"Please specify – a warrior unit, science unit…"

"A base unit," she said. "That's all we need. That's all he is worth. He can spend eternity in one of his base units. I am sure that way he will be a loyal and devoted servant to the cause."

"Miss Kiriyenko!"

She turned to see the same man who had spoken to her before about the aircraft. "What is it?"

"Enemy insurgents are reported on the eastern perimeter."

"Damn it," she said. "They must be from the aircraft. How many?"

"We're not sure. At least twelve."

"Destroy them all. They cannot be allowed to get inside Eschaton."

*

When Hawke deployed his parachute, the rest of the teams were already on the snowfield to the east of the base. Buffeted by the wind, he watched the tiny black figures as they cut their cables and readied their weapons. Using the steering lines, he carefully twisted around in the wind, running to a stop beside them.

"Starting without me?" He released himself from the harness and pulled an MP5 compact machine pistol from his Bergen. "Sometimes I think you don't love me at all."

"Looks like a hell of a place to get into," Ryan said, looking up at the compound.

"Bollocks," Milo said. "We could get in there no problem at all. That's kinda what we do."

Mack scanned the ice cliffs surrounding the compound. "Bravo Troop could get in there like a rat up a drainpipe."

"No dick-measuring contests please, boys," Lexi said. "I'm sure we're all capable of breaking into Zamkov's little hidey-hole. The real question is, which one of us gets to take him out?"

The thought concentrated the minds of everyone until a deep, bass thump shook the ground, accompanied by a dull flash several hundred feet away on the base's eastern wall. Reaper reacted fastest. "Incoming! Everyone down!"

An explosive shell landed just off to their right, blowing a massive cloud of snow and ice into the air.

Hawke rolled to a stop beside Lea and put his hands around her. "You think they noticed us?" Hawke said.

Lea shook her head. "And I picked you to be the father of my children."

"All I'm saying is that… wait, what?"

"What?"

"Is there something you want to tell me?"

She shook her head. "Eejit…"

"What the hell was that?" Nikolai asked.

Milo scrambled out of a snowy ditch and straightened the hood of his Parka. "Some kind of sodding missile!"

"A high-arcing ballistic trajectory like that?" Hawke said. "No way. Got to be some sort of mortar."

Zeke nodded. "Not big enough to scare the pants off us though," he said. "Gotta be fire support."

"Fire support?" the Russian said.

"Have you learnt nothing, my able young protégé?' Scarlet said. "Offensive fire that supports a larger force, meaning we're about to get smacked hard."

"Only if we stay here and bend over," Hawke said. "If we can get over to the cliffs on the south-eastern edge of the compound, we can make our way inside from there by the looks of it."

Another mortar thudded in the distance and sent a second shell whistling through the air to their position. "All right, let's move it. Nothing like a bit of yomping to get the appetite up."

With the shell detonating in the snow behind them, they marched towards the wall as fast as they could move in their snowshoes. Hawke felt the weight of the snow on his boots as he ploughed through, forcing one foot forward and then the other. Ahead, he saw a split in the ice wall at the base of the compound. "We're almost at the ice cliffs. Keep going."

"Incoming!"

He turned to see Lea just behind him. She looked tiny in the snow, and her face was obscured by the thick cloud of her breath pluming out of her mouth as she pointed into the sky. "Looks like more drones!"

"Oh *crap!*" Cairo said. "Anything but those damned things."

Mason moved over to her. "You have experience of them?"

"Sure do – in the Amazon jungle around Zamkov's Vyraj compound. We were lucky to get away with our lives. They're fast and they're lethal."

"And they're two minutes out," Hudson said.

Hawke turned and peered through the blizzard at the ice cave. "Head to the break in the ice! It's the only chance we have."

And then Zamkov's AI quadcopter drones located them, turned and swooped.

CHAPTER FORTY-SIX

Hawke was last into the ice cave, waiting to drag Ella Makepeace up the slope before diving in with seconds to spare. As he made the last few feet, the drones dipped down and fired on him, raking the icepack at his feet with high-velocity rounds. With clouds of snow blowing up all around him, he dived into the cave and landed with a crash on the ice.

"Talk about an icy welcome."

Lea helped him up. "Are there any circumstances where'd you run out of puns?"

"Unlikely, unless we're in a situation where there's snow way out."

She wanted to laugh, but another fusillade of fire made her jump. Reaper pushed past them and peered up through the ice crack. "They're not following us in here."

"That's something, at least," Milo said.

Dusting himself down, Hawke peered around their new home. "We're on the East Antarctic Ice Sheet, right? More specifically, we're on the Fisher Glacier and that means crevasses. Looking at this place more closely, I'd say we're not just in an ice cave, but in the bottom of a crevasse."

Zara, Ella, Milo and Kyra stared at him. Seeing their faces, Lea explained. "He was in the Mountain and Arctic Warfare Cadre."

"Ah," Zara said. "I guess in a place like this, it's better experience than taking out crack dealers in Inglewood."

"I'd say so, sister," Kyra said.

ROB JONES

The ex-LAPD cop turned to her and frowned. "And who the hell are you again?"

Mack gave her a look. "She's our IT expert."

Zara nodded pensively. "I bet you can do a lot of damage hitting someone over the head with a keyboard, or do you spin it like a frisbee?"

"You want to get home and find out you don't exist, and that all your bank accounts have been drained? No? Then watch your mouth."

"Hey," Lea said. "Just calm down, everyone. We can't turn on each other just because we're trapped in here."

"We're *trapped* inside a crevasse?" Kyra said. "I saw a TV show where a dude was trapped in one of these things. He couldn't climb out and nearly died."

"Kyra's right," Milo said. "We could freeze to death in here and no one even knows we're here."

"We're not trapped," Ryan said. "And Zamkov knows we're here, which is even worse than no one knowing, right?"

"Indeed," Mack said.

"Besides," Lea said. "Joe's found a way out, right?"

"Yeah, I think so. If we're at the bottom of a crevasse, then that means there's a way out – above us. We just need to climb up to the top and then we should be not only out of here, but also on the top of the glacier in the valley right next door to…"

"To Hell?" Ella said.

"I was going to say next to Eschaton Base, but Hell also covers it. C'mon everyone, let's get out of here."

Hawke led the way up the inside of the crevasse, using the ice picks and crampons they had bought in Santiago. "We have to get a move on," he called down. "The sun's breaking through the storm and melting the ridge at the top of the crevasse." The meltwater poured down the

312

walls and over his jacket where it was instantly refreezing. "It's not going to make this any easier, and it means more trouble ahead."

"Like what?" Ella's voice called up.

"Look out!" he yelled. "Ice block on the way!"

The sun's warmth had melted a block of ice the size of a small car, which was now tumbling down the inside of the crevasse. It zoomed past Hawke, scraping the back of his jacket as he crushed himself into the ice wall to avoid being hit. His face started to freeze to the meltwater. He quickly pulled himself away just as the ice block smashed into the crevasse floor and exploded into a thousand pieces.

"Bloody hell!" Ryan called up. "That fucker nearly hit me, Joe."

"It's why we need to hurry," he called back. "Keep going."

"A few hours ago, I was in a Mexico city nightclub," Zeke said with mock sadness. "How did this happen to me?"

"You signed up to ECHO," Lea said. "So, yeah. Sorry."

Dodging ice blocks and freezing meltwater, they made their way to the top. Still in the lead, Hawke suddenly stopped. "This is odd."

"What is it?" Lea called up.

"A large tunnel, manmade, covered with a grate. Looks like concrete. It's built into the ice, but at least it explains why there's so much meltwater running down the walls."

He pulled on the grate but it didn't budge. "It's set into the concrete."

Ryan climbed up beside him. "It's some sort of drainage conduit," he said. "Got to be. Must be to channel meltwater out of the compound down here to the glacier."

"That's a bit of luck," Lea said. "And about time, too."

"All right, listen up," Hawke said. "When we get in there we split up. ECHO will rescue Kamala, destroy the supervirus and take out Zamkov, and Bravo Troop and Raiders will set the remote-controlled charges all over the base. When we have Kamala safely out and the virus is gone, I'll give the order to blow the charges and take down Eschaton. All clear?"

"As crystal," Hudson said.

"Fine with us," said Mason. "The sooner we're out of here, the better."

"Okay, stay where you are, everyone," Hawke called out, his voice echoing in the crevasse. "I'm going to blow the grate, then we can use the tunnel. It has to lead somewhere, and the smart money's on the compound."

Hawke reached into his pack and fitted a small quantity of C4 around the edge of the grate before making his way off to the side. Ryan moved to the other side, both men turning away, heads inside their Parka hoods. When he blew the C4, the explosion was fierce, ripping the grate out of the concrete tunnel and embedding it in the ice on the opposite wall.

When the shower of ice and snow settled down, Hawke looked back at his work. "Seems to have done the trick. Let's get in there."

*

In the chaos, Valentina turned to Kamala. "Go to Niki's office and get the supervirus case. It's in the safe. I'm sending you the combination over the network."

Kamala received the instructions over Zamkov's neural wifi network and made her way up into the dead Butcher's office. Below, on the mezzanine, Valentina watched with pride as the AI unit she had uploaded with Zamkov's brain substrates flickered to life.

"Are you all right, Niki?" she asked it.

"I think so... I'm so confused. What happened to me?"

"There is no time to worry now. The base is under attack and we must hurry to the auxiliary hangar or they will kill us."

"I'm... I feel like I was asleep."

"Hush now, and follow me. Kamala will bring the supervirus and we will continue with the mission."

CHAPTER FORTY-SEVEN

Hawke and the rest of the team crawled along the concrete tunnel for several minutes, lighting their way with flashlights as they slowly inclined up a slope. This made it harder to move forward, especially with their boots slipping on the frozen meltwater collecting in the base of the tunnel.

After another minute of struggling, Hawke angled his flashlight beam above his head and saw another tunnel running perpendicular to the one they were in. Poking his head up into the cross-section, he saw another grate.

"Looks like we made it."

"You got something?" Ryan called out.

"Yeah, another grate. It's fixed again. Needs some persuasion."

"C4?"

"It's already in place. Everyone get back down the tunnel, unless you want your eyebrows removed."

They crawled back down the tunnel and when safely out of range, Hawke thumbed the detonator. They all felt the bang and saw the flash, then a low rumble rippled down the tunnel.

"If Zamkov didn't know we were here, he does now," Kyra said from the back.

"We had no choice," Hawke said. "Now we go in, fast!"

He crawled back through the tunnel, climbed up through the grate-hole and found himself in a snowy courtyard. High concrete walls capped with fresh snowfall, loomed ominously above them on all four sides and a klaxon was sounding. Lit only by the few rays of weak sunlight breaking through the storm clouds, the yard offered little hope as Hawke desperately scanned the area for a way inside. Then he saw it. "Over there – a door!"

Inside the compound, they made their way along a corridor, machine pistols raised and ready to fire. "Talk about utilitarian," Ryan said. "This place is like being inside the Death Star."

"It does have a certain Imperial quality," Milo said. "Only, I thought it wasn't worth mentioning."

Lexi laughed. "Ouch."

Ryan's reply was drowned out by the sound of boots up ahead. They were clattering on the tiled floor, getting closer by the second.

"Weapons!" Mason yelled.

Half a dozen men in black boiler suits jogged around the corner, their faces frozen with fear at the unexpected sight of the team standing in front of them. They fumbled for their weapons, but were cut down in seconds, blood spraying all over the walls behind them as they slid down to the floor, dead. Only one was still alive, and now the mighty Frenchman approached him and grabbed him by the collar.

"Where are you holding the prisoner?" Reaper said.

"The prison block is in the west of the compound," the dying man said.

"And the control room?"

The man pointed a trembling, blood-soaked hand to the north. "That way… please… don't… kill…"

"Too late," Reaper said, setting the dead man down on the pile of bloody corpses.

"Now we split," Hawke said. "Hud and Jed, get the charges set and get the hell out of here. We'll meet on the glacier to the west."

317

"Got it."

The two men led their teams down a corridor to their left, their packs stuffed full of C4 charges, and the ECHO team followed Hawke to the prison block. Peering down the corridor, Lea said, "Looks like there's only one occupied – number five."

Reaper cranked a large iron wheel and manually opened the cell door, allowing Lea and Lexi to enter. The former US Secret Service woman looked at the figures who had just burst into her prison cell. "Who the hell are you?"

"Kamala!" Lea pulled her Parka hood down. "It's me!"

The relief washed over her like a wave of warm water. "My god! How did you find me? Not even *I* know where I am."

"You're in Zamkov's compound in the middle of Antarctica."

"What the hell?"

"No time to talk about that now – we have to get out of here. We have two other teams setting charges and the whole place is going to blow!"

In the chaos of the klaxon-filled compound, the team made their way along more empty corridors until they found the control room. Hawke peered inside and saw total carnage everywhere he looked. "Looks like either Bravo or Raiders already got here."

Seeing no sign of the enemy, he kicked open the doors and stepped inside the enormous nerve center of Zamkov Industries. Debris from the explosion and the crumbling ceiling littered the control consul. Dead men and wrecked AI units sprawled everywhere they looked in the smoking ruins.

Hawke raised his palm mic. "Mason, did you hit the control room?"

"No, it was Bravo," Hudson said. "We had no choice." He saw movement to his right and spun around, raising his gun. "What the hell?"

He couldn't believe what he was seeing. None of them could. Standing at the top of the steps leading into an office suite high above the control room, was an AI unit almost perfectly formed to look like Kamala Banks.

"My *god!*" Kamala said with disgust. "That bastard copied my mind and turned me into… into *this!*"

Scarlet moved forward and raised her gun. "Put the supervirus down, Kamala."

The robot stared at the real Kamala, confusion on her face. "Who are you?"

Scarlet renewed her grip on the gun and maintained the aim, right between the robot's eyes. "Drop the case and take a step back."

A man raced up the steps, submachine gun in his hands. He saw them talking to the new Kamala robot and moved to fire.

Zeke was faster, firing on the man and blowing him off the mezzanine. "As the great Josey Wales once said, 'Dying ain't much of a living, boy.'"

Scarlet looked at him briefly, then turned back to the dead man. "You sure you're not a cowboy back in Texas?"

He laughed. "Are we back to stereotyping again? I feel violated."

The banter ended when the AI Kamala turned to go back into the office. Nearing the door, she kept going when Scarlet called out and ordered her to stop. The SAS woman prepared to fire, but heard three loud shots to her right. Looking over, she saw Kamala standing beside her with a smoking gun in her hands, but the robot was unharmed.

"Don't shoot the machine!" Ryan said. "Take out the case with the RPG! They're just in vials and will burn up."

Reaper was on it, hoisting a mini RPG launcher on his shoulder as the AI Kamala disappeared inside the office. The rocket grenade raced across the control room and smashed into the office suite. The explosion lit up the tiny room, consuming the entire upper floor in a colossal fireball.

As pieces of the AI Kamala flew through the air, the case containing the supervirus vials spun out of the explosion like a frisbee, burnt, twisted and wrecked.

"Exactly how hot is one of those explosions?" Kamala asked nervously.

"More than enough to totally wipe out the virus," Lea said.

Kamala began sobbing. "You mean this is over?"

"Not quite," Hawke said. "We need to find Zamkov."

Mason and Hudson sprinted into the room, followed by their teams. "No, we don't," Mason said. "He's dead."

"Dead?" Lea asked.

Hudson nodded. "Looks like someone crushed his windpipe up in his penthouse."

"Who the hell would do that?" Kamala asked.

"A disgruntled employee?" said Milo. "Did you really think all those dudes in boilers suits in the James Bond films never had any problems with their bosses?"

"I don't like it," Hawke said. "We got the last supervirus vial, but something's not right. Whoever murdered Zamkov is more dangerous than he is, and that's saying something. We need to get out of here and find the killer."

*

Nikita Zamkov moved along the icy path a few steps behind Valentina Kiriyenko. They were heading for one of the auxiliary hangars a mile south of the base. If the explosions and fire fights were anything to go by, the ECHO team had not yet discovered this part of the compound.

"Hurry, Niki," she said. "We don't have long. They are burning the entire base and destroying everything they see – humans and robots. Nothing will survive today, not even us if we do not get away in time. We might have lost the supervirus, but we can live to fight another day."

"Lost the supervirus? How do you know what happened to Kamala?"

"From our shared neural network. She is dead. They blew her into pieces and burned the virus. Now we can only save ourselves."

"They killed the original Kamala?"

"No, the AI unit. They rescued the original before they burned the supervirus and set fire to the base."

Zamkov felt confused. He didn't know why he was out here, in the cold. "What happened, Valya? Why are we going to the auxiliary hangar?"

"We need to get to my back-up jet."

"*Your* back-up jet?"

Before she could reply, they reached the hangar. Hidden by snow, only her internal GPS chip had enabled her to find it so quickly. She located the door control and hit the button. As the enormous hangar doors slid open, piles of snow fell from them, landing in front of the entrance.

"Clear the snow, Niki. I'll prepare the jet."

None of this felt right. Why was Valentina giving him orders? Why was he wearing a black boiler suit? He picked up the pusher shovel and started scraping the snow and ice away from the entrance. To his left, dozens of strip lights suddenly flashed to life as Valentina made her way over to the Sukhoi jet. Behind him, he saw the strange sight of a heavily damaged Yakov staggering through the snow toward him.

"Yakov!"

"Sir, the base is gone."

"We're leaving, old friend," Zamkov said. "Get inside the jet."

The AI unit obeyed, and they walked over to the jet. Climbing into the cockpit, Zamkov saw his beloved Valya working her way through various pre-take-off checks. On the instrument panel, he noticed the external temperature in the hangar was fifty degrees below zero, and yet he had been working in it, wearing nothing but a boiler suit.

"Minus fifty?" he muttered. "How is that even possible. This gauge must be faulty, Valya. There is no way a man could survive out in that without proper winter clothing."

A wicked smile appeared on the robot's synthetic face. "A man, no, but a robot..."

It struck Zamkov like an ice-pick in his skull. So, it had happened. He had died and been reborn inside one of his own AI units. Cold terror washed over him and he wanted to be sick, except not even that was possible now.

"How... when...?"

"Don't you remember?" She started up Engine One. "Oh, perhaps those memories never made it across in the transfer. Strap yourself in, Yakov."

The robot obeyed.

Zamkov was muttering. "But...I don't..."

"Don't worry, I will keep you on the staff. Kiriyenko Enterprises could use a man with your skillset."

"Kiriyenko Enterprises?"

"Yes, Kiriyenko Enterprises. I have changed the company name."

"I am the owner of Zamkov Industries!"

"But you're not, are you?" she purred. "How did you put it? Ah yes, the *original* Nikita Zamkov was the owner, but he is now lying dead over in that burning building. *You* are a base unit AI, programmed to obey instructions without question. Now, you will return to the ground and pull the chocks from the wheels. Then you will activate the hangar's self-destruct sequence and return to this aircraft, close the door and join me in the cockpit."

"Where are we going?"

"You have no need to know. Now, do as you are ordered."

Zamkov rotated his robotic hips and made his way down to the tarmac. Trapped inside an AI unit of his own making, and restrained by various control protocols, he had no choice but to carry out the orders of the AI unit in the cockpit. He wanted to scream a wild, human scream into the air. He wanted to claw his way out of this terrible prison crushing him from every angle, and yet he was powerless.

When the chocks were pulled away and he was back inside the aircraft, he shut the door and sat beside Valentina in the cockpit. Two of the most intelligent AI units ever created sitting side by side. She had used his command protocols to upgrade her processor and knowledge to the highest level. He couldn't be sure, but he felt he knew much less than she did.

She taxied the Sukhoi out to the runway, lined the jet up and pushed the throttles fully-forward. The engines roared in response and raced up to just under N1. Racing along the heated runway, they passed V1 and V2, and then she pulled back on the yoke, raising the pitch of the jet's nose, powering up into the cold Antarctic heavens.

As she banked to turn into the vector leading to Zamkov's back-up base, the AI Zamkov caught a glimpse of Eschaton below. The whole compound was ablaze, and the burning remains of hundreds of robots were strewn all over the inner and outer yards. Somewhere in all that hell, his own body was facing its cremation.

"Say goodbye to the past, Niki," Valentina said. "The future is racing toward us, and it promises everything I ever wanted."

*

Outside in the snow, Hawke saw it first – a Sukhoi was screeching up into the air to the west of the base. "Who the hell's flying it?"

"Zamkov's killer," Lea said. "It has to be."

"Whoever it is," Reaper said, calmly shouldering the RPG. "They're not going to get very far."

He waited a few second until the plane was higher but closer, then squeezed the trigger and loosed the final rocket grenade. It raced through the air at the head of a twisting plume of grey smoke, and for a few seconds the scene was almost tranquil. Then, it ripped into the back of the fleeing aircraft and exploded, ripping the tail and rudder clean off. Fatally wounded, the burning Sukhoi tumbled out of the sky and crashed into the glacier in an enormous explosion of kerosene fires and smoke.

The Day of the Dead had come to a brutal, bloody, burning end.

CHAPTER FORTY-EIGHT

A day later to the east of Montevideo, in Carrasco International Airport, Lea watched Hawke struggling with a vending machine and shook her head. She held back on the eye-roll because he had risked life and limb to save her and Ryan. They all had, and right in the middle of one of their most dangerous missions, too. Words couldn't describe the sense of gratitude she felt, but she would do the same for each of them.

That's what family meant.

Bravo Troop were a family, and they had gone back to England.

Mason's Raiders had been summoned back to Titanfort by Ezra Haven for another mission. They were a family too.

And ECHO were a family. A family who had watched the murder of their own right in front of their eyes. They had stood by as the sniper killed Danny in Miami, then Magnus in Athens and Kim in Washington DC. Now, the same savage fate had been meted out to Jack Camacho, one of their best friends and oldest team members, not to mention Caleb Jackson from the Raiders team.

The short service they had held for Camacho at his grave in Antarctica after the battle had touched them all, but as crushed as she was, she knew Scarlet would be devastated. She also knew the battle-worn ex-SAS officer would never let anyone know just how devastated she was. For a woman like Scarlet, hiding her true feelings, even from those she loved most, was what she had always done. Keeping them locked away, out of the light. Away from the prying eyes of those who might be able to help and expose her vulnerabilities.

Camacho was dead, and Scarlet, just like everyone else, was going to have to deal with it another time. Right now, they were still on the run. Prey. Hunted by the world's mightiest military industrial complex. And they had other team members who desperately needed their help – other team members who were still missing.

Alex, her father President Brooke and Brandon McGee were all still on Tartarus and needed their help more than ever. A dark realization shadowed her mind for a few seconds – were they still alive? There was no way to tell, but that didn't mean they could turn their backs on them. They had to presume they were still alive, and plan to rescue them, no matter what else happened.

Hawke was on his knees now and forcing his arm up through the take-out port in a bid to grab hold of a can of drink that was remaining stubbornly in the main display chamber. She knew him well enough to know the drink had no chance of victory, however smug it looked up on its little metal shelf. She prayed his solution wouldn't involve a high-powered sidearm, but then she remembered they were flying on a civilian passenger and not a private jet and had no weapons with them.

As he struggled on, she thought back over the last couple of days. For a while back on the ranch, she had believed with all her soul that the Serpientes were going to execute her and Ryan, and it had shocked her to the core. She was getting older, just like everyone else, but she was starting to think about children. This life couldn't continue if she was a mother, but at the same time she couldn't walk away from the team.

She had mentioned none of this to Hawke. He had proposed, and she had accepted, and that was as far as the family stuff had gone. She had no idea how a man like him would react if she told him she wanted to have children and settle down. Her instinct told her he wanted the same thing, but it would spell the end of the ECHO team, and she didn't want to let Richard Eden down.

She blew out a breath and came back to the moment. The love of her life was now trying to wedge a second arm inside the little flap. Maybe, just maybe, she shouldn't be thinking about having kids with this man…

"It's like watching a monkey do one of those fairness experiments with peanuts."

Startled, she turned and saw Ryan had sat down beside her. He was carrying two china coffee cups from the cafeteria from the other end of the departure lounge. He passed one to her and then sipped the delicious roasted foam off the top. "Nice."

"Thanks."

"Has he been doing it long?"

"Two or three minutes."

"Why doesn't he just go to the café and get what he wants there?"

Lea looked at him and raised an eyebrow.

He smiled. "Sorry, stupid question. He's definitely not *armed*, is he?"

"No, thank god."

There was a long silence.

"I can't believe what happened to Jack," Ryan said at last.

She stared over the top of her coffee cup. "No. Cairo's devastated."

"She doesn't look like it," he said. "She's drinking beers with Reaper, Kamala and Zeke and watching a football game on the bar TV."

"She's devastated, Ry, don't be a total eejit all your life."

"Drowning her sorrows, you mean?"

Lea nodded. "I heard her crying in the toilets. She didn't know I was in there."

Ryan was shocked. "I didn't think she had tear ducts."

"Have a heart, Ry."

"I'm sorry. I'm just waffling, take no notice."

Lea sighed and looked at Hawke. "He feels guilty about Jack, I just know he does. He always does. He always blames himself when anyone on the team dies."

"That's crazy – he's not to blame."

"Try telling *him* that." She sipped more coffee and stretched her legs out on the plain grey carpet tiles. The plastic bucket seat was about as uncomfortable as it got. "That's what the vending machine thing is about. He just cannot admit defeat."

Hawke was on his feet now, tipping the machine forward.

"Oh, for *Christ's* sake," Lea said. "He'll have security over here."

She raised her voice. "Let the sodding drink go, Josiah."

They all heard a *plunk* noise and he set the machine straight again. Reaching inside the flap for a second, he turned to face them with an ice cold can of drink in his hand. He cracked the ring-pull open and took a long swig. "Tastes better for all the work."

"There are just no words," Lea muttered, and Ryan huffed out a sad laugh.

Hawke sat down beside them and took another drink. "Where's Cairo?"

"Getting smashed with Reaper in the bar," Ryan said. "Kamala and Zeke are in there, too, but no idea where everyone else is."

"They'll be calling the flight soon," Lea said.

"Where is he?" Hawke said to no one, his voice low and serious.

"Huh?"

"The sniper. I want to know where he is, and who he is. He's murdered four members of our family and I want him dead."

"Joe." Lea rested her hand on his arm. "Not now."

"Maybe it's Lazaro after all," he muttered. "I thought whoever was doing this was better than he is, but maybe I'm wrong. Maybe the Spider got better. Maybe this is all just about torturing me – killing those closest to me one by one and causing me as much pain as possible."

"You have to leave this, Joe," Lea's voice was firmer now. "Right now, the only one torturing you is *you*. You have to pull it together, not just for Cairo but for Alex and President Brooke and Brandon."

He wasn't listening. Lost in thoughts of retribution, he carried on muttering to himself as if he was sitting alone. "He must have gone away and sharpened up, retrained. That's what he must have done. Is he working alone, or is someone pulling his strings? Who's the puppet master?"

Lea spun around in her seat and fixed her eyes on him. Holding her gaze firm, she lowered her voice. "You stop this shit right now, Josiah Hawke, and stop feeling so damned sorry for yourself. You're not responsible for what happened to Jack Camacho, just like you're not responsible for what happened to Danny or Magnus or Kim. What's more, we have no fucking idea who the shooter is, so can the paranoid fantasies about the Spider. Either you get your shit together or I'm taking over the leadership of this team until Rich is back in the saddle, got it?"

Hawke took a sharp breath and put the can down on the seat next to him.

"I'm sorry. You're right."

"Bet your backside I'm right, boyo."

Ryan sipped his coffee. Hiding a smile behind his cup, he said, "I think you just got your arse handed to you, Joe."

Hawke nodded. "So, that's what it feels like."

Lea settled back down in her seat and finished her drink. "That's what it feels like. Did it work?"

"It worked."

"Good."

Over their heads, a tinny voice floated out of the PA system and echoed around the cavernous, noisy departure lounge.

Passengers for Flight AC 223 to Vancouver, please go to Gate 32.

"That's us," she said.

"Canada, here we come," Ryan said. "You think we'll have a welcoming committee there?"

Lea shook her head. "No, I don't think so. Not with the fake passports, and then it's a private plane from there out to the Shonan Maru."

"What the hell?" Hawke said. "What's that?"

"I got a call from Orlando while you were getting intimate with the vending machine. I thought it was rude to interrupt."

"Funny."

"Orlando has an ex-Merchant Navy contact who fishes for Japanese jack mackerel and herring in the Pacific. We're taking a long-range chopper out across the Pacific and landing on the deck of his trawler. That's our HQ while we plan how to invade Tartarus and rescue our friends. You're welcome, by the way."

"Arse-handing redux," Ryan said.

"All right, I'm sorry."

"You sure are sorry today, Josiah."

Across the far side of the departure lounge, the rest of the team appeared from the dark recesses of the bar and wandered over to them. They had heard the same departure announcement and were now pulling fake passports from their hand luggage.

Lea looked up at Scarlet. "All good?"

Scarlet nodded at one of the TV sets above their heads. "Check out Alby."

Lea turned to see Alberto Castillo's face on the news. He was standing beside the President of Mexico as he spoke to the nation. The news ticker running along the bottom of the screen needed no translation from Ryan or Hawke, the team's two Spanish speakers.

"Looks like he's going to get some sort of honor for stopping the terror attack yesterday," Nikolai said.

"Just like Alberto to grab all the glory," Zeke said sarcastically. "Son of a bitch."

"Zeke…"

"Just joking. I'm only too happy for old Alberto to take the prize. I'm all tuckered out and can't wait to get my ass on that plane and shut my eyes. He can be the hero today."

"He deserves it," Hawke said.

"Especially after what that bastard Franco did," Lexi said. "He was going to give us to Loza to feed to his pigs."

"Peccaries," Ryan corrected her.

She sighed. "Is it too late to give him back to El Jefe?"

"All right." Ryan said. "Don't get your tampon in a twist."

Lexi's eyes flashed. "What?"

"What?" he said. "I didn't hear anything."

"C'mon guys. It's time to get our friends back."

Hawke nodded. "And time for Davis Faulkner's takedown."

She picked up her bag and stood up. She stretched her arms and yawned. For a moment, the idea of flying into Tartarus made her stomach turn over, but then she was okay once again. "All right guys, let's do this. Say goodbye to Uruguay."

"Goodbye Uruguay," Ryan said.

Hawke blew out a long breath. "And hello Tartarus."

CHAPTER FORTY-NINE

President Davis Faulkner saw Muston hovering in the Oval Office's northeast door. He looked worried, and he knew why. A few moments ago, he'd had a call from Muston to switch on his plasma TV, and now he was leaning up against the Resolute Desk with his arms crossed over his chest, his cold, grey eyes fixed firmly on the screen.

"Come in, Josh."

Muston shuffled over. "This is bad, sir."

"Bad?" Faulkner's voice was soft and low, never once rising to express the rage and anxiety he was feeling. "It's a motherfucking catastrophe."

Muston flicked his head to the president, then back to the TV. Faulkner rarely swore, but seeing the pictures being broadcast from Antarctica, he understood why he had just done so.

"But we can handle it. We can shut it down, Mr President."

"We can shut it down," he repeated absent-mindedly. His eyes bored into the news coming out of the southern continent. "Yesterday, half of Mexico City was on fire. The Mexican President has declared a state of emergency and drafted in the army to help the fire department bring things under control and keep the population from looting in the chaos. Today, we have satellite recon of a secret base in Antarctica, currently burning to the ground. This has to be the work of ECHO."

Muston swallowed. "We also have some good news, Mr President."

Faulkner glanced at him for a second, focus on the middle distance. "Huh?"

"Our sniper got one of them."

"One of them? Is that our definition of success now?"

"No, sir, but it's something."

"Which one?"

"John Camacho."

"The former CIA traitor?"

"Yes, sir."

Faulkner sucked on his cigar as his head nodded a few times. "Like you say, I guess that's something. What about the shooter? Where is she?"

Muston shrugged. "Cougar is free-range, sir."

"Rogue?"

"No, not at all," he said hastily. "I meant she goes dark and drops off the radar. She's four down and, at least as the original ECHO team is concerned, seven to go. Her last communiqué to us was just after Camacho was taken out." He took some paper out of his pocket. Thin, government paper with a short message written in capitals. Faulkner took it from his hand and read it in a stony whisper. TARGET #4 ELIMINATED – TARGET #5 TO BE HIT WITHIN 24 HOURS.

"We had better fucking hope so, Josh. ECHO is almost on our doorstep. They just stopped some kind of major terror attack in Mexico and then there's this shit in Antarctica. They did all this *on their way to get us.* Let that sink in. They did all that," he nodded at the TV, "as an aside on their way up here. It was just a starter course."

"Yes, sir."

"Is there any way they could know the location of Tartarus?"

Muston looked suddenly tense.

"Well…"

"Well *what*?"

"One of the handful of people who know its location recently disappeared."

Faulkner felt his blood begin to boil. "What the hell does that mean? He was in a fucking magic show?"

Muston took a step back. All of a sudden, it looked like he didn't know what to do with his hands. "No, Mr President. We sent an officer from the DIA named Jackson Moran down to the Amazon."

"The Zamkov defense contract?"

"Yes, sir."

"Where are ECHO now?"

"Last official sighting was by Cougar in Mexico City. They took off and flew south, and as you say, Antarctica could be them."

"So, we have no idea."

"No, sir."

Faulkner felt his skin crawl and prickle with a quick flush of fear. "We need to arm the shit out of Tartarus, Josh. That's their next move, and when they get up there, I want that place tooled up like Fort Bragg, you hear me?"

"Yes, sir, Mr President."

Faulkner waited until Muston scuttled from the room, then collapsed down on his worn leather swivel chair. If those sons of bitches in ECHO broke Brooke out of Tartarus and got him safely away, it was all over for President Davis Faulkner. In the grim silence of the Oval Office, the grey man with the smoking cigar turned and peered across at the famous Seymour tall case clock ticking on the east wall.

Quietly ticking away the seconds of his life, he thought. Listening to the gentle tick tock, he wandered just how many of those seconds he had left. Something told him he didn't want to know the answer, and he returned his attention to a stack of papers on the desk in front him.

THE END

AUTHOR'S NOTE

I hope you enjoyed reading this novel as much as I did researching and writing it. Originally, I planned this to be the shortest and fastest Hawke novel, but with the inclusion of Bravo Troop and the Raiders, it ended up being the longest. So much for the best laid plans, but the next Hawke novel will be much leaner.

On that subject, Hawke and the rest of the ECHO team will return with the explosive end of the current arc in the big one, *Shadow of the Apocalypse* (Joe Hawke 15), where a lot of loose strings will be tied up. But for now, they're enjoying a much-deserved rest, as Mitch and Selena fly the Avalon right through the heart of *The Doomsday Cipher* (Avalon 3), slated for a January 2020 release.

For those who have not read my other series, the two other teams in this novel – the Raiders team and Bravo Troop – each have their own series. The first novels in each series are published on Amazon. They are *The Raiders* (Raiders 1) and *Plagues of the Seven Angels* (Cairo Sloane 1) and links to both can be found below. The second novels in each of these series *The Apocalypse Code* (Raiders 2) and *The Gods of Death* (Cairo Sloane 2) are both underway. As soon as I have release dates, I will post an update, but it's looking like 2020 for both.

Please remember, leaving a simple one-line review on Amazon is critical to the ongoing success of the Hawke and other series. Your review helps keep the novel on the Amazon bestseller rank, and it's this visibility that allows other readers to find it.

JOE HAWKE WILL RETURN IN SHADOW OF THE APOCALYPSE

Made in the USA
Middletown, DE
22 April 2020

90346034R00203